FROM THE
SAN JOAQUIN

· Also by Barry Kitterman ·

The Baker's Boy

FROM THE
SAN JOAQUIN

Stories

BARRY KITTERMAN

SOUTHERN METHODIST UNIVERSITY PRESS
• DALLAS •

This collection of stories is a work of fiction. Names, characters, places, and incidents are either the product of the author's imagination or are used fictitiously.

Requests for permission to reproduce material from this work should be sent to:

Rights and Permissions

Southern Methodist University Press

PO Box 750415

Dallas, Texas 75275-0415

Cover photo: "Ivanhoe Hardware Store" by Richard Harrison

Jacket and text design: Marisa Jackson

Library of Congress Cataloging-in-Publication Data

Kitterman, Barry.
From the San Joaquin : stories / Barry Kitterman. — 1st ed.
     p. cm.
  ISBN 978-0-87074-569-0 (alk. paper)
1. San Joaquin Valley (Calif.)—Fiction. I. Title.
  PS3611.I89F76 2011
  813'.6—dc22   2010051608

Printed in the United States of America on acid-free paper

10   9   8   7   6   5   4   3   2   1

•

for Lyle and Audrianna,
and for Jill, always

•

· Contents ·

· Acknowledgments ·

MY GRATITUDE TO FRIENDS AND FAMILY who may find small pieces of their lives in these stories; to my teachers along the way, in and out of the classroom, Frank Bell and Peter Facanti, and to William Kittredge at the University of Montana; to Kathryn Lang, Keith Gregory, and George Ann Ratchford at SMU Press, who gave me a place at their table; to anyone who has lived in a town like Ivanhoe.

Earlier versions of these stories appeared in the following magazines: *Cutbank*, *Carolina Quarterly*, *California Quarterly*, *Zone 3*, *Green Hills Literary Lantern*, *The Long Story*, *Oxford Magazine*, *Gihon River Review*, *Chariton Review*, *Turnstile*, and *Flyway*. Generous grants toward the completion of this work were provided by The Fine Arts Work Center (Provincetown), Tennessee-Humanities, and Austin Peay State University.

The Man
· Who Raised Rabbits ·

TRY AS HE WOULD, Cy Franklin could not come up with the name of the woman from the county, the one he had just let into his house. She was tall and plain, and she wore her hair cut short as a man's, and she was sitting in his kitchen now, drinking coffee and talking to Ostie about the boy, about Isaac. The woman wasn't from Ivanhoe. She had never run through the town's vacant lots as a girl, or walked the highway kicking up the summer dust underfoot. If she had grown up in Ivanhoe, she would have done those things. If she had grown up in Ivanhoe, Cy would have remembered her name.

He finished feeding and watering his rabbits in the backyard before slipping around through the side gate and heading downtown. He didn't want to go through the house again, not this morning, but he stopped at the gate, looking out across the adjoining schoolyard to where the Sierras rose up against a distant sky. Ghost mountains. The fog had burned off, and fresh snow from the storms of the previous week outlined each peak. Sawtooth, Mt. Whitney, Split Mountain—there had been a time when he could name all of them, one by one. The air was better then, or his vision was better. If he got in the car and drove for four hours, first to the foothills then up into the park, he could be in the middle of snow and redwoods and manzanita by noon. He couldn't remember when he had last packed children into his car and made a trip like that.

He didn't care for snow, and he didn't care much for anyone who would go to work for the county, although he was sure Ostie would see the situation differently. He was hoping she would. Ostie had that county woman parked at the kitchen table by now, sitting in Cy's chair, drinking from his best coffee cup. Ostie would listen to a complete stranger when she wouldn't listen to her own husband. And it was true; they had to come to a decision about Isaac.

There wasn't any traffic in Ivanhoe of a morning. Cy made his way along the side of the road in the thin black coat his wife had tried, twice now, to put in a bag and take to the store in Visalia where the retarded people worked. The morning had turned cold, and he noticed the children at the grade school had all been taken indoors. Most mornings the playground spilled over with screaming red-faced boys and girls playing ball and beating each other up. This morning the schoolyard sat quiet and still, except for a new flag, too bright, too red and blue next to the California flag, the bear flapping in the wind.

Cy liked quiet places: the backyard with his rabbits, the Tack Room. He had moved to the San Joaquin after the war, leaving San Francisco in search of a small town like the ones he remembered in Iowa, towns made up of aunts and uncles and aging grandparents with accents left over from the worlds their own parents had left behind. Iowa was all right, but there was no going back there. San Francisco was all right too, in its way. He couldn't have moved to this hot and dusty crossroads directly from the fighting in the Pacific. He needed to step down from the war, first the year in San Francisco, another in Sacramento, only then making his way south to this place, Ivanhoe. It was a grand name for a town that even now, twenty years later, had half a dozen streets. The people he'd met here when he first drove his Studebaker into town, the people in the gas stations and the feedstore, were just a generation removed from the farms and stores of the Midwest and Oklahoma and Texas. He found that comforting. During the war, the men he fought beside talked of California as if the whole place was a long sandy beach shaded by giant sequoias, one tree so big you could drive your car through it. But Cy's California, Ivanhoe, was as familiar as the eighty acres he'd grown up on in Iowa.

Cy knew his friend Tommy would be waiting for him downtown at the Tack Room. Tommy practically lived there. He sat at his favorite table most mornings with dominoes or checkers, marking time until the afternoon when he would nurse a single beer with his lunch. When he was good and ready, Tommy took his nap leaning against the wall in the winter sun, or, in the summer, slipping farther back to the cooler recesses of the tavern. The Tack Room attracted old men, claimed them, especially during the World Series when the daytime bartender brought a black-and-white Philco out from beneath the bar and dusted it off. The place smelled of tools, and tobacco, and damp clothing left to dry on a rack near the door.

Cy stopped outside the post office on Main Street, looking north past both barbershops and the feedstore, then in the other direction to where the Sunkist packinghouse sat crowded up against the railroad tracks. He was warm from his walk and the two sweaters he wore beneath his coat. He shielded his eyes to see in through the post office window, though he knew it was too early for the mail. That Miss Whitefield who ran the post office gazed seriously out at the street, pretending not to see him. She was so short she had to stand on a box to work the counter. The checks were late, and it irritated Cy, who had things to buy, wire to mend the rabbit hutch. He would have to charge what he needed at the feedstore. He thought about asking the Whitefield woman about the mail, when she thought it would ever arrive. He'd known her since she was a little girl staring out the window of her father's pickup with dirt on her face. Cy didn't want to ask her anything. He didn't want to give her the satisfaction.

He rubbed his chest where he felt heartburn coming on, a reminder of the bacon he'd found in the icebox that morning, a thick slab, mostly fat. He had dropped four pieces in the bottom of a pan and thought, if you fed bacon to a rabbit that had just thrown a litter, she wouldn't eat her young. He wondered why that was so. Cy had wanted something special to add to the eggs, and he'd taken an onion from on top of the icebox, one of the last onions from his garden, and chopped it up until tears came to his eyes and he cut the tablecloth. He'd stopped for a moment, staring bleary-eyed at the sampler Ostie had hanging beside the kitchen door. As long as they'd been married there had been a sampler on the kitchen wall, one that read GOD BLESS THIS HOUSE. Of late there was another one hanging next to it, a new one with a couple who looked like George and Martha Washington standing over a rhyme.

> *Women's faults are many.*
> *Men have only two.*
> *Everything they say*
> *And everything they do.*

"You cooking?" Ostie had asked. She'd brought Isaac into the kitchen, letting the back door slam. The two of them had been out in the yard. A faint odor, the last linger of fallen oranges and lawn clippings, had come into the room with them. "Cy?"

"I guess I can fry an egg," he'd said, at once sorry for the tone of his voice, but not willing to apologize for it, not first thing in the morning.

"Grandpa cook!" the boy had said. His voice crowed like a little rooster's.

"Grandpa's burning the bacon," said Ostie. She had settled Isaac into a tall chair, tying him in snugly with a dishtowel around his waist. "Watch this baby while I get dressed."

GOD BLESS THIS HOUSE, read the sampler above the door.

"Goddamn that woman," Cy had said. He'd thrown the onion into the skillet with the eggs, making a note not to give any of the big pieces to the boy.

Now, as he neared the Tack Room, Cy stopped in the middle of the sidewalk. Through the weeds of a vacant lot, he could see the back of the Baptist church, the white stucco and one broken window with a piece of cardboard in it. He thought it was the Baptist church. Maybe the Nazarene. Maybe he should know. Ostie had belonged to both of them, one time or another. He could have asked for help from one of those churches, but he'd called up the county woman instead. The county woman, a social worker, would be telling Ostie now, making her accept that the two of them were too old to raise a child. Someone like her would have been to college. Ostie would respect that, and would be able to understand the situation better after talking things over with the woman. Ostie would see the brochures for the place in Bakersfield; the county woman would quote some famous words she'd read in one of her schoolbooks. Ostie wouldn't be speaking to Cy when he got back home.

Cy swallowed painfully, wishing he hadn't put onions in the eggs. He hoped the day would stay clear. He was sick to death of fog. He hoped Tommy had waited for him at the Tack Room.

"You're late."

Tommy sat in the sun that filtered through the front window, his glasses reflecting the midmorning light. His sparse white hair stood on end—there wasn't enough to comb anymore—and he wore a clean work shirt, which meant Tommy's granddaughter had driven over from her fancy house in Oak Ranch to do his laundry. Those were new houses in Oak Ranch, just two streets so far, carved out of the orchards near the dry river. Cy didn't care for the idea. You might as well live in Visalia.

"I couldn't get away," said Cy, pulling up a chair. He made a face and exchanged his chair for one with four sound legs. "Had to tend to the rabbits."

"Those rabbits," said Tommy. He laughed quietly.

"What's funny?" said Cy.

"I like to think of it," said Tommy. "Your backyard, the walnut tree, the garden. The rabbits in their hutches."

"It's nothing to laugh at."

"You let the boy help you?" said Tommy.

"Sure," said Cy.

"You better," said Tommy.

"He's a big help," said Cy.

Isaac begged to go along every morning to feed the rabbits and change their water. He always wanted to be the one who carried the coffee can full of green pellets. "Don't eat those," Cy had to tell him. The can made a rattle when he walked, like rain on a tin roof, though it hardly ever rained in the valley, nothing like the rains Cy had grown up with. He had to keep an eye on the boy, who was only two, and who had slipped some of the rabbit food into his mouth once. The pellets must have tasted odd. They must have tasted *green*. Cy hadn't interfered with his grandson's curiosity that morning, not even when Isaac tried the little round turds that fell through the wire onto the ground.

"You're lucky to have the help," said Tommy.

"I know," said Cy. "Lucky as hell. Lucky's my middle name."

Isaac had made a sour face, had tried to spit the whole mess out. When the boy began to cry, Cy had only meant to hush him up, but Ostie heard and came out the back door, that wooden spoon in her hand as though she would use it to defend her grandson against anyone who would dare make him cry, against the devil himself, or God. Seeing the green stain on Isaac's lips, she railed at Cy, Isaac cried louder yet, and Cy finally had to go to the house and bring the boy a glass of milk and a graham cracker.

"How's the old buck?" asked Tommy.

"He's all right," said Cy. "He's lost some interest in life. Sort of like us."

"Speak for yourself," said Tommy.

Cy pushed the dominoes around the table to mix them up. He stopped once to wipe away a ring of water with his sleeve. "You're still interested in all that?"

"In what?" said Tommy.

"Rabbit business. What rabbits do."

"I'm pretty interested," said Tommy. "For eighty-four."

"Eighty-seven," said Cy. "And you're a liar."

"It's a lot to remember," said Tommy. "A lot to think about."

"You're right about that," said Cy. "Remembering is the hard part."

He had heard a rabbit scream in the middle of the night: the buck. Lying in bed, Cy had listened for it again, half prepared to get up and take a look but hoping he wouldn't hear anything more. He could picture the night outside the walls of his house, the moon hanging just over the top of the nearest orange grove. Orchards butted up against the town on every side. Unable to fall asleep again, Cy had pulled the blankets closer against the cold, and he'd found himself thinking about the buck, about the day he'd bought the rabbit from a man at the fairgrounds. Four years ago—it surprised him to count it up. The buck was older than Cy had realized. Could be that was why the others, the does, were kindling such small litters. This last time, the little doe had pulled her fur and made a nest, but she hadn't been pregnant, unless she did away with her young before Cy was able to check on her. He didn't think it likely. There wasn't any blood on the wire.

The new bartender, a man with skin so pale it was slightly yellow, brought two cups of Sanka to the table. Soon the only sound in the Tack Room was the click, click of the large white dominoes Tommy brought downtown with him every day in a cloth bag. His bones, he called them. He wouldn't let Cy slam them down on the table too hard, or line them up on end and tip them over in one long rush. Cy thought of dominoes as a child's game; he'd bought a set for Evelyn the first summer she spent with her hip in the brace. His daughter wore her brace five years, a lot longer than she maintained any interest in dominoes. Ostie took her up to Fresno to go shopping for new clothes the day the doctor said the girl could take the brace off for good, as if the stores in Visalia weren't good enough. Evelyn hardly limped after that, only a little when she got tired, and Ostie wanted her to dress up a little, look pretty for the boys at school. Cy hadn't said anything then, when he could have.

"I guess I decided, Tommy." Cy played the five-six on the end of a long train of white tiles. He thought about cheating and saying it was the double five, but he didn't cheat. You didn't have to do a thing just because you thought about doing it.

"What did you decide?" said Tommy. He picked up one of his dominoes, holding it close to see it better.

"I'm sending Isaac down to Bakersfield. They got that home there. Place is supposed to be clean. He'll have kids to play with. The woman from the county is telling Ostie about it this morning."

"What county?" said Tommy.

"Our county."

"Which woman?"

"From the county," said Cy. "I think she's the one in charge of children. That tall woman. She's got a haircut like a man. A flattop."

"Don't know her," said Tommy. He turned his face toward the window and looked intently toward the gray front of the post office across the street. Cy knew he couldn't see past the curb.

Cy drew a tile from the boneyard. "I suppose you think I'm doing the wrong thing."

"I don't know any woman with a flattop."

"I can't raise him, Tommy. I've got too old for it."

Tommy nodded as he tallied Cy's score with a large X on a paper napkin. He slid a domino into place and marked his own score.

"I'd be almost ninety before the boy was ready to vote," said Cy.

"Pretty old," said Tommy. "Awful old."

Cy looked up from the table. He tried not to look at the electric beer sign that hung on the back wall, a cartoon bear with a fishing rod, a sign so hypnotic he could lose entire afternoons due to its influence. "About as old as some folks I know," said Cy. He let himself glare into Tommy's eyes.

"You know what your trouble is, Cy?" Tommy took off his glasses and polished them on his shirt front.

"You told me before," said Cy. "You're always telling me. I'm a son of a bitch."

"You're not just a son of a bitch," said Tommy. There were dents on the bridge of his nose that looked sore and red. He rubbed at them gently, as if he could make them go away. "You're a wrongheaded son of a bitch is what you are. You're just about one of a kind."

"Could be," said Cy. He played his domino and drew another. "Could be they don't make them like us anymore."

At noon, Cy walked down the street to the Jolly Kone, where he ordered hamburgers and milkshakes for himself and Tommy. He stared up at the sky, daring it to cloud over, but all he saw was the vapor trail of a jet from the air station to the north. He told the girl behind the window to hold the onions on the burgers, thinking he should recognize her. He was sure he knew her people.

"You're one of those Whitefields."

"Hell, no," she said. She leaned a little ways out the window. "I'm nothing to them."

"Well, no onions," said Cy, "whoever you are."

"Why not?" she said. "You got a date?" She winked at him, and it was all she could do to keep from laughing at her own joke. Cy thought it would be okay if somebody smacked her. Not hard. Not really. He was sorry for the thought. He made himself think about the milkshake, how cool it would feel to his tormented stomach. While she grilled the hamburgers, he walked to the post office to see if his check had come. Only one of the customer windows was open. Once in a great while Miss Whitefield opened two windows, and she had the key to a third window too. They'd be growing oranges in hell before the woman would open a third window. Cy took his place in line, leaning against the long metal table to read the vital statistics and the crimes listed on a sheaf of wanted posters. An angry young face reminded him of Evelyn, although Evelyn wore her hair different now. His daughter was thirty-four, at least that, not so young anymore, not the queen of the carnival she'd been the summer her brace came off. Her forehead had been creased just so when she'd last stood in the driveway with her bags, waiting for her friend to come and drive her to the bus station. Cy read the poster, how the unknown face on the wall was wanted for tampering with the mail. He wondered what Evelyn's poster would have read: *fornication, forgery, child abandonment.*

The line was moving too slow, so he left the post office without asking about his check, stopping to pick up the burgers on his way back to the Tack Room. Tommy had dozed off while Cy was out on his errands, and by the time he woke up enough to eat, the thin gray hamburgers were cold. In the end, Cy took most of Tommy's lunch out to the alley and tossed it over the fence to a collie bitch in the next yard. He had hardly been able to finish his own lunch, he was so used to having Ostie fix sandwiches for him and the boy. He could picture Isaac in the tall chair at home, the dish towel holding him in place, another one draped around his neck for a bib. Cy wondered if they had waited for him.

Cy and Tommy played cribbage in the afternoon, and Cy won when he could keep his mind off Isaac. When he had taken three games in a row, he offered to buy his friend a beer.

"Why not?" said Tommy, shuffling the cards slowly.

The bartender set two drafts on the bar and punched the keys on his cash register, and Cy handed him a creased bill, counting the money remaining in his wallet, wondering if the mail had come. Tommy bent over the cribbage board, his hands in his lap. When Cy placed the beer on the table in front of him, waiting for Tommy to raise his glass, Tommy closed his eyes instead.

"I need to go to the washroom." Tommy ran his tongue over his lips.

"You sick?" said Cy. He set his beer down without tasting it. "You haven't eaten anything all day."

"I'm aware of when I do and do not eat," said Tommy.

Leaning over his friend, Cy smelled something sour. It made him think of the hospital, or that store with the used clothing. It was an old smell, a borrowed smell.

"Come on," he said softly, drawing Tommy's chair back from the table. "I'll help you."

He steadied Tommy to the back of the tavern and into the men's room, where he locked the door behind them. He sat Tommy down in the only stall.

"Can I get you anything? You want a drink of water?"

"Hand me some paper towels," said Tommy.

Cy felt his throat tighten from the odor of urine and disinfectant as he went to the sink for towels. He turned on the tap and looked up into the mirror, where Tommy sat watching him. Cy was alarmed at how white his friend's face had turned.

"You didn't pass any blood?"

"No," said Tommy. "I'm all right."

Cy folded one of the paper towels in half and wiped the sweat from Tommy's forehead. He gave the other towel to Tommy and returned to his place at the sink to comb his hair, then use his handkerchief, then comb his hair again, wondering if he would have to help the man with the buttons on his trousers. Tommy's pants would be worn thin and at least three sizes too big.

Tommy tried to flush the paper towels down the toilet.

"Don't do that," said Cy

"I don't know why not," said Tommy.

'You'll plug it up," said Cy. "You'll plug the whole damn town."

Tommy waved his hand dismissively. "I don't know about that."

"You know what I'm talking about. You know a thing or two."

"I don't know so much," said Tommy. "I don't know why anybody would be in a hurry to get old."

Cy avoided Tommy's gaze as best he could. He let himself think about pleasant things, about cold drinks and warm days, then about the job he once worked at, the packinghouse that sent oranges all over the country.

He tried not to think about bacon, or onions, or children. He tried not to think about getting old. He thought about his check waiting for him at the post office, and he thought about rabbits.

He'd brought the first rabbit home when Evelyn was nine, a black and white Checkered Giant with a droopy ear. One of the men at the packinghouse had given that one to him. Cy built a makeshift hutch for the doe out of odds and ends lying around the garage, and he told Evelyn the rabbit wouldn't make a pet, but Evelyn gave her a name anyway. She spent hours tracing the black and white patterns in the rabbit's fur with one of her fingers. Twice that summer, Cy waited until the sun dropped low in the sky and it was cool enough to carry the doe in a cardboard box to a commercial breeder on the other side of Visalia. When the rabbit failed to conceive the second time, he told Ostie not to buy anything for Sunday dinner. He wanted to ignore the way his wife frowned at him. His daughter came home from Sunday school as Cy was finishing up the butchering. Evelyn had known it was going to happen, but knowing didn't make any difference. Cy was stern with her, then ended up taking her into his lap to comfort her, ignoring the way her brace pressed into his legs.

"Good lord," he'd said through his daughter's tears, "she was just a rabbit." He felt his daughter hated him. "Just a rabbit," he repeated, rocking her back and forth.

He raised white rabbits after that, New Zealand Whites. He'd been to New Zealand during the war, but he hadn't seen any rabbits there. He thought at times about experimenting with other breeds but always decided against it. Colorful rabbits were harder to kill.

The collie Cy had fed earlier whined at him from behind the redwood fence. Two boys on bicycles raced down the alley, blue fenders flashing in the sun, and the collie ran along the fence barking and snapping at them. Cy stood in the alley as still as he knew how, remembering the bicycle he'd bought Evelyn the summer her hip got bad. It had been blue too, but she hadn't learned to ride it. You had to bend your leg to ride a bike. He wanted to go home now and lie down. That was what old people did in the afternoon. It was what Isaac would be doing too, in the middle of the big bed. But Cy wasn't ready to face his wife, not over the boy.

He found himself circling down a familiar street, then turning onto another alley, a shortcut, until he came to the packinghouse, wondering if he would find anybody he knew in the parking lot. The men would be quitting soon, and when they quit work, five o'clock, he could speak to one or two of them and walk home just like he had for the twenty-eight years he worked for Sunkist. Ostie would have dinner ready, and there would be a newspaper. He would feed his rabbits.

He thought about the day a boy named Toland got crushed on the loading dock. Just a young kid, not very bright. The whole place had shut down for the rest of the day, the only day Cy could recall going home from work early. He had walked up the driveway that long ago afternoon, surprised at first to see the car was gone, but it was Thursday, and Thursdays Ostie visited her mother at the rest home. The front door was locked. Cy wasn't sure if he had a key to the door on his key ring, and he had to try several before he found the right one. As he stepped into the living room, he heard the screen door shut at the back of the house, that familiar sound. Someone had tried not to let it slap against the doorframe. He thought he smelled cigarette smoke. He went through the house slowly until he came to Evelyn's room.

"Daddy," she said, red-faced. He nudged her door open, but he stayed outside in the hallway. She was dressing, her bed unmade. "What are you doing home?"

"There was an accident," he told her. She was only fifteen. He wanted to tell her about the accident, and he wanted to ask her what she was doing in bed in the middle of the day. He could do neither. She asked him to leave the room so she could finish dressing. He had sat down heavily in the kitchen, too tired to pour himself a beer.

Cy kicked the fence that ran around the packinghouse. He thought of Isaac and the children's home in Bakersfield and his daughter, who wasn't coming back. The five o'clock siren blasted from the firehouse, and Cy heard the conveyor belts inside the packinghouse as one by one they shut down.

"Goddamn Sunkist too," said Cy.

When he walked up his driveway, he saw the boy standing on the couch looking out the big front window. Cy watched Isaac run to the front door with the coffee can they used to carry food to the rabbits in their hutches, and he wondered if he was supposed to go into the house and speak to Ostie. He decided instead to feed the rabbits first, before it got dark.

Isaac had been looking out the same window the afternoon his mother left. She had stood beside the hedgerow the last day of the long Fourth of July weekend, refusing to look over her shoulder at her son, just as, the night before, she had refused to acknowledge the fireworks exploding from a yard down the street.

"Ostie thinks you're coming back," Cy had said.

"I might come back," said Evelyn. "Or I'll send for the boy." She was impatient, the noon sun unbearably close in the sky above them. Her ride was late.

"At least tell me one thing." He'd pointed a long finger at his daughter in an effort to hold her in place. "Say who this boy's father is. You could at least tell me that." But she remained silent, her eyes on the scorched lantana that grew beside the road.

"Don't you know?" said Cy.

Trembling, she turned on him.

"Daddy," she said. Her voice wanted to break. "Maybe I don't amount to much. But you don't want to raise him either. How are you any better than me?"

A green Chevrolet had pulled into the driveway, a woman Cy didn't know behind the wheel, a woman whose hair needed to be washed and combed. Evelyn quickly opened the car door and climbed inside. She rolled her window down.

"You'd rather raise those stinking rabbits," said Evelyn, "than your own grandson."

Cy heard his daughter's words again each time he crossed the driveway, each time he watered the grass and those orange and white flowers at the edge of his yard. He heard the other woman's laughter and the sound the car made as she backed out to the road. The flowers were a reminder that he lived in a desert really, a desert valley where every growing thing wanted constant attention. And now Ostie kept Evelyn's postcard on the kitchen table. It was a picture of two kids riding a motorcycle across that desert, with Evelyn's writing on the back. "Sorry. Best this way. Try to send some money." Cy didn't know who was supposed to send money to who.

He opened the door to the garage, and when he turned on the light, a mouse ran from the sack of rabbit chow, its feet making a whisper across the garage floor. Isaac's eyes grew wide as the boy pointed under the tool bench where the mouse had disappeared.

"It's all right," said Cy, dipping the coffee can into the green pellets. "They don't eat much." He started to hand the can to Isaac, then hesitated.

"How about you?" he said. "You get any lunch?"

Isaac reached for the can impatiently, and Cy gave it up, letting the boy run on ahead of him through the side gate.

The hutch was built against the back fence, where a few slow flies floated up over the manure under each cage. While Isaac watched the old buck twitch his nose and stamp his feet on the wire, Cy fed the does and the three young fryers. He wiped the green scum from the sides of their water dishes, letting the boy hold the hose as the dishes filled up again. He showed Isaac how to turn the water off when they were finished. There was no wasting water, even in a good year.

The sun had dipped to a place just above the top of the fence, but Cy didn't want to go in yet. He watched the young fryers feeding, two does and a buck. They were three and a half months old and needed to be put up. He had waited longer than he should have. It would be silly to dress them out now, just after feeding them. A lot of things were silly. He left Isaac playing with a trowel in the garden, digging in the soft rich soil Cy had been building for more than thirty years. Cy went to the garage, returning with a bucket and his skinning knife and a newspaper that he unfolded and spread out on the grass.

He set the bucket down beneath the walnut tree that grew beside the hutch. When summer returned, the tree would shade the rabbits from the worst of the sun. Cy walked to the farthest of the hutches, reaching into the pen of fryers and grasping one of the does by the loose skin at her neck. He carried her over to the tree, where he set her down on the grass, checking to make sure Isaac wasn't watching. A short length of wire hung from the lowest branch, alongside a few walnuts still clinging to their blackened husks. He hardly cared anymore about the walnuts that grew in his yard. To gather them in the fall when they lay like a blanket on the grass was more trouble than it was worth. He raised a short length of pipe and brought it down hard behind the rabbit's ears. He waited for her to stop kicking, then hung the rabbit by a hind leg from the wire. When Cy was younger, he had been able to break a rabbit's neck with a turn of his wrist, but he had lost the strength in his arms.

From where he worked, he could see Ostie standing at the kitchen window, her eye on the boy. Over her shoulder, he could just make out the sampler on the wall, the one with George and Martha Washington.

> *Women's faults are many.*
> *Men have only two . . .*

He pulled the entrails from the rabbit and dropped them into the bucket at his feet, careful to remove the tiny sac of bile so he could save the liver. Cy had laughed the first time he saw Ostie's needlepoint. Then the thing started to bother him until he took to sitting in a different chair in the kitchen, one with its back to that sampler. He laid the liver on the newspaper next to the skinned and gutted carcass. He would have to work quickly to finish before dark.

Pulling another of the fryers from the hutch, he carried it to the tree, where he turned it over and saw that he had the other little doe. Her white fur was thick and smooth. When he saw one this nice, it made him regret he had never learned to do anything with the fur. This fur was prime, and he would bury it in the garden. Setting the rabbit on the ground, he broke her neck with the pipe as he had the first one, careful to make a sure kill, not wanting to injure the rabbit and cause her to make the same chilling scream he had heard the night before. He worked with an economy of motion that came from having done the same chore many times, looping the wire around one foot and letting the rabbit hang for a moment. He remembered the first time he had heard one scream: the Checkered Giant. He hadn't known how to kill them then. After gutting the second little doe, he severed the feet and dropped them into the bucket with the skin, then laid the meat on the newspaper alongside the first.

He removed the last fryer from the hutch and carried it to the base of the walnut tree. As Cy searched in the dark for the length of pipe he had been using, the rabbit moved to the Bermuda grass that grew thick along the fence. Isaac came out of the garden and tried to catch the young buck, following it across the yard one step at a time, afraid to reach out and grab it. Cy caught the rabbit behind the ears and held it while the boy slid his hand along the white fur, then touched the long ears tentatively. He smiled up at his grandfather, running off a string of syllables Cy didn't understand at first. The boy wanted to hold the rabbit.

"Isaac," said Cy softly.

From inside the house, Ostie had turned on the back porch light, spreading long shadows across the yard, gathering the moths from the lawn to fly against the bare bulb. Cy stared at his hands, covered with blood and fine white hair from the fryers. He set the boy down on the grass and placed the rabbit in his arms, knowing the young buck would soon slip away, back to the Bermuda grass, knowing Isaac would follow him slowly along the garden fence. Watching them, Cy wiped the knife on his pant leg. The boy was a lot like his mother, thought Cy, wanting to hold the rabbit, wanting to change people's plans. Nothing Cy did ever turned out according to plan. The right answers eluded him. His life was like the algebra problems he'd wanted to help Evelyn with, the ones she brought home with her on the school bus from the high school in Visalia. No matter how hard they worked, often as not they couldn't come up with the number written in the back of the book. It never bothered her. "I'll find out tomorrow," she'd say, drifting from the room. And he would stay at the kitchen table until one or two in the morning, when he would finally go to bed muttering to Ostie, "This time the stupid book's wrong."

Cy looked down the row of cages until he came to the old buck.

"We're wore out, you and me," said Cy. "You can see that." The buck loosed a long stream of urine into the manure under the hutch, as Ostie's shadow moved at the kitchen window. She would be wondering why it took him so long to come in from the rabbits. She would want to give the boy a bath. Cy watched the buck. He stared right into the old one's pink eyes and tried to think. This was like a story problem from Evelyn's book. Take a man named Franklin and let him be A, and his woman, make her B. Leave them in a house in the valley, C, alone for twenty years. Then put a two-year-old kid in that house and call him D. No matter how you stacked the A and the B against the C and the D, some on this side of the equals sign and some on the other, some in the merciless June sun, some in the greasy fog of January, it would never come out right. Cy heard Isaac laugh in the dark, and he felt a thing in his chest a little bit like indigestion and a little like his heart was skipping a beat. He held on to the rabbit hutch with both hands and refused to feel what his heart was doing. He wanted to blame the bacon, but it wasn't bacon he was feeling, the warmth that spread through his chest when he listened for the boy. It wasn't a bad feeling. It wasn't and it was. It was like being lost and wrong, and finding your way, and being lost all over again. It was like being wrongheaded. There were worse things than being wrongheaded.

"You could be finished," said Cy. "You could be all done," he said to the buck. He was used to talking to the rabbits, the same way he was used to the smell of the orchards, the sight of the mountains in winter.

"Worse yet, to be wrongheaded and all done at the same time," said Cy. "And a son of a bitch." Those last words were followed by an unfamiliar sound. He must have laughed at his own joke. It had been a long time since he had laughed at anything he had, himself, thought to say.

"Lord," he said. Somewhere in the yard he heard Isaac moving across the grass. Cy stopped laughing and listened for Isaac's voice. He expected to hear it from the garden, or maybe from a far corner of the yard where together a week ago they had watched a large gray toad, too big and too slow to be afraid of either of them. When he didn't hear the boy's voice, he took a step in that direction.

"Isaac?"

There was no answer. Cy moved along the fence until he could see the last of the carrot tops and the broken cornstalks, the garden hose coiled against the faucet.

"Isaac," he called again, not loud.

He wasn't worried. He knew he hadn't lost the boy, that Isaac couldn't have left the yard. Cy turned and walked back along the fence, feeling his way in the dark. He looked for Isaac under the hutch, then walked around the walnut tree twice.

"Boy," he said. He wondered if he'd left the side gate open. He moved over the uneven lawn toward the garage, trying to look calm in case Ostie was still watching out the window. But when he got to the gate, it was shut, the latch fixed in place. He thought of his skinning knife, pictured Isaac running with it, holding the blade at a frightening angle, and he crossed the lawn again as quickly as he could. Cy tripped over one of the walnut tree's thick roots and fell onto his knees. He searched the grass until he found the length of pipe and the knife where he had left them. Out of the shadow the walnut tree cast over the backyard, he saw Isaac crossing the lawn towards him. The boy had his arms around the young rabbit, was half-carrying it to his grandfather. The rabbit kicked once, and Isaac hesitated, but he didn't cry. He tightened his grip and carried the rabbit a little farther.

"Come on then," said Cy. He bit on his thumb, surprised to find that his heart was pounding. "Set him here now."

He eased the rabbit away from his grandson, holding it against the ground until the animal grew calm, until he himself grew calm. He put one arm around the boy pulling him close to his side, and it came to him with an unexpected sureness, with the scent of shampoo and sweat and child. He saw his wife in the light of the kitchen, her back to him as she stirred a pot at the stove.

"Some of those problems never had any answers," he told Isaac, "not like that." It was the thing Evelyn had known.

Cy reached into the buck's cage and stroked the old one gently behind the ears before he lifted him out of his pen and set him down beside the walnut tree. He laid the bloodstained pipe down and knelt over the rabbit, looking away for a moment to the house lit up against the evening. He thought he heard the radio playing from the kitchen, or it was Ostie singing to herself. Cy tightened his hold on the buck and tested the edge of his knife against his thumb to see that it was still sharp. When he was done with this old one, he would put the young rabbit in the buck's cage before he went inside to Ostie. He'd watch the look on her face when he told her what he'd done. He would call the county tomorrow himself, tell the county woman how sometimes an older person made a mistake, tell her right out. There was nothing for Isaac in Bakersfield.

So many other nights like this one, so many nights with Isaac and the rabbits. He couldn't say how many nights. That would depend on how much time he had left, how much time was left in the whole world. "The whole world," said Cy, weighing the words, finding them heavy on his lips.

He watched the boy move toward the back door and his grandmother. He watched the moths against the porch light. They made him happy and sad at the same time. Isaac reached for the doorknob, and somewhere in the night, a few roads over, Cy heard a familiar sound. It wasn't close, but it was clear and sure. It was the sound of a small engine, and voices laughing, like boys guiding a motorcycle across the desert.

· Someone Like Me ·

MY MOTHER TELLS ME from reading the paper how Nick Deems has been killed. I keep thinking about last year's revival and Nick sitting in the pew in front of me, both of us wondering what we were going to do about Jesus. Nick was nineteen and he wore his uniform and he knew he was going to the war pretty soon. I was eight and I was a coward, but I decided I would do whatever Nick did about getting saved. It was my sister Coral Ann who played the piano every night at the revival, looking over her shoulder every chance she got so she could smile at Nick. Now Coral Ann won't even leave the house. She's crying over Nick because he's dead.

I don't go near the piano anymore. My mother gave up on me last year when I couldn't learn the "William Tell Overture," at least not the right way, not by heart. I had William Tell for my lesson five weeks in a row and finally my mother said to forget it. She was tired of wasting her money. I don't have as much music in me as other people do. Coral Ann goes to high school in Visalia, and she can play a lot of songs off the radio, anything she wants. She can play all the hymns, even the ones nobody wants to sing, and my other sister, Lettie, can play too. Lettie's a year older than me, but she's three years ahead of me at the piano. She can almost play "Clair de Lune."

If it hadn't been for the time I fell off the roof of our neighbor's garage (don't ask, I'm not talking about it), I could have made it at the piano. Even if I wasn't supposed to be up on Miss Whitefield's roof, nobody got hurt, and anyway, Miss Whitefield could have had that car fixed if she wanted to. It was a minor dent I made where I landed on the trunk. But after that, instead of going home every day after school where I could practice and discover if I had a musical talent, I had to ride the school bus to Lanny Spellman's house. Lanny's father has a thousand acres of orange trees. He raises trees from seedlings in his nursery and buds the trees when they get big enough and puts them out in one of his groves to do their job growing oranges. My mother's job is to work in his nursery, and I had to go out there so she could keep an eye on me. Last year Lanny Spellman was the tallest boy in my grade, taller than half the boys in the fourth grade, even taller than one kid in the seventh grade, J. W. Patterson. J.W. has a glandular problem. Lanny had bad teeth and he was sometimes hard to understand, but I thought we were friends. I was surprised that first afternoon when he pulled me behind an orange tree and slugged me three times, twice in the stomach, once on my jaw. I hadn't done anything to get on his bad side, and there he was riding me like a horse in the dirt and the dry leaves, kicking me in the ribs with these boots I never saw him wear before that day. He wore them special for me.

At home that night I couldn't stop thinking about the way he jumped me. I was supposed to be practicing, but all I wanted to do was watch television. It was my third week of William Tell and I had a lesson on Saturday. You can't play serious music if your heart isn't in it. It wasn't the first time I got beat up either. I was popular that way, but I was tired of it.

"Play that Lone Ranger song," said Lettie. Lettie twirls her baton all the time, a dreamy look on her face like she's heading up the Christmas parade or the halftime show. I saw those majorettes at the football game in town in their white boots and something like swimsuits. They looked like girls from a bigger town. They gave Lettie ideas.

"Look out with that thing," I told Lettie. "You're not even supposed to bring it in the house." Lettie is prone to accidents. She wears glasses that look like they were meant for a grown woman, and she thinks her brother Pauly Hubbard is a gift from God so she can have someone to take charge of. I am her brother, Pauly Hubbard. I heard her praying one night, "Thank you, God, for Pauly Hubbard. He's a trial to me."

"Play something for me, Pauly," said Lettie. "Play anything." Only I couldn't. It was Lanny Spellman's fault I couldn't play. When he knocked me down, I'd shoved a thorn in my palm, and I'd been trying to dig it out ever since, trying to remember what Coral Ann told me last summer about lockjaw. She said it runs in our family.

"I don't hear a piano," said my mother from the kitchen. "You'd think I'd hear a piano if someone were playing a piano."

So I acted as if I couldn't find the right book, and when I found it, I let it fall back behind the piano and had to sweep it out of there with the broom. I was hoping my father would come home. He works at the locker plant in Visalia, and he works too hard. He likes peace and quiet when he gets home. He pretty much felt the way I did about William Tell.

Lettie was humming a song like you might hear a marching band play. She said it made her twirl better.

"It's very hard to practice if people have to hum," I said.

My mother went to the drawer by the sink and started rummaging around after her pancake turner, the one she uses to get a person's attention. Even with my mother preparing to come after me, I wasn't doing justice to William Tell. That thorn in my hand was like a knife in my palm. I would say I was being crucified, but it's not right to say it. I thought I'd see that thorn poke between my knuckles at any minute. I kept after it until I managed to work it loose. A thing like that, I wanted to save it and look at it later, so I opened the hymnal to the song in the middle of the book, "Amazing Grace," and left the thorn there. It resembled a quarter note only it was bigger than a quarter note and not shaped right for a quarter note. I bent over the keys and gave William Tell my best, knowing my mother would find what she was looking for sooner or later in her kitchen drawer.

She meant to help me keep time with the pancake turner, but before she made it to the piano, I was frightened off the bench by a sound like an earthquake would make (a real earthquake, not the phony one they're always having over by Hanford). I heard glass falling all across the living room. My mother stood a moment with her eyes closed. It was a sound we had heard before. It was no earthquake.

"I didn't mean to," said my sister. Lettie was crying real tears, holding her baton in one hand, looking at the overhead light fixture, what was left of it. It wasn't overhead anymore. Mostly it was on the floor.

"She's supposed to keep that outside," I said. My mother gave me one with the pancake turner. I yelled a little, mostly because she surprised me, and my book fell off the piano again, and Lettie cried harder, hopping around on one foot because she had glass in the other one. That's when the front door opened, and in came my father, looking as though he wished he'd worked late again. Ronald Reagan was the first one to greet him. Ronald Reagan is our dog.

That night was the first night we went to the revival. My mother said we should have gone sooner, how it was only a one-week revival and not a two-week like the year before, and we were lucky to get a revival in Ivanhoe, and my dad said one week felt about right to him. I was glad I didn't have to go before that night because this was a serious revival with a youth choir, and the choir was going to be sitting up behind the preacher. I didn't want to find myself in their shoes. If they tried to get me into the choir, I was going to tell them, "I sure would like to, but I missed the first three nights and I don't know the songs. I don't want to hold the rest back." I practiced saying it a few times in the backseat of the car on the way to the church. My mother kept checking the rearview mirror to make sure Coral Ann made it to the revival with Nick Deems. They were riding in his pickup. Nick had been coming around our house for a year, ever since Coral Ann started to wear short skirts and act hateful in the morning. He used to give me enough money to go for sodas, so I liked Nick pretty much. One night my mom thought she smelled beer on his breath. She asked my dad to talk to him, but my dad got mad at her and went to bed. He liked Nick too.

We made it to the church without losing Nick and Coral Ann. I didn't figure we would lose them. We only lived four blocks from the church. And we didn't have to wait outside on the sidewalk until they got out of his truck and came to the big front doors either, but nobody asked me. Before we went inside, I read the title of the sermon on the wooden sign in the churchyard: THE BLOOD OF THE LAMB. I had been hoping they might not have a sermon, just show slides the way they did sometimes of *Lottie Moon, Missionary to China*, or *The Sunnyview Boys' Home*. That's the one down in Bakersfield. We went there once, the whole Sunday school, to take them some used clothes, and Isaac Franklin refused to get out of the car. He was only four, a little kid, and he thought we were going to leave him there. You couldn't blame him.

It looked to me like a long night. Coral Ann went up front to play the piano, leaving Nick by himself. He sat straight as a board and let the old women eyeball him and whisper to each other, except for Grandma Roberts, who looked the other way while she fished around in her bag for a handkerchief. We sang four hymns before they took the offering, which was one hymn more than I wanted to sing. Nick slipped a dollar into the plate and passed it to me. I passed it on. I got the pancake turner once for taking money out of the plate. It was Lettie who saw me do it. You don't take money out of the plate, not in my family.

I looked for Brother Slade in his wooden chair up behind the pulpit, but Brother Slade wasn't there. Maybe he was in another town somewhere, helping to revive some other church who needed it more than the Ivanhoe church. A different preacher, someone I didn't know, was sitting in Brother Slade's chair. When he stood up and came to the pulpit, this visiting preacher was a thin man with a raspy voice, as though he needed to cough if he just would. But he could preach. He told about Jesus dying on the cross, the nails in his hands and the nails in his feet and the crown of thorns on his forehead, and pretty soon that preacher had me feeling like I was the one who did those things to Jesus. He told about the soldier who plunged a sword into Jesus' side and all the blood and water running out. That's when Nick started to sweat. Nick was a big person, taller than my dad, and with him sweating and shivering, I felt like we both might be coming down with a serious illness.

This preacher wasn't a long-winded preacher, one thing I will say for him. He preached until nine o'clock, when he asked Coral Ann to play the piano so we could sing the invitation. As she played the first few chords, the preacher asked how many of us were sorry for making Jesus suffer, and I was going to raise my hand, but I saw it wasn't a question you had to answer like that. The preacher said if we were sorry, we should come down and be saved. We started singing "Just As I Am without One Plea," and I never felt so terrible. I was about to go down the aisle when I thought to look at Nick, standing as if he was at attention, not bothering with the words in the hymnal, the sweat running down his forehead. I told myself I'd get saved if Nick did. But pretty soon the hymn was over, and Nick went out of the church and waited for Coral Ann in his pickup.

I made up my mind the best thing to do was to put some distance between myself and Lanny Spellman, so the next day at school, I stayed away from Lanny, and I asked Rudy Valendez if he wanted to throw the baseball around after lunch. Rudy's folks worked for Mr. Spellman too. Lanny said they were wetbacks, but my mother said she never saw anyone work in the oranges as hard as Mr. Valendez did. As soon as I started to ignore Lanny, he came around as if we were old friends. He didn't exactly say he was sorry, but he let me try his new baseball mitt and he gave me a fancy candy bar out of his lunch. When it came time to ride the bus at the end of the day, he saved me a seat.

The bus had pulled onto the highway, and I was looking out the window at the orange groves. Seems like oranges is all anybody wants to grow in our county. There used to be other fruit, and more olives, and cotton.

My mother said she liked oranges a lot better than she liked cotton. Lanny was looking straight ahead at the seat in front of him, his forehead wrinkled up. He was about to have a thought. Some people, you can tell.

"Anybody at your house know how to swear?" asked Lanny. It's funny the way when you drive past an orchard, for just a second you can see all the way down each row, like if you looked hard enough you could see to another part of the world. "I mean, really *swear*," said Lanny. Only when he said it, the word came out funny, like *shvear* or *shemare*. A little like *silverware*. I kept my eyes on the window and the trees we passed. Sometimes there were pickers on tall ladders or somebody's foreman driving a forklift. There's money in oranges. Lanny's father is building a new house.

"You mean, like cussing?" I said. I kept my guard up. With a person as hard to figure out as Lanny, you wouldn't say yes or no to a question like that. I knew some words, but I didn't know all the really big ones. I was trying to learn what I could from the radio. I can't always make out what those guys on the radio are singing. Lanny got out his ball glove so he could pound it. He was working on the pocket, the only kid in my school with a first baseman's glove.

"You still go to church?" he said. It wasn't really a question. More like he was accusing me of something. I've got this pin at home that says I went to church every Sunday for two years and never missed a day. I keep it attached to my sport coat, what I wear on Sundays. After I got the pin, I did miss church one time to go fishing with Nick Deems, but my dad said I could go and we didn't catch any fish and so I still wear the pin. I knew what Lanny Spellman would think about all that. Lanny would call me a choirboy or worse, the way he called Marvin Wallace a morphodite because Marvin's parents were Jehovah's Witnesses and nobody in that family would ever salute the flag. Still, I couldn't lie about it. The night before, I'd been feeling bad about what happened to Jesus.

"I go sometimes." I made my voice sound low and rough the way Nick's did.

"We used to go," said Lanny. "That church with the cross." He was studying his mitt like it was the *World Book* encyclopedia. "When I was a kid," he said.

I looked out the window and tried to figure out where we were. It's hard to know if you're coming or going when you can't see anything but orange trees and telephone poles and the highway. The bus stopped in front of Lanny's house, and we bailed out, Lanny and me. He looked at me strange again. I knew what that look meant. I felt like running, but Lanny was faster than me, and I knew he would love to give me a head start so he could tackle me from behind. It was the sort of thing he liked to do. It wasn't until I heard the bus move away that I thought to say anything to the driver. Mr. Mullins was an old man with white hair, but he was bigger than Lanny Spellman.

"You ready to fight?" said Lanny.

I was trying to think of an answer when he hit me hard in the face. He stood over me, rubbing his hand, then touching it to the side of his jaw. I guess he wanted to remember how it felt to hit me there. It seemed the best thing to do was just to lie still and wait for him to go away.

When we got home late that afternoon, I surprised my mother by going straight to the piano and giving all my attention to William Tell for the better part of an hour. I didn't try to sneak away or knock my music book off the rack. While I played, I was thinking about my problems. I was thinking about the Bible, and I was trying to figure Lanny Spellman out. It didn't come to me at first because I was still in the New Testament, but once I shifted to the Old Testament, it was easy. Lanny Spellman was a Philistine. I know about Philistines, and Samson. That's one of my favorite stories in the Bible, that and the time Joshua blew his trumpet so hard the walls caved in around the city of Jericho. My mother once said she'd buy me a trumpet if I made progress at the piano, but it wasn't looking very likely.

There's a lot to the Old Testament. What I liked about Samson was the way one time he killed close to a thousand Philistines and all he used was the jawbone of an ass. Ass is a word that's in the Bible, but I used to wonder why Samson would use a thing like a jawbone to kill Philistines. Of course, they didn't have guns in those days, or good knives. While I played my best and thought about life, Lettie hung over my dad's recliner, staring at the side of my face. She'd had her baton put away after breaking out the lights one time too many.

"What happened to you?" Lettie had to ask. My mother was in the kitchen frying a chicken, trying not to listen to something awful that Coral Ann said Nick Deems said. I could have told my mother Nick never said anything that stupid in all his life.

"Somebody hit you pretty good," said Lettie. Her glasses were broken, and she'd taped the two halves together with adhesive tape. My mother would have to take her to Visalia to get a new pair. You can't get your glasses fixed in Ivanhoe. You can't get anything but oranges and revivals in Ivanhoe.

"Get lost," I said, the way I'd heard a guy say it on television. My stomach trembled, and I knew I was about to cry, or maybe go crazy. Sometimes getting beat up isn't as bad as thinking about it afterward. Pretty soon I couldn't tell the white keys from the black ones. The way I was playing, it sounded like William Tell had just shot an arrow straight through his son's head.

"That's enough for today," said my mother from the kitchen. I thought her voice sounded tired. It was a long day for everyone.

"I know all about it," said Lettie. She rolled her eyes behind her glasses and hung a little farther over the back of the chair, as if she was going to tell me something important. What it was I never heard, because the recliner unfolded and Lettie went headfirst into the coffee table. She knocked Coral Ann's books onto the floor and my father's Bible and a big bowl of plastic fruit, and she opened up a pretty good cut over one eye right about where William Tell's arrow would have gone in. My mother came and stood in the kitchen door with her pancake turner to make sure Lettie got all the grapes and apples out from under the couch. I heard my father's truck in the driveway, and Ronald Reagan came flying through the living room. My mother barely missed him with the pancake turner.

Lettie managed to get the recliner back to its normal position before my father made it to the front door.

"Lanny Spellman," she said. She didn't know her head was bleeding. She could have been set on fire and she wouldn't have known it.

"Yes," I told her. "He's a Philistine."

"What I thought," said Lettie.

That night we went back to the revival. We were almost late. Nick didn't show up until the last minute, and Coral Ann kept refusing to get in the car with the rest of us, saying Nick had promised to come for her.

"I hope he shows up," said my mother. "A lot of people are praying for that boy."

Coral Ann groaned and turned red, but I knew she was one of the people praying for Nick. I noticed she wasn't mad at him by the time they got to church. We made it inside just before the doxology, and Jewel Reynolds, who was at the piano, had to get up and let Coral Ann take her place because everyone knows Jewel Reynolds can't play anything like my sister can. Sometimes Jewel fakes it with her left hand. I've seen her do it. I looked in the bulletin and saw the preacher was going to preach on *The Wages of Sin*. I didn't want to think about that kind of wages, so I watched Nick, who sat down in front of me. He was studying the baptismal behind the preacher, where there's a picture painted right on the wall of a lake with two mountains. That picture made me think about the time me and Nick went fishing. After we sang "The Old Rugged Cross" and "The Lily of the Valley," they took the offering and Nick put another dollar in the plate. We sang "Love Lifted Me," and the youth choir sang a song about heaven. I kept hunched over drawing battleships and orange trees on my bulletin so nobody would notice I wasn't in the youth choir.

Then the preacher started in about *The Wages of Sin*. And I had to give it to him—he knew the Bible. He brought up the part about the last judgment and the fiery furnace and never having a drink of water. And more than once he stopped and prayed for the lost souls in the church. When he had Coral Ann come play the piano real soft, everyone was supposed to close his eyes and look into his own heart. I raised my head and kind of squinted at that preacher, and he was staring right at Nick, and Nick was staring right back, not pretending to pray.

We sang the invitation, "Why Not Tonight?" I saw Coral Ann look at Nick and smile, but Nick wouldn't look at her. He wasn't looking at the preacher anymore. He just stared at the painting in the baptismal like he knew there were fish in there. We didn't get saved that night either.

The next morning I thought about telling my mother I was too sick to go to school. I'd had all of Lanny Spellman's friendship I could stand for the week, but there was a dent in the trunk of Miss Whitefield's car that said I wasn't old enough to stay home alone. (I don't know how Miss Whitefield even drives that car. Her feet barely reach the pedals.) I knew being sick wouldn't solve my problems. If I was sick, I'd have to spend the day with one of the ladies of the church, like the one time I did fake being sick, and I stayed with Grandma Roberts, who isn't really anyone's grandmother that I know of. We just call her that. A strange thing happened. First she went to the store and brought back chicken soup and saltine crackers and two bottles of 7 Up. I finished most of it by nine o'clock when *Jeopardy* came on the TV. She gave me some aspirin and asked me if I would like to try some Pepto-Bismol. I said yes, thinking Pepto-Bismol looked good, like strawberry soda. Just before *Password* came on, she brought out this ancient vaporizer from the closet and filled it full of hot water and a big gob of jelly. She told me to breathe deep and I'd be feeling better in no time. God, if I didn't get sick for real. My mother took off three days from work to look after me.

I forced myself to get dressed, and I ate a bowl of cereal. The guy pole-vaulting on the cereal box reminded me of Nick Deems except this guy on the box was skinnier than Nick. Lettie told me to hurry up or I'd be late. She'd found her baton, and she gave me a quarter when I sneaked it out the back door for her. We walked to school together, Lettie chewing gum and twirling, and every now and then throwing her baton way up into the sky. She could throw it pretty good, but she didn't have much idea where it would land. As soon as I got my quarter, I let her go on ahead.

It wasn't an exciting day for a Friday. We had a spelling contest, which Lanny Spellman came close to winning because of his crooked teeth. The teacher couldn't understand him any better than the rest of us could. The contest finally came down to Lanny and a Japanese girl in our class who can spell anything, even some Japanese words. The teacher told Lanny to spell *friendliness*, and he couldn't manage it. Marvin Wallace, who sat right behind me, gave a little laugh from inside his desk, and Lanny thought it was me laughing. So when the teacher sent everyone to recess, I stayed inside and cleaned the chalkboards.

I was thinking about the talk I'd had with Nick the night before, after we all got home from church. Coral Ann was mad at him because he wouldn't get saved, so I got a chance to talk to him by myself for a change.

"So Nick," I said, "tell me a good way to beat up somebody who's bigger and stronger and meaner than you are."

He laughed and said I should try to settle things without fighting, the way I was taught in Sunday school. I told him yes, I could do that, but things never work out like they say in Sunday school. He said I was right, and always would be right, but there was no future in being right all the time. He asked me if I wanted to go fishing with him again some-time soon. He left without saying goodnight to Coral Ann.

I cleaned all the chalkboards in the classroom, and I beat the erasers in the sink. I could see Lanny outside the window waiting for me. It was cold outside, and he had his hands tucked into his armpits to keep them warm. I started scrubbing the sink with cleanser, and I had my eye on the Drano. I was reading the label on the can when my teacher saw what I was thinking. She took the Drano away from me and asked if I felt okay, and I told her yes, only I'd noticed for a long time the sink needed to be cleaned and maybe the drain was about to develop a bad clog. She looked out the window at Lanny Spellman pounding his baseball mitt, and she smiled at me, a little sadly I thought, as she went back to grading papers.

I prayed then. I prayed that God would protect me from people like Lanny Spellman. For one thing, he could make it so Lanny missed the bus. That wouldn't be too hard for God. I could just see Lanny running to the bus, the bus already moving, Lanny tripping on the asphalt and getting crushed underneath the back wheels when Mr. Mullins shifted gears and drove out the gate. I didn't know, though, if prayer would work for someone like me. Two nights in a row I'd gone to the revival and I hadn't got saved. I thought God might keep track of things.

That afternoon when Mr. Mullins brought the bus out of the garage, I was the first one to get on. I slid way down in my seat and held my breath and watched the bus fill up, hoping someone would sit next to me, anyone, before Lanny showed up. Rudy Valendez ran past without seeing me, followed by the Japanese girl, smiling because she won the spelling bee. I was still praying when Mr. Mullins started the bus, and I told myself prayer was really something and I'd have to do it more often, and read my Bible more too. I looked out the window and saw Lanny running for the bus with his ball glove tucked under one arm like a football.

"Go," I shouted to Mr. Mullins, but he only stared through the windshield the way old people do sometimes. Lanny climbed the steps and sat down next to me. Lettie was the last one to get on the bus. She went all the way to the backseat where she could twirl her baton and maybe not hit anyone, where I couldn't ask her why she was leaving school an hour early instead of staying for baton practice.

Lanny didn't say a word to me. He worked on his glove and whistled through his crooked teeth. I thought about getting off the bus at the first stop sign and running home, or running in the other direction, into the foothills, over the mountains. I wouldn't quit running until I was in Nevada. But I knew I wouldn't get away with it. Mr. Mullins had memorized everyone's stop and he'd never let a person get off the bus anywhere else. So when the bus pulled up at Lanny's house, I pretended I was asleep.

"Come on," said Lanny. I sat there as long as I could. Lettie passed me in the aisle as if she didn't know me, and I could see Mr. Mullins looking at me in his big mirror. I smiled at Mr. Mullins, and he frowned at me, and I got off his bus.

Lettie walked down the road, twirling her baton and throwing it into the air, eyeballing it and either running after it or running to get out of the way. I decided to duck into the nearest orange grove and slip over to the nursery through the trees. If Lanny came after me, I could crawl up under a tree and hide there in the dry leaves. I could stay there for days if I had to, living off the fruit the pickers had missed. But I barely made it into the orchard when I collided with Lanny. He'd run to his house as fast as he could to get his bicycle, and he was riding through the orchard to cut me off. His bike, red with chrome fenders, had raccoon tails hanging from the handlebars. I'd bet you any amount of money Lanny Spellman cut off those raccoon tails himself.

"Can you steer?" asked Lanny. It wasn't what I expected him to say. He caught me by surprise. I told him I couldn't steer, and this time I wasn't lying. In fact, I don't know how to ride a bicycle. Lanny knew that too. You can't keep that sort of thing a secret. I was going to ask Nick to teach me, but he went away.

"I'll pump you," said Lanny. He had two big rocks, one in each hand, and I could see another one sticking out of his pocket. He held the bike steady while I got up on the handlebars the way he told me to, and Lanny pedaled, steering with the tips of his fingers.

"When we get close to your sister," he said, and he showed me one of the rocks he was holding, "you take over. I'll let her have it with one of these."

"I can't take over," I told him. "It's me. Pauly Hubbard. I don't know how to steer a bike. I could kill us both. Give me a different job." I didn't want to be a partner to Lanny's meanness, but I couldn't just refuse. I wasn't brave. I wasn't Samson or William Tell. I wasn't Nick Deems.

"You're going to do it," said Lanny.

"But I can't."

"Steer!" he said.

He took his hands all the way off the handlebars, and at first we continued in a straight line just like he was still in control. Then I guess I leaned too hard to the right because we started to go off the road toward a big dusty orange tree, its leaves powdered white with pesticide. A sign hung from one limb.

PARATHION—POISON—KEEP OUT

I leaned hard as I could the other way, and there we were going back across the road, Lanny hanging off one side of the bike, me hanging off the other. He took his feet off the pedals and slid them on the ground to make us slow down. He started to swear.

"Stop now, damn it," he said, "will you stop? You damn homophiliac." Lanny would have hit me, but he didn't want to put down either one of his rocks.

"Pauly," he said. He spit on the road. "You must have venereal disease, the way you steer a bike."

He made me get off his bicycle, made me hold it for him. Lettie was watching from the side of the road. She could see right away what he had in mind, the way he crossed the blacktop toward her with a rock in either hand, and I thought sure she'd turn and run. She was a good runner for a girl with glasses. Instead, she took the gum out of her mouth and stuck it on the end of her baton.

"You get out of here, Lanny Spellman," she said. "You go right back to hell where you came from."

I wanted to go help her, but I couldn't get the kickstand down on Lanny's bike. I watched him throw all three of those rocks at her, watched him miss twice, which surprised me. He'd never have missed, throwing at me. He nailed her the third time though, right above her knee and the birthmark she's been praying will go away before she's old enough to march in parades. He should never have thrown that third rock. He gave up his advantage.

Lettie swung her baton back and forth, slow, like some big-league ballplayer waiting his turn at the plate, and she started after him, calling Lanny Spellman a lot of words I didn't think she knew how to say. She described things I never imagined a boy doing to himself. I couldn't believe my ears, the way she came charging out into the road shouting new and more terrible language. She laid one good blow to the top of his head with the fat end of her baton, all the time repeating what the preacher had said the night before: "The wrath of God, the wrath of God."

Lanny yelled some too, but he didn't yell anything I recognized as words. It was one time he couldn't think what to say. He took a step or two backwards, and then he was running through the orchard, forgetting about his bike, forgetting about Lettie in the road crying. She always cries when she's mad.

"You better come on," she said after a minute, wiping at her face with the hem of her dress. I kicked at the stand on Lanny's bike so I could prop it up beside the road, but I looked around and Lanny wasn't watching, so I pushed his damn bike over on its side right on top of the white line, and I left it there. A car might not come along for two or three hours on that road, but when it did come along, I hoped it would drive right over Lanny's fancy bike. I pulled at one of the raccoon tails, but it was tied on too good. When I caught up to Lettie, I could see her baton had a big dent in it. She wouldn't be able to twirl it anymore, and that was my fault too.

We got home late that afternoon, too late for me to practice the piano. My lesson was the next morning, and I knew I was going to catch it when Mrs. Nickels found out I still couldn't keep up with William Tell, but we barely had time to eat dinner and get ready for the revival. Coral Ann was already dressed when the rest of us got home, and she sat at the piano playing "Whispering Hope" real quiet. She had borrowed some of my mother's perfume, and she smelled all grown-up sitting there by herself. She stopped once or twice and looked out the window, wondering if Nick Deems was going to take her to the revival or if she had to ride in the car with the rest of us. I could see Coral Ann was mad enough to burst when Nick pulled up in his truck. Nick smiled at me and messed up my hair that I had taken a long time to get right, but I didn't mind. Coral Ann said, "Sometimes I think you come over to see Pauly." The thing about Nick and Coral Ann, they never could stay mad at each other for long.

When we got to the church, the first thing I did was check and see what the sermon was going to be. YE MUST BE BORN AGAIN said the sign in the churchyard. Nick stood outside by that sign for a long time, smoking a cigarette and listening to Coral Ann play the piano. I stayed outside with him, but it was as if I wasn't really there. When we heard the first chords of the doxology, we went inside.

The preacher and Nick started right in staring at each other even before we were done singing the hymns. The harder the preacher stared at Nick, the taller Nick stood when we sang. When we were supposed to be praying, I looked at the preacher, and it was just what I thought. He was staring at Nick during the prayers too. Nick stared back for a while, then started cleaning his fingernails with a little pocket knife he carried with him. It had the words *Sequoia Park* etched in the side. I know it did because the day we went fishing, he gave me a knife just like his, only my mother put it up until I'm older.

When they took the offering, Nick put another dollar in the plate. I put in the quarter Lettie gave me that morning. We sang "Send a Great Revival" and "Blest Be the Tie," and there was special music by Alta Reynolds with Jewel playing for her. All that, before the preacher started in.

"What must I do to be saved?" he shouted. And he answered his own question. "Ye must be born again."

I went to work drawing battleships as fast as I could all over my bulletin, battleships blowing up orange trees in a sea full of fish that looked like Lanny Spellman, and as soon as I filled my bulletin up, I started in on Lettie's bulletin. The preacher told us to imagine the world could end tomorrow morning at six A.M. "Are you right with Jesus?" he asked. I knew I was the blackest sinner that lived. That preacher's voice went straight to my heart, and I thought about all the times I'd cheated and said bad words and stole money out of the offering plate and picked up the other phone to listen in while Coral Ann was talking to Nick. I realized I needed to get saved, for if the world ended at six A.M. tomorrow, I'd go to hell while Lettie and Coral Ann and my mother and father and Grandma Roberts and Alta Reynolds all went to the opposite place. I know Nick was thinking hard too. He put his knife away and folded his arms and stared down at his feet. When the preacher asked Coral Ann to come play the invitation while the rest of us prayed, I told God all I needed was for Nick Deems to get saved and I'd be right behind him.

We started singing.

> Softly and tenderly, Jesus is calling,
> Calling for you and for me.

The preacher asked everyone to sing quietly, and while we were singing he kept on pleading with the sinners in the church.

> See by the portals He's waiting and watching,
> Watching for you and for me.

Coral Ann played better than I'd ever heard her play the piano before. She moved her right hand up to play the high notes pure and clean and sweet. I watched Nick edge toward the aisle. He was sitting near the righthand aisle, and I was closer to the left. Every inch he moved toward his aisle, I moved an inch toward mine.

Come home, the song said, sweet as could be. *Come home. Ye who are weary, come home.*

The preacher started to sing, and when he sang there wasn't a raspiness to his voice like when he preached. He knew the words without looking at the book. As he sang, he closed his eyes, and he didn't see Nick ease into the aisle on his side. I saw it, and I knew it was time. I got out into the aisle on my side and headed for the preacher. I felt relieved. That's what I'd have to call it. I felt relieved when I got out in the aisle, and I felt relieved when I got down in front. Then I saw Nick wasn't there, and I didn't feel relieved anymore. I looked where he had been sitting, and I saw him slipping out the double doors at the back of the church. The preacher stood by the pulpit holding out his hand to me, but he was staring at those doors too. The back of Coral Ann's neck turned red, and she wasn't playing so well. I don't know what got into me. I sidestepped the preacher and ran up the aisle and out the door after Nick Deems. But I was too late. I just saw the taillights of his pickup leave the parking lot as I ran down the steps. Inside the church, I could hear folks singing even though Coral Ann had quit playing. Pretty soon the voices stopped too. I could see my breath when I yelled for Nick. After that, all I could hear were the wind machines running in the orchards somewhere beyond the dark, and I knew it was supposed to freeze.

That was last year's revival, when I still played the piano and Lanny Spellman got beat up by my sister and Nick Deems used to come over to the house every night. I never did get saved, but there's a new revival starting up Monday, and this year, without Nick around, I probably will do it. My mother says Nick is dead. I guess it must be true. She would never lie about it. A lot of things are different from last year. Lanny Spellman's father had a heart attack, and Lanny got braces, and Ronald Reagan got hit by a car. Lettie may need an operation on her eyes. After that, my mother's going to let us join the swim team.

I liked it last year having Nick around all the time. I thought once he got out of the army, he'd come back and see us, just say hi. But he never got out of the army, and we never heard anything from him. I know they have chaplains in the service who are kind of similar to preachers and kind of similar to regular guys, and I wonder sometimes if Nick Deems maybe got saved over there before he died. It doesn't have to be a revival after all. You can get saved anywhere.

· Crazy People ·

PEOPLE GO MISSING AROUND HERE all the time. It doesn't matter how old they are. I'm out looking for my mother's dog the morning Corky Rollins finds a body down where the railroad tracks cross the Visalia highway. A lonely place to find a body, no houses close by in either direction, the orchards crowding right up to the edge of the right-of-way. It's the missing girl, the Fuller girl. She's fourteen and everybody knows her. She sold hamburgers all summer at the Jolly Kone, a little standoffish, didn't make friends, but she worked hard and kept on working there as much as they would let her even when school started up again. They've been looking for her for a week. Corky Rollins, on the other hand, is the sheriff's deputy in our town, and he's exactly my age. Corky came back from Korea thirty years ago with his arms and legs all taped up, and as soon as he got well he went to work for the county. As far as I know, he's never been missing. Then you have my mother's dog: he's sort of a setter, not a bad dog, and I can't tell you how old he is. He lacks a sense of direction. I don't know how long he's been gone.

I know enough to hide behind an orange tree while Corky takes a blanket from the trunk of his car and unfolds it over the body. You might wonder about it, why I would choose to hide. I don't trust Corky is why. I saw what he did to Thunderbird Wells one night, a cold winter's night when the fog was so thick you could look out the window of the Tack Room and you couldn't tell if the post office was still across the street or if someone had come along and moved it. It's tule fog does that, no sweet little fog like they write songs about up in San Francisco. The fog was too much for T-bird, who wasn't an Indian or anything. He wasn't that smart. He got his name from a bottle of wine, and Corky took advantage of him.

As soon as I can, I slip through the orchard for town, figuring a missing dog can just as easily be going through the garbage behind Main Street or waiting outside the elementary school for a handout, could be anywhere there aren't dead people lying in the weeds. I feel bad about the girl, though I've known she was headed for trouble from the day she and her mother arrived in Ivanhoe. Her mother works at the café, the one with the sign that flashes BREAKFAST-LUNCH-&-DINNER. I don't think the place has a name, but nobody cares about it. They lived in a room upstairs. The woman never looked after her daughter, let her run around town in all kinds of weather in a sweatshirt with the fuzzy side out and Levi's cut off so short the white part of the pockets showed. Cold days, you could see the hard points her breasts made against the sweatshirt. Ivanhoe's not the place for that. People dress that way up in San Francisco, but that's a different story altogether, San Francisco.

I get to Walt's barbershop by nine-thirty and take the last empty chair just inside the door. Walt's shop is the one across the street from the Jolly Kone, not the one over by the drugstore. That other one belongs to Fergie. I have never been to Fergie's. Fergie is not for me. It's Walt who stops hacking at Floyd Grissom's hair long enough to squint at me through his photo gray glasses.

"Didn't I cut your hair Wednesday?" says Walt.

"You did." There's a scab on my left ear to prove it, but I don't say that out loud. "I'm looking for a dog," I say.

Floyd Grissom has a girly magazine in his lap, one finger stuck between the pages to save his place. Floyd is not handsome. The barber chair at Walt's sits in the middle of the shop between two large mirrors, and when Floyd smiles, his teeth are reflected across the room more times than I care to count.

"What dog?" says Floyd.

"Kind of a setter. Blind in one eye. You've seen him around."

Walt turns Floyd's head away from the light.

"What did you do to me?" says Floyd. As if Walt could do anything to detract from Floyd's appearance.

"Nothing," says Walt. He lathers the back of Floyd's neck extra thick and adjusts the barber chair up a notch. A pickup truck goes by, its radio tuned to the Mexican station. We all hear the ranchero music from the truck, but we don't say anything about it. We don't look at Floyd.

"Sit still," says Walt, and I decide to speak up.

"Corky Rollins was out by the railroad tracks this morning."

"How do you know that?" says Walt.

"I know what I know. He found the girl, her body. She's dead."

Floyd Grissom takes his finger out of his magazine and pushes Walt's arm away. A little spot of lather from Walt's razor flies to the mirror and sticks there.

"How?" says Floyd. "How did she die?"

"Somebody did it to her."

The barbershop goes quiet except for Walt sharpening his razor against the strop he keeps hanging from the chair. The sound he makes is terrible. Pretty soon Floyd turns around and looks at Walt, and Walt leaves the strop alone.

Now, Ivanhoe is not what it seems. It's a funny town, rotten clear through, and everybody who lives here has something to hide. There are two halves to this town. The poor people live on this side of SavMor, and on the other side of SavMor is where the poorer people live. They call that Okietown over there, six or eight blocks of shacks and crummy houses. It's worse than living on Main Street, a little worse. There's a lot of crazy people in this town too. A woman named Ida appears in front of the post office every other day or so where she makes dog noises at the pickup trucks that go by. Ida is supposed to live over in Hanford.

She only moved to Ivanhoe because she heard it's a good place for crazy people. This morning, I do not have crazy people on my mind. I have something I am trying to accomplish. I am in search of a dog named Hershey. I look in the alley behind the drugstore where Mr. Herbert, the pharmacist, sometimes puts out food for stray cats. Hershey might be there. Cat food, dog food, I don't think he can tell the difference.

"Good morning, Ben," says Mr. Herbert. He sees me through his screen door, the one that opens onto the alley.

"You haven't seen that dog?" I ask him. In his position, Herbert sees a lot of things before anyone else. He's a smart man. He subscribes to several magazines, and he gives out awards at the eighth grade graduation. He's the first one who got suspicious of Dr. Simpson and how many of his patients were on Demerol. Herbert blew the whistle on Dr. Simpson.

"What dog is that?" says Herbert.

"You know, my mother's dog. Kind of a setter. Walks with a limp." I let myself in the back door and go around to the customer side of the counter. Herbert is counting a pile of long white pills, sliding them by twos into a plastic jar. Three boys read comics at the magazine rack. They look like they're getting up the nerve to buy a rubber.

"You boys go home," I say.

"Now, Ben," says Mr. Herbert. "They're not hurting anything."

"I guess you heard about the Fuller girl?" I say it soft, so only Herbert can hear me. I don't want the boys to hear.

"No," says Herbert. "They found her I hope."

"Oh, they found her." I take a Fresno newspaper from the pile next to the candy bars. There's a picture on the front page, a bunch of kids playing in the sprinkler, kids not much younger than the dead girl. They run that same picture every year in July. It seems to me they lack imagination at the Fresno newspaper.

"She was . . . how do I say it . . . she was stabbed to death."

Herbert's face, all but the liver spots on his forehead, turns white as the pills in front of him. "Are you sure about this?"

"I'm sure. I was down by the tracks this morning." I put thirty-five cents on the counter for the paper and watch Herbert's fingers dance through the pills until he catches two and pops them into his mouth. It doesn't surprise me. Maybe that's the way with all pharmacists. Maybe they all dip into their stores once in a while. A woman comes in after those boys, and it's like I suspected: they weren't supposed to be here. They move on out of the store one step ahead of her, and I'm not far behind.

On my way out, I pass Mrs. Fenton, possibly the oldest person in town who is still on her feet. She refuses to speak to me. She's a perfect example of what's wrong here. She moved to Ivanhoe in the sixties with a retarded daughter she kept in the house for seven years, in the back bedroom most of the time, until the gal from the welfare department found out about it. That tall woman found out. It's illegal to keep a retarded child locked up seven years in California. Mrs. Fenton was surprised to hear it. She said it wasn't illegal in Missouri.

Alneta Fenton may be off her rocker, but there are worse people in this town. She probably never killed anybody, unlike T-bird Wells, who stood six foot nine and who was seriously crazy. He made Mrs. Fenton look like an amateur. T-bird lived upstairs over the Tack Room Bar and Grill, and he used to invite the old pensioners up to his room to drink wine. I saw him carrying a body on the handlebars of his bicycle more than one night before Corky Rollins caught on to him. And it's just when I get my mind on something else, the dog runs down Main Street not more than a hundred yards away. I whistle, but he doesn't hear well. Maybe I don't whistle so well. Hershey gets to where the railroad tracks cross the street, then takes a left and heads for Porterville. That's forty miles from here. The way he has to stop and rest, I may catch up to him before he gets there.

When I think about it, it seems to me there's been a lot of murders in Ivanhoe. T-bird Wells took the lives of three winos; at least, three's all the bodies they found in the orchard behind the grammar school. Some little kid was out there running around with his BB gun, and he stumbled over the bodies, fell right in among them. They could have been buried better. Maybe the men who searched that orchard didn't find all the bodies, but I don't think T-bird was responsible for more than half a dozen at the most. Even winos count for something. There's others, though. Marna Walker's husband killed her, his own wife, by confusing her medications on her. She had kidney failure and heart trouble. He gave her the kidney medicine when she had heart pain and the heart medicine when she had kidney pain. He did it for years, then just played dumb for the coroner. And there was the Mexican kid who was dating Floyd Grissom's daughter on the sly. They found the boy and his motorcycle in the ditch one morning, and Floyd Grissom had to sell his pickup right away. Floyd's daughter went to stay with her aunt in Modesto.

Counting the Fuller girl, that makes six murders at least, and for a town of twelve hundred that's a lot of murders. One for every two hundred people. But what can you expect with all the crazy people who are running around? There's a man in a wheelchair named Deward who sits outside the library all day and reads books out loud. He would probably rather kill somebody.

I walk down the railroad tracks to where they intersect the highway, where I saw Corky park his car that morning. The gravel between the railroad ties has been stirred around, and a shallow depression in the weeds still holds the shape of the girl's body. There isn't any clothing left behind—Corky's gathered all that up—but a shiny blue comb lies in the weeds where the girl dropped it. I slip the comb into my pocket. There's also a piece of paper in the weeds, a page torn out of a Bible, from Revelations. I leave it there. It won't help. There's no way to understand Revelations, although people will try, church people.

The only thing this town has more of than crazy people and murderers is churches and church people. We've got Baptist, Presbyterian, Nazarene, Pentecostal, Church of God, Church of Christ, Church of God in Christ's Name. More churches than bars. There's the Highway Tabernacle down by the Korean woman's beauty salon. No Catholic, though. You go to Visalia if you want that. They've got a colored Baptist in Visalia too, but no colored Baptist here. No colored live here is why. Who can blame the colored people? Think about it. Every one of these churches has a preacher and a congregation and a softball team. And in every one of these congregations, there's at least one crazy person. Although murderers probably don't go to church much. Corky Rollins doesn't.

From where I'm standing on the tracks, I can just see a farmhouse where it wavers in the heat rising from the railroad bed, and I have to wonder if that dog has ducked in there for a drink of water or a quick one-two with some little bitch dog. I'm also wondering if no one in that house heard the girl scream. Maybe they had the television on. I can tell you who lives in that house: it's a crazy woman named Louise who goes to the Baptist church.

I went to the Baptist church when I was a boy. The Baptist preachers are the best at making a young person feel guilty, with the possible exception of the Pentecostals. The trouble with the Pentecostals is, just when they've got you feeling pretty bad, they start speaking in tongues and let you slip off the hook. Say what you want about the Baptists, they don't make that mistake. Louise is a case in point, a fully developed woman in every respect except for her mind. Basically, she's an idiot, but she has a Baptist sense of guilt. Once a month she gets saved during the invitation at the close of the service, more often than that if her people let her attend evening services too. One of the Baptist preachers left the church on account of Louise. Some folks say he'd borrowed a little too much from the goodwill offering, but I think he just got tired of saving the same woman over and over. Plus he didn't care for softball.

When Corky Rollins and I were boys, we played a lot of softball for the Baptist team. Corky was more of a Nazarene than anything else, but Nazarenes are terrible softball players. There never was a Nazarene in Ivanhoe who could pitch, and Corky needed to play for a winner. The last game before he went to Korea, Corky hit three balls over the right field fence and stole home on a wild pitch. It was against the rules to steal home on any kind of pitch, but they let him do it since he was going to Korea. It didn't matter anyway. We lost the game when I struck out in the last inning with a man on base.

I roll the newspaper I bought at the drugstore into a little bat and start swatting gravel across the railroad tracks, missing as many times as I connect. I decide to quit when I realize that's just the sort of thing your crazy people do. There's a guy in Tulare who sits and fishes in his folks' driveway 365 days a year, Christmas included. When you go to their house, they make you use the back door so as not to scare the fish. I stick the newspaper in my pocket before I start walking the tracks back into town. If I hear anyone coming along the gravel in a car, I can dodge into the orchards. That's how the man who killed the Fuller girl got back to town without being seen. He went from tree to tree, staying in the shadows. I wonder if Corky has figured that out.

When I get home my mother is settled in at the kitchen table drinking coffee she's doctored up with whatever she's got in the house. She's a regular drinker, and it has fallen to me to look out for her.

"Did you find him?" she asks, as soon as I walk in the door. I ignore her, go to the sink, and open up a can of tuna fish.

"Drain the oil in his dish," she says. "You know he likes that." So I drain the oil in his dish, even though I know it gives him the runs. His stomach's not good.

"They found that Fuller girl," I tell my mother as I lay the tuna between two slices of bread. I know without looking that we don't have anything to go with it.

"Probably ran off with some man," she says. I can tell she's watching me through the uppers on her bifocals. I know my mother pretty well.

"She didn't run fast enough. Somebody stabbed her."

"Is she . . . ," says my mother, "is she dead?"

"Bled to death. Multiple stab wounds."

"Dear God," says the old lady, and I can see for once in my life I've got her sitting up and taking notice.

"You have to find Hershey," she says. "No telling what that man might do next."

I choke a little on my sandwich.

"Poor Hershey," says my mother. "I'm worried." She pours herself another cup of coffee and taps her fingers on the kitchen table. I know she wants me to leave so she can get out her bottle.

After lunch, such as it was, I'm out walking again, which is what I do a lot. It passes the time. I walk past Corky Rollins's house and make a left onto Main Street. Corky and his wife, Evette, live in a ranch-style house with a stucco front, a lot nicer than any house Corky lived in when he was a kid. When we were kids, I spent half my time at the Rollins house. We were always going fishing or playing softball or chasing girls up and down the street. Evette was my girl before she was Corky's. Then Corky came back from Korea, one big bandage, and I could see he loved her too, so that was that.

Nobody in town seems aware that anything's amiss. Leon is standing outside the feedstore, trying to tune in his transistor radio that's been broken now for ten years. Leon is a three-hundred-pound boy who's always got that radio stuck in one ear. Thing is, he's deaf in that ear. So maybe it doesn't matter if his radio's broken. Old men are playing dominoes inside the Tack Room Bar and Grill, and Ida, the dog person, is barking in front of the post office. Carl Speakes, the school principal, is walking door-to-door smiling and selling raffle tickets. He tries to sell me one, but I'm too quick for him.

"Heard the news?" I ask him. "Heard about the Fuller girl?"

The smile falls from his face. He tries to get the smile back up there, but he can't.

"What about her?" says Carl. Everyone calls him that. Just plain Carl.

"They found her body this morning," I tell him. I watch his eyes twist up. "It wasn't pretty."

Just plain Carl looks as if he might toss his lunch if I tell him any more. I leave out the sex part.

"Do they know who did it?" he wants to know. He clenches his fists, and I can see how he's crumpled his raffle tickets into a wad.

"Looks like one man," I tell him. "He must have followed her out there when she was taking a walk. I saw her walking the tracks plenty of times. Have you seen . . . a dog?"

"Lord," says Carl. I point out to him that he's ruined most of his raffle tickets.

"I better talk to Corky," he says.

Carl isn't worried much about those tickets, not so you would notice. The principal's an okay guy, though. He's not from around here, which is a thing in his favor. He could be a pillar of the community if it wasn't for that thing going on with his secretary. Everyone knows about it. This community could use a few more pillars. We don't have a mayor or a city council. We have a water district, but everybody knows they're corrupt. The only law we have is Corky Rollins. And Earl Stone's rent-a-cop agency. One of those rent-a-cops turned out to be crazier than Leon and T-bird and Ida, the barking lady, combined, started wearing plastic gloves and a surgical mask all the time, even on the job. He claimed the Communists had spread large quantities of germs and viruses all over the United States, said the John Birchers proved it. The man was especially worried about rabies in the public schools.

"Carl," he says one afternoon. He went right to the Ivanhoe school and pulled Carl Speakes out of his office. "If any of these kids starts to foaming at the mouth, I want you to call me." He took his gun out and showed it to Carl. It was winter and Carl's face turned pale as the snow on top of Mt. Whitney. They had to tie that security cop up finally and take him to the hospital at Springville. That's very crazy when they won't let you live in Ivanhoe. They didn't even do that for T-bird Wells.

I head over to the schoolyard where there's supposed to be a softball game between the Church of God and the Church of Christ to decide the church league championship. I don't care which team wins. I'm just figuring Hershey likes ball games and he might show up there, along with the murderer. If you just murdered someone, you'd be too nervous to stay home by yourself.

Those softball games can be interesting anyway. There's always the possibility of a fight along about the sixth inning when the losing team sees the whole thing is hopeless. They don't use umpires for church league. Everyone says using umpires would be the same as admitting good Christians can't get along. So instead of umpires, folks fight. Usually in the sixth inning.

I remember one game, Jim Biggs, who was playing for the Nazarenes (those losers), threw a punch at the Presbyterian preacher's son, which was a mistake and started a regular free-for-all. We didn't have any ecumenical Christmas service that year, no giant tree set up in the street across from the Jolly Kone, and no ecumenical Easter service the following spring. The town probably never would have pulled itself together if someone hadn't called for an ecumenical support-our-boys-in-Vietnam service. One thing the war in Vietnam did that few people are aware of, it saved the ecumenical movement in this part of the valley.

When I get to the school, the Church of God is at bat, the Church of Christ is ahead by a score of 6–2, and a familiar-looking dog is running at an angle across right field, Carl Speakes coming along behind him sort of shooing him away from the school buildings. He can't run in a straight line anymore, the dog can't, not Carl, something to do with his balance. Word of what Corky Rollins found by the railroad tracks has already made it to the ball diamond, and the game has come to a complete halt. Miss Whitefield, who has left the post office early to come down and keep score, looks like Humpty Dumpty in her plastic lawn chair, her stretch pants pulled up over her stomach. Her feet won't touch the ground. I ask her why the game is delayed. She puts a Rolaids in her mouth and nods over her shoulder to the county patrol car parked alongside the school fence.

"Corky's asking about the Fuller girl. How she died."

"Buck knife." I watch her raise her eyebrows, one at a time.

"You talk to Corky, you know anything," she says.

I've not talked to Corky since he came back from Korea and married Evette, and Miss Whitefield knows it. There are grown men in this town who weren't even born then. It seems to me it's been too long for us to just start talking again. Like friends. Though we were the best of friends once, Corky and me. There wasn't anything we wouldn't share. I did most of his homework in high school, and he wanted to teach me how to do the high jump, and hit home runs, and ride a bicycle standing on the seat. I'm not as good at those things, but one thing I could do, I always could outfish Corky. I learned that early, how to sit still, and how to think like a worm-hungry bass. Corky can only think like Corky Rollins. I can imagine what it's like to be someone else.

"Ben," says Corky. "Can I see you a minute?"

I walk over to the patrol car. My mother's dog is taking a leak on second base. It's his kidneys. Nobody seems to care. There's another man with Corky, a man from Visalia who I don't know, and I realize for the second time this day how it's hot, how I'm sweating big moons under my arms.

"I guess you heard about the Fuller girl," says Corky.

I nod and take the newspaper out of my back pocket. I should have left it at home. There's black ink all over my hands, and you can't read the front page of the paper anymore.

"You know anything, Ben?"

Oh, I say to myself, the things I could tell you, Corky. The things I know about my little town. I think about the night, seven years ago, when they were looking for T-bird Wells on account of those three dead men buried in the orchard. It was Halloween night and foggy as the devil's backyard. All the little kids were going door-to-door for their candy, slipping in and out of the whiteness, and it seemed every other one was dressed up as a hobo or a wino. Someone tossed a pomegranate against the side wall of the BREAKFAST-LUNCH-&-DINNER, but there wasn't much ordinary meanness that night. Kids here don't get mean until they're fifteen or sixteen. Folks were trying to get their children in off the street, but the kids thought it was a game and went running into the fog, laughing, invisible as ghosts, especially the ones who were ghosts. I saw T-bird duck down the alley behind the drugstore. He was trying to get out to the railroad tracks, catch a freight maybe, leave town. He was afraid of Corky Rollins. A great big man such as T-bird, afraid of Corky.

I saw it when Corky surprised T-bird behind the feedstore, and nobody was ever going to believe what I saw after that. Corky gave the man a pistol. T-bird didn't want it—he acted as if he was afraid of guns—but Corky made him take the pistol, and Corky got back behind the wheel of his car and gave T-bird a ten-yard head start before he ran him down. He got out and checked to see if T-bird was still breathing, then Corky got back in the car and drove over him again. The car high centered on T-bird because he was so big. That part made me sick. Everyone said what a brave man and fine officer Corky Rollins was to catch a dangerous criminal like T-bird Wells in the fog and on Halloween night. I didn't say a thing.

Corky is looking at me. He's waiting on me.

"Can you make these people go away?"

There's no one left watching the ball game. All the spectators are crowded over by us and the patrol car, along with the entire Church of God team, which is supposed to be at bat. The Church of Christ team is moved into the infield the way they do when they're expecting a bunt. They want to hear what I have to say.

"Go on back to the game, folks," says Corky. They all pretend he's talking to someone else, and he has to ask more than once to get them back on the ball field. Miss Whitefield takes a new pack of Rolaids from her purse and half turns her lawn chair so she can watch Corky and me and keep score at the same time. I wait until the Church of Christ pitcher starts throwing again, wait until he has two strikes on the batter.

"I did it, Corky."

I watch him bite at the point of his pencil. The man from Visalia blinks his eyes several times, like that's going to clear his ears so he can hear me better.

"I killed her."

Corky breathes slow and keeps his face calm, but I can tell he's shocked, the way I've always been able to tell what Corky was thinking.

"What are you saying, Ben?"

"She was a little tease. That sweatshirt, Corky. I couldn't take the sight of her breasts anymore."

The man from Visalia opens the back door of the patrol car and motions towards it, meaning I should get in, but Corky makes him wait. It doesn't matter. I look Corky straight in the eye, one murderer to another, and let him know I'm ready to go to Visalia. In Visalia, they don't have as many crazy people. Fewer idiots, spastics, fewer retarded children. Very few homicidal maniacs. The divorce rate is low, and they don't let you play certain card games in the taverns. It's pretty boring over in Visalia actually, though they do field some good softball teams.

"How'd you do it?" says Corky.

"Buck knife," I tell him. "Ten times with the big blade. I didn't want her to talk."

"What the hell," says the other man. His voice is angry. I'm thinking I want to keep my eye on him. It's a long ride to the county jail.

"Sorry, Ben," says Corky. "You got it wrong. She wasn't stabbed."

"Well, maybe not ten times," I tell him.

"Not even once," says Corky.

It's funny, the things you remember in a spot like that. I can hear the sound of a wooden bat being tapped against home plate. The bat is broken, and I remember how it makes your hands sting to hit the ball with a broken bat. Corky puts his little notebook and the stub of pencil back into his shirt pocket. He turns to the other man and shrugs his shoulders.

"This is Benny. Nothing to worry about. You know how it is." He looks away, sees Hershey running across the schoolyard barking at a tetherball pole, sees Carl Speakes running along after him, sees the blackbirds rising altogether in one cloud from the telephone lines beside the road.

"Benny and his dog," says Corky. He points his forefinger at the side of his head and twirls it in a little circle. I hate that. I can see Miss Whitefield shake her head. She pushes her chair around again, puts her back to Corky and me.

"You better take that newspaper home to your mother," says Corky. He isn't even looking at me. He's watching the ball game instead. "She'll be wondering what happened to you."

A freckle-faced boy with red hair hits a ground ball to third and tries to beat the throw to first. There's an argument at first base.

"Did you see that, Corky?" yells Miss Whitefield, who obviously, for all her fine ways, has not been paying attention. "Was that safe or out?"

"How can you even ask such a question?" says the Church of Christ catcher, who is turning blue in the face. "Are you blind?"

"Just wait for Corky," says Miss Whitefield, "and don't get smart. Corky saw it all."

The catcher takes his mask off and throws it down in the dirt. The Church of God batter says something he should not have. It's not even the sixth inning yet.

I'm a little mad at Corky, watching his back move away from me toward first base, where batters and runners and infielders are all yelling and stomping on the grass. There are a lot of things I want to say. I guess I'm the type to keep my thoughts to myself. The main thing that bothers me, though, is Corky's attitude. I mean, okay, so what if it didn't happen the way I said? It could have happened my way. I could have killed someone. They should grant me that. They think they're so much better than me. Anyway, just because a thing never happened doesn't mean it isn't true. It doesn't mean I'm crazy.

· A Place in the Opera ·

THE OPERA ONLY COMES to this part of the valley in the winter, when the days are shortest and the highway disappears into the fog at every bend in the road. I turned nineteen this winter. Sometimes I feel old, like I'm the only person my age living in Ivanhoe. I may tell people to call me James from now on, instead of Jamey. I may be spinning my wheels. I may learn to play the saxophone, or take to drugs. I would love to see the opera again.

I was eleven when I saw my first one, *Madame Butterfly*. We rode to Visalia on the school bus, fifty of us yelling and tearing up that bus the whole way in. We had the mean bus driver that year. We were the ones who made him mean. I yelled with the rest on the way to town, but on the way home I sat by myself and thought about what I'd just seen. Most people couldn't follow it, all those white actors made up to look Japanese, singing in Italian. At one point two women were dancing on stage, whirling around pretty good, and when they collided, everything they owned flew up into the air, silk and rose petals and Japanese fans. I loved it when they hit the high notes, and then the colors, like fireworks, when the women fell on each other.

Maybe they shouldn't show opera to children. It didn't bother most people, but I was always different from most people: like in high school, how I got into the choir my first year. I had some pull from my aunt Reba, who lived in Visalia and worked as a school aide. Reba was okay, trim for her age, with wild gray hair that made you think of angry birds out to kill. She played the piano for free for the choir director, Mr. Muncy, this elegant white-haired guy with a face like a funeral home. It was Muncy who scheduled the opera, and Reba had a thing for him.

Muncy just about killed me that first year when the show came to town, *The Barber of Seville*. I saw the yellow buses pull in from all the elementary schools out in the county, and the little kids file into the auditorium the same way I used to. I heard the sopranos warming up behind the stage, but Muncy said I wasn't allowed to see this opera. He said I was in high school now, and I had to go to U.S. History where they were having the civil war. I was so mad I pulled the fire alarm next to the stage door; I swear to God it was the first time. I was crazy about opera.

That's why when Muncy told us the next winter the Great Central Valley Opera Troupe was coming back to do *Hansel and Gretel* and they needed a few voices to help out, I jumped at the chance to be in the show. I was a cinch to get in. It's all kinds of people in a high school choir. Those guys in the back row didn't know an aria from the Avon lady. They were after the credits they needed to graduate, a lot of fifth-year seniors like Tavio Ruiz, who spent some time at the Youth Authority. Tavio was big as the courthouse, and he'd take your head off if that was what you had coming to you. Before he went to the Youth Authority, he was on the wrestling team in the unlimited weight division. He sang as well as he wrestled.

Plenty of girls volunteered for the opera. Muncy had the tenors too, since I talked the show up in my section, how it was written by Engelbert Humperdinck. The other tenors who volunteered, the Holbert brothers, were new to opera, and they thought it was the same Engelbert Humperdinck from their old man's country-western tapes. Tenors could be a little mental. But the basses were the real problem. Muncy had two guys who would volunteer for anything—car washes, donkey basket-ball, religious films. All he wanted was one more bass. He usually got the warm bodies he needed, but he was having trouble with this one.

It surprised the man, it startled him really, when Tavio Ruiz smiled and raised his big right arm.

"Octavio?" said Mr. Muncy, as if he thought Tavio maybe had a cramp.

"I'm in," said Tavio.

Muncy didn't want to let him in, I could tell. But it would have looked bad if he kept someone out of the opera just because he was a big Mexican delinquent. That's why Muncy wrote the name Octavio Ruiz down with the other names. I figured it out later when I saw the costumes, the real reason he didn't want Tavio in the chorus. That's getting ahead of the story. Muncy chose three sopranos and three altos, and he tried not to make it obvious, but he was going for the ones who were small and pretty, which I figured was on account of Muncy was a pervert the way some other Tule High teachers were perverts. There was more to it than that, which I will also tell you about as soon as I get to it.

What I have to tell next is embarrassing. I was lovesick in those days. I was falling in love every week, playing the field with my affections. I was crazy about an Italian cheerleader who was a senior, but short like me. It wasn't so ridiculous if you would have seen the way she smiled when I passed her on the bridge between classes. Then I got stuck on a girl my own age, a swimmer with broad shoulders who I used to dream was crushing me half to death, just squeezing the sputum out of me. A new girl moved to our school from Argentina of all places, with a long braid that switched back and forth as she walked, right above her pockets. When she went home to Argentina I wanted to go with her. I didn't know how to bring it up.

But as soon as I saw who the altos and sopranos were, I excused all other women from my mind. It was the chief alto who did it, the first one Muncy chose, a beautiful Mexican girl named Teresa Cruz, not five feet tall, who I had never spoken to, yet had dreamed about before and after the swimmer. Those were decent dreams, such as moving to Visalia to meet Teresa's family, where I would speak perfect and respectful

Spanish, which I could not do, and turn Catholic for the sake of the wedding. I should have realized Tavio Ruiz was in love with her, too. Love has always made me forget things and neglect my parents and chores. This was a hard love for me, the worst.

We had to give up our lunch hour for three weeks to learn the music. The chorus was going to sing backup when Hansel and Gretel, all lost and pathetic in the forest, out of bread crumbs, did their big prayer: "Now I Lay Me Down to Sleep." It was a sweet melody and it satisfied the Humperdinck fans. Even in that hot choir room, which smelled of pastrami (no reason *Muncy* couldn't eat), and with my aunt Reba right in view playing the piano, I still got carried away listening to the piano swell up, watching Teresa outshine the other altos. The hard part was this dance we had to do, a two-step sort of thing. Tavio picked it up right away, and Teresa was a wonderful dancer. I was the one who couldn't get it right. Muncy asked a couple of the girls to stay after school to help me, and Tavio offered to stay too.

"No," said the Munce. He had to look up when he talked to Tavio, the way we all did. It made him nervous. "Just Jamey," he said, meaning me. I was embarrassed, but Teresa was there so I didn't let on.

Something was up with Teresa. I watched her all the time, the way you do when you fall in love. One minute she'd smile and laugh with the other altos about how the three of them were practically midgets, and the next minute she'd go sit by herself and stare into space, her legs drawn up into one of those red padded chairs they had in the choir room. Once, when we were getting our Hansel-and-Gretel number more or less right, she started to cry. She was definitely troubled, and she avoided Tavio. She didn't avoid me at all, which I took as a bad sign. Girls don't avoid you if they don't see you.

As soon as we had our parts memorized, we mixed ourselves up when we sang instead of having the tenors all together and the basses all together and so on. It was different this new way. It meant I could hear my own voice for a change, not just Tavio and some overheated soprano,

but it was nice too, once I maneuvered myself next to Teresa. I was singing better than even I thought I was capable of, and for a while I was
convinced I was the one who made Teresa get choked up, me and not
E. Humperdinck. So where, you ask, was the fly in the ointment, the
hair in the potato salad? It was foggy most mornings when I woke up,
and fog can suck the life out of you. But it wasn't the lasting kind of fog
that makes people afraid to come out of their houses. I had everything
going for me: music, a beautiful girl my own height to sing next to, a
place in the opera. I hadn't pulled a fire alarm in two months.

To be honest, which I'm trying, one of the problems was Spanish.
It was a language I could not get the best of, and I needed a foreign
language. I thought I'd go up to Fresno State for college. We all did. The
summer before I started high school, I asked my aunt about foreign lan-
guages. She took Russian when she was in school, and as far as I could
tell she spoke it like a regular Warsaw native. Reba showed me one of her
Russian books and told me to try to pronounce a few words. She started
me out with the American alphabet. After she heard me say a thing or
two, she closed the book and made a face like heartburn. She didn't try
me on the Russian alphabet.

"It's Spanish for you, Jamey," she said. "Two years ought to be enough."
She had her Russian book clamped tight under her arm, as if she was afraid
I'd see a word in there that might disturb me.

"Get Mr. Perez," she said, "and you'll survive." She talked about
Spanish like it was a long hot desert I had to cross. It made me feel weak
in the knees.

"It's going to be that bad?" I asked. But she was already out of the
room. I was hurt. I didn't think my Russian was that much worse than hers.

The more I thought about it, Spain vs. Russia, the more it burned
me up. That night, I caught a ride into Visalia, where I pulled three fire
alarms—one at Teen Heaven, where they have that bogus hotline, and
two at the Presbyterian church. They leave the doors unlocked all the
time at that church: they deserved it. I took care of stress that night. But

when the new school year rolled around and I got into my Spanish class, I found out Aunt Reba was right.

Spanish was worse than she said it would be. The first day, Mr. Perez, this tall guy but not as old as most teachers, droopy around the eyes, he explained how there was a portion of your brain where you stored all the foreign words you knew and how some people had a very small doorway to that part of their brains while others had gates up there you could drive a truck through. I could feel the door to my brain shrink as he talked. All the Mexican kids in the class had spoken Spanish since they were born, some even before that. A few of them pretended at first they didn't have a good grasp of their native tongue so Perez wouldn't bump them up to the next level. A couple of the boys made their pronunciation match mine, which frosted my butt, but there was nothing I could I do about it. I was short even by Mexican standards.

After Christmas, before Muncy started to rehearse for the opera, my Spanish class got better and worse at the same time when the beautiful Teresa Cruz transferred in. The class was better because no matter how lost I was, I could look at Teresa sitting up near the front. She was there like a fire alarm to keep me from losing control. But the class was worse too. When Perez called on me, all I could think about was how I was embarrassing myself in Teresa's eyes. I couldn't keep it straight in my head about *usted* and *nosotros*, and I never could roll an *r*. Perez used to make me say *ferrocarril* in front of the whole class, which is Spanish for freight train or steam engine, one of those, but when you say it right, you have to make the letter *r* about thirty-seven times. He made me stand up and everything, and freight trains or no freight trains, I felt the doors in my brain slam shut and the windows, too, curtains get drawn and dead bolts thrown. A house down the road from us in Ivanhoe was quarantined once, and the county put a giant plastic bag around the whole place. That's the way it was up in my brain. When I said *ferrocarril*, it sounded like I'd caught hold of the whole of Pismo Beach through a straw. Even Teresa laughed.

I went to Perez's classroom after school to beg him not to make me speak in class again. Aunt Reba had assured me he was the easiest of all the Spanish teachers, so it wouldn't do any good to change to a different Spanish class. I wasn't thinking about a different class. I was thinking I'd change to a different school, go live in some other town, learn to cook for myself, pick up a trade, all of that. Only I didn't want to stop seeing Teresa every morning. She was even prettier in Spanish than she was in the choir. She spoke the language well enough she could have taught the class. Sometimes she and Perez talked on the side and she made him laugh, but in a good way, not the way I made him laugh.

I knew they were more or less buddies. Still, I was surprised to see her in his room after school. I had to knock on the door, which was locked, and when he let me in she was sitting at his desk marking papers for him, which I was pretty sure was illegal. Perez was embarrassed to see me, and God knows I was embarrassed to be there begging for a break. People had started to call me *Jameycarril, the little Spanish freight train.* Only Teresa wasn't embarrassed. She was a cool one that afternoon, or I would have realized what was up. The part of your brain where you understand about love is right next to the part where you store foreign words. Or maybe all the roads in my head were under repair.

You understand what was going on? I was in love, I was in the opera, and in Spanish class all at the same time. Tavio Ruiz was in love and in the opera. Teresa Cruz was in the opera and in Mr. Perez's Spanish class, but Teresa was not in love with me, or with Tavio Ruiz either. Teresa was in love with my Spanish teacher, Frank Perez, and I think he was in love with her, and as I figured all this out, it broke my heart to pieces. It was like they'd tied me to the tracks in old Mexico and drove over me with the biggest train they make down there. I couldn't stand it. I was at home on a Friday night without a ride into town. I walked down to SavMor and pulled the fire alarm.

I used to wonder how they got started, Perez and Teresa. We had International Day every February, and Perez didn't care about that sort of thing, but he could have used it as a pretext to get her to work on posters or to plan the food they would sell in the schoolyard. The Spanish classes made a lot of money selling tacos and tortilla chips. You had to feel a little sorry for the French students who tried to make you eat snails. Or my aunt's Russian class back when she was in school. They cooked beets.

Perez asked Teresa to stay after school, and he gave her a task that would take hours to finish so they would be alone in the building, the sun going down. He didn't turn on the lights in the classroom. He let it get dark, pretending he was absorbed in their work together. They were painting when he noticed how late it was, as if he hadn't planned it that way. They had to go to the little washroom at the back of his class to wash the paint off their hands. When he noticed how the paint wouldn't come off, he took her small hands in his and softly cleaned the nooks and crannies she had missed. She didn't say no to him since nobody at her house paid that kind of attention to her, and Perez was smooth the way a lot of older guys are smooth. She wasn't the first to stay late. He dried her hands for her too, since he kept the towels up high where she couldn't reach them. Then he made up some story about the harshness of the soap, and he brought out a bottle of lotion that smelled of lavender or orange blossoms. In the dark, he rubbed the lotion on her hands and pressed her against the wall. She didn't want him to kiss her; then she gave in, thinking it was just this once, only it wasn't just once. She found that out later.

That's probably how it happened.

As soon as I realized Perez was way ahead of me with Teresa, I got my love for her under control. I would have quit the opera, but I'd already learned my part in the chorus. I couldn't let Muncy down. My aunt could tell I had lost my opera enthusiasm, and she asked me why, and I told her it was because of Spanish. She'd heard the stories about *Jameycarril, the human freight train*. She tried not to act amused.

I was burning with love before, but now I cooled off enough to notice how whenever I stood next to Teresa in the choir room and sang the Hansel-and-Gretel song, Tavio Ruiz was standing on the other side of her. And the way he sang amazed me. If you're a bass, you get better as you age. I went around for a week trying to make my voice sound rich the way Tavio's did. I wasn't ready for it. Muncy still looked at Tavio as if he was a problem, but Tavio was carrying the show.

One day my aunt, who had a cold so bad she was sneezing in Russian, took out a yellow tape measure and said she wanted to size us up for costumes. The boys were apprehensive until I calmed everybody down. I trusted Muncy in things of that nature. I had seen enough pictures of opera, I knew we would be decked out in tuxedos or dressed like guys in the Swiss Alps who wear hats with little feathers in them—woodcutters in knickers and suspenders. The truth is, I couldn't be bothered. I'd just had this vision of Teresa and Perez in the back of his classroom groping and clenching at the sink, and my heart all but stopped. I let myself be measured for a costume, but I didn't care about any of it. Aunt Reba wasn't much interested in me either. She didn't pay any real attention to what she was doing until she got to Tavio. She put down her handkerchief and measured him twice every way she could get away with until he got embarrassed. It took a lot to embarrass Tavio, who had witnessed things at the Youth Authority.

See, what I'd had was more than a vision. It was a revelation. I was sitting there watching Reba measure the altos and sopranos, first their hips, then their waists, then their busts. The girls acted as though they'd done this sort of thing plenty of times before. I would have memorized the numbers, only my aunt didn't say the numbers loud enough for me to be sure. Those numbers could have been valuable. When she measured Teresa, I couldn't bear it. I had to stop up my ears. Teresa had a beauty mark on one side of her mouth, and when she blushed, her cheeks turned crimson, like the rosé wine Reba and my mother drank on special occasions. Teresa's hair came down past her shoulders. She had to scoop it out of the way so Reba could get that last measurement. The girl smiled, all poised and full-to-bursting with just being Teresa Cruz. That's when I realized how it must have happened with her and Perez. She was the one who started the whole thing.

It was when they were working after school on those posters, or making phony sombreros out of construction paper. No, they were building the piñata they made every year out of paper mache. Perez wanted to go home. He was married and he had three kids, all of them in grade school, and his wife ruled their house. He was thinking it would be nice to be a student in high school again where you didn't have to worry about house payments and the dentist's bills, and where you didn't have a wife who was disappointed in the way her life turned out. That's when Teresa took advantage of him. She got him back by the sink and told him she didn't want to go home anymore because it was horrible at home. Nobody in the world was good to her except Frank Perez. Every time she spoke Spanish, she was speaking from her heart to his, and when she sang in the choir she was thinking about him too, not some little kid named Hansel. Then she burst into tears and looked up at him so pitiful and kind of raised her hands so he knew he could hold her if he wanted to. He realized when he felt her breasts pressed against him that he wanted to hold her, and more, but he would have run from the room if she hadn't rested her head against his chest so he could smell her perfume and her own smell. She had him then. He didn't get home until awful late and then only after he rubbed dirt all over his shirt so he could tell his wife he had a flat tire.

I'm pretty sure that's how it happened.

A week before the opera, Tavio disappeared for three days. When Muncy heard us sing without Tavio's voice, he considered having a stroke, and I dreamed of little red boxes that said "Break glass in case of fire." Without Tavio to give them courage, the other basses were going to bolt. And in the tenor section, the Holbert brothers were not what you would call reliable. Tavio was back in school on Thursday, which relieved a lot of people since the opera was scheduled for Friday, but the boy didn't look good. Muncy should have realized Tavio was in trouble. I should have realized it myself, the way Tavio kept looking at Teresa, as if he had a pain behind one eye that was about to kill him. When Tavio sang our prayer, it sounded as if Hansel and Gretel had both died in the woods after all, and he was their father and had just found out about it.

That afternoon, Aunt Reba had us try on our costumes. Always before, because I'm short, I'd shied away from costumes. I never liked Halloween, and I didn't take part in International Day. The band director once asked me to dress up as the school mascot, some kind of cat with whiskers on my face, but I told him I would not let him rob me of my dignity even if I were seven feet tall. I had complete faith in Muncy (who excused himself and left the room), but you can imagine my nerves when Aunt Reba opened the big trunk, the clothes she started to pull out of it. She brought out a pair of green tights, which I wasn't worried about because I didn't care what the girls wore. But then she pulled out another pair of green tights, and another and another, twelve pair in all, and twelve green smocks with buttons down the back, and finally pair after pair of wings that looked like giant coat hangers covered with Reynolds Wrap.

"The hell," said Brian Holbert, tallest of the tenors, who was all knees and elbows even with his regular clothes on. The rest of us were struck dumb. Aunt Reba stopped and looked at us slowly, one after another.

"Didn't he tell you?" she said, stopping to wipe her nose. Reba wasn't over her cold.

"Tell us what?" said Teresa. She wasn't worried. Teresa could have dressed up in anything and still looked beautiful as the queen of Spain, or maybe a princess.

"You're fairies," said Aunt Reba. "Or angels. It's hard to say. I never thought about it."

Nobody moved. Brian Holbert handed Tavio a pair of the tights, a ridiculously small and green pair, and Tavio stared at them like they were a strange woman's underwear.

"What about Tavio?" said one of the sopranos. "This stuff won't fit him."

Reba turned red in the face. Tavio smiled at her, and he kept smiling even when his shoulders fell. He wanted to be in the opera more than any of us, more than I did now that I saw what I had to wear. Aunt Reba went over to where she'd set down her coat and purse. She opened a box, the kind they give you when you buy a new sweater. Inside was a giant-size pair of green tights wrapped in tissue paper. There was a smock in the box, too, big as a tent. All the other costumes were frayed and stained after hundreds of fairies from hundreds of high schools had sweated in them and wadded them up and stuffed them back into the trunk. Tavio's costume was new.

"Don't tell Muncy I told you this," said Aunt Reba to Tavio. "He had me make these things for you. He knew none of their stuff would fit you."

"Gentlemen," said Tavio, as he watched the girls slip into the robe closet to try on their tights. "Come with me."

He led us down the hall to the boys' bathroom. The other basses wanted to ditch their green costumes and head for the great outdoors, and the Holbert brothers wanted to take me behind the building and work me over because of those costumes, and because I hadn't told them how there could be two E. Humperdincks. Only Tavio didn't care about the tights and the wings. I kept close to Tavio.

Everything fit, sort of. Brian Holbert tore the crotch out of the first pair of tights he tried on, but with Tavio's help he found a pair that wasn't too short. None of us wanted to put on our wings, but Tavio said we better because we didn't want to discover any problems the day of the performances. We had two shows scheduled in the morning and one after lunch. To fix our wings, we had a box of diaper pins. Nobody mentioned it. We'd just got the wings pinned on and were standing around looking sideways at each other, trying not to be faint of heart, when Tavio announced he had to take a leak. His costume was better than ours in every way. Aunt Reba had given him a zipper. He stepped into a stall, and it was touch and go if he was going to get the door to close behind him with his wings sticking out, but he did.

Hearing him make water made me have to go too. It was tight quarters in that room with six of us and our wings, our clothes piled here and there, and I was trying to maneuver around the others to get within shouting distance of a urinal when the door to the hallway opened and it was like, by God, someone please change the picture, because there they were, some kind of nightmare: three senior boys in Levi's and white T-shirts straight out of Okietown, looking for a quiet place to have a smoke. All three of them needed a shave. The last guy to come through the door could have passed for twenty-five, a little old even for Tule High. These were Ivanhoe boys; they don't make them that homely in Visalia. The one in front wore shades and he had his cigarette lighter out, but he forgot what he was doing with it.

"This," he said, staring at the lot of us, "is ugly." He tried to catch his cigarette as it fell out of his mouth. One of the tenor fairies went to pick it up for him. When he bent over, his wings hit me in the chest, and that sent us all shifting about, giant green birds looking to roost. The Okie who dropped his cigarette lowered his shades to get a better view of us.

"Tell me I'm on acid," he said.

"What is this shit?" said the oldest one of the three. He kept his hand on the door like he wanted to leave. "What building are we in anyway?"

The boy with the lighter stared me dead in the eyes. "Who are these fuckers?" he said, as if one of his friends would know. We bowed our heads. We were out there, lost in the woods with Hansel and Gretel. He flicked his lighter into a flame and held it in front of him.

"We're the chorus," said one of the basses, a boy who had starved himself over the summer so he could lose thirty pounds and walk around school with his stomach sucked in, hoping girls would notice.

"For the opera," he added. A weight loss such as that must give a person brain damage.

"The opera . . . ," said the boy with the lighter. He reached out and fingered the material of my smock with awe. He took a handful of it and flicked on his lighter again, meaning to torch me. I heard a toilet flush, the sound my soul would make when it left my body.

"Make way," said a deep voice. "I'm coming out."

The five of us in green squeezed into the space in front of the urinals as the door to Tavio's toilet stall swung open. Somehow, though he was dressed the same as we were, he didn't resemble a fairy. Unless he was the king of the fairies. He looked more like the Green Lantern, or Robin Hood's friend, Little John. His tights fit him snug and his stomach filled out his smock so he didn't have to be pinned together in the back the way the rest of us did.

"Tavio?" said the boy who had grabbed hold of my shirt. He let his lighter go out again. "You're in the opera?"

Tavio stepped up to the mirror and straightened the collar on his smock.

"Give me a cigarette," he said.

"Sure thing," said the boy. He looked around at his friends. "Give him a cigarette."

The boy who looked the oldest took a pack out of his back pocket. It appeared he'd been sitting on it all day.

"In fact," said Tavio, "give cigarettes to all these guys."

The Okie with the lighter, the head Okie, took the cigarettes from his friend and passed the smokes around the room. Some of us had never had a cigarette in our mouth before, but we didn't let on. We shuffled around the tile floor and tried not to poke each other with our wings. When the boy had us all lit up, he was out of smokes. He didn't have one for himself.

"Here," said Tavio. He knelt down gracefully and picked up the cigarette that had fallen to the floor, wiping it off and straightening it out as well as a person could. "I know you didn't mean anything with that lighter."

"No," said the boy, "I didn't mean nothing."

Tavio held the cigarette out like it was a small offering.

"Nothing wrong with this one," said Tavio.

"No," said the boy. He hesitated a second before he put it into his mouth. "Nothing at all," he said.

We had our smoke, the nine of us in that small room. Tavio pulled the smoke detector from the wall so it wouldn't go off, and I watched him do it so I'd know how. Before we were done, we felt as though we were old friends, and some of us fairies felt a little sick, but that was okay too.

When we turned in our tights and wings to Aunt Reba, she wrinkled her nose and made a wisecrack about what fairies do in their spare time. I was nervous about the smoking, and I was nervous about the opera. But those were not my big worries. I was feeling powerful from the moment I'd shared with Tavio and my new friends, Randy, Sammy, and Lon. I wanted to take Tavio aside and tell him what I knew about Perez, but I didn't know for sure who was responsible for this thing between Perez and Teresa. I had to get to the bottom of it.

I decided to confront Frank Perez. I was going to demand that he stop humiliating me in his class, and I was going to threaten to unmask him for his affair with Teresa. Walking across campus to his room at the close of day, I wished I had another cigarette, or a whole pack so I could offer Perez one and we could talk things over as men. I didn't care if he got away with it, no matter whose fault it was. I was in love with Teresa Cruz. I didn't want her to suffer.

Everything Teresa ever did surprised me, like when I got to Perez's room and she was already there ahead of me. I guess it was sneaky not to knock on the door right away. I pretended I was getting some books from an empty locker out in the hall, and I listened to them.

"It has to be tomorrow," she said. Teresa was pleading with him. "It's the only day I can leave the house with a suitcase. Because of the opera."

"I want to," said Perez. "You know I do." His voice was full of torment.

"But you have to be sure. You don't realize what you're giving up. You'll want to come back someday."

"I won't come back," said Teresa. "I wish I'd never seen this place. This shithole."

I'd never heard anyone talk that way to a teacher. She sounded old, except I never heard an old person say shithole. I leaned up close against the locker door, and right away they stopped talking.

"Someone's there," said Teresa. She had anguish in her voice, as if she might scream any minute, or break down and cry.

"I'll look," said Perez.

The door out of the building was at the end of the hall, a mile away, and if I'd made a run for it they would have seen me and known I was listening. I was standing in front of the tall kind of lockers, the kind they never give you until you're a junior at least, or a major suck-up, and it pissed me off to see two or three of those good lockers standing empty with their doors open. I could have used one of those big lockers. I kept a lot of stuff at school. There wasn't time to worry about it. There was barely time enough for me to slip inside a locker and pull the door in after me.

Teresa and Perez both came to the doorway of his classroom. I heard them breathing on the other side of the locker I was hiding in.

"I don't want to wait anymore," said Teresa. She was talking quietly again, but she was still close to hysterical. I could tell he had his arms around her: the row of lockers moved as they leaned against it. They could have heard my heart beat if they hadn't been so busy with their own hearts.

"*Pues*," said Perez in a whisper. "*Mañana. Vamos a ir mañana.*"

My Spanish was bad, but it wasn't bad enough. I knew what he said. I didn't know where they were planning to go, but I knew they were leaving town together. They were in their own opera.

It wasn't until they left, Teresa first and then Perez a few minutes later, that I realized the fix I was in. It was five o'clock and already getting dark outside, the way it does in this valley in the winter, and I was supposed to meet Aunt Reba in front of the music building. She was going to give me a ride home. Only I wasn't waiting for my aunt in front of the music building. I was hiding in a tall locker outside of Frank Perez's classroom. I'd been careful not to let the door latch, but Teresa had bumped the locker with her shoulder on her way out, and now I was trapped. I waited until I was sure Perez was out of the building before I called for help. I didn't want him catching me in there. When I figured the coast was clear, I yelled and I yelled some more until my voice grew hoarse, and then sweet relief, I heard the distinctive jingling the custodian made when he walked down the hall. Mr. Larry. I was cooking up a reason for being in the locker as he came closer, dragging his floor waxer behind him. When he turned it on, it started humming away, and I yelled again, this time as loud as I could. Mr. Larry was half deaf. He waxed that whole hallway from one end to the other before he turned off the lights and shut the door to the building behind him.

I wondered if Reba would look for me. She told me more than once that if I wasn't in front of the music building at the appointed hour, she was going home and I could walk the six blocks to her house or I could walk the ten miles to Ivanhoe, she didn't care. She told it to me in English and she told it to me in Russian to rub it in. I was ready to give up, but I heard voices, people whispering. I thought it was the ghosts of students probably who had died in my school. Lots of them had died, more than you can imagine. One of those voices tried a locker at the end of the hall, then another and another, as he worked his way toward me.

"These are empty," said this gruff voice like a dead man would have. I didn't even breathe. The voice was the voice of a grave robber. It was the voice of death itself. Someone jerked on the door of my locker, but I was holding it closed from the inside, and so he had to jerk it again, this time so violently I fell out at his feet.

"I got you," said that voice, and I looked up and saw it was Lon from Okietown. He had a short crowbar in his hand.

"Don't kill me," I said. "I've got money. I'm rich."

"I ain't going to kill you," whispered Lon. "I came looking for you. That wild-haired woman is calling your name."

"Aunt Reba?"

"Hell no," said Lon. "I ain't related to her."

He helped me to my feet and we shuffled down the hall to where the door to the outside had been propped open a crack. I was shuffling because my legs had fallen asleep in that locker. I don't know why he was shuffling. I could hear Reba calling for me. I didn't shuffle after that. I ran as fast as I could to her voice, and Lon ran the other way. I thought I saw a shadow at the corner of the building, a shadow big enough to belong to a huge Mexican delinquent, but when I passed it, that shadow melted into the night.

The next morning when I reported to the auditorium for the first performance, I thought I might throw up. I still had the cigarette smell inside my head, so of course I was thinking about cancer. And I was thinking about the shadow from the night before, and about the fact that I hadn't slept all night, tossing and turning and trying to see my way to doing right by all the people who were making my life so complicated. By the time Aunt Reba had the music started up for the first show, I knew what I had to do. Sometimes you have to stop everything and start all over. It's a lesson in life. I was going to wait until Teresa and Perez were about to make their getaway, wait until he had her suitcase in his car, and I was going to break every fire alarm in the auditorium. I wanted to see the cops come seal off the school and hold everyone right where they were until I could point out a real criminal, the man who meant to ruin Teresa Cruz's life. I wanted to see Frank Perez get arrested.

The first performance was nothing to brag about. We had only practiced our song once or twice with the opera company, which was smaller than I'd figured it would be. Just the two of them actually, Hansel and Gretel, and both of them women, which wasn't right, but they seemed like nice women. Hansel wore a white shirt and leather shorts. She was flat-chested enough to play a boy, and Gretel was pretty, if a little old. Her dress had a small white apron that made me think of cookouts. We stood in the wings when the curtain opened, the boys on one side of the stage and the girls on the other, and even though we knew those were just grade-school kids out there, and even though the lights were turned down low so we couldn't see them anyway, the twelve of us were scared to death. In the middle part of the opera, the first time we were supposed to do our bit, I never would have gone on stage if it hadn't been for Tavio. When he stepped out into his place with all his sadness, the soprano who played Gretel gasped. She hadn't realized how big he was. She sang and then we sang, but the only one of us you could hear was Tavio; twelve green fairies stood up there and moved their lips, and it sounded like one mournful bass. When we did our dance, I took Teresa's hand. It felt different from anything I had ever touched, so cool and heavy. The life had gone out of it.

We had a lunch break. Hansel said it was in her contract. But it was too much trouble to get out of our costumes, and nobody was going out of the building dressed the way we were. Muncy brought in oranges and water and told us how great we sounded, how it made him think of the New York City Opera Co. He heard them once on tour in Bakersfield. Hansel, who was taking a long drink from a silver flask, snorted all over her leather shorts when Muncy said that about the New York City Opera Co. Muncy pretended he didn't see her flask.

"Ah," he kept saying, "the opera, the opera." Muncy was a good guy, but I was hoping I wouldn't turn out like him.

I saw Perez come to the stage door, and Teresa walked over cool as you please and handed him her suitcase. It wasn't any overnight bag either, but a big leather thing with a strap cinched around the middle. She was leaving our town forever. Tavio saw her give the bag to Perez, too. He'd been sitting all alone with his head in his hands. When Teresa came away from the door, Tavio grabbed hold of her by the wrist.

"Please," he said to her. "Don't do it."

She didn't lose her composure. She laughed and made her voice sound hollow and tenor, exactly the way Muncy's voice sounded.

"Ah," said Teresa, "the opera."

Everyone laughed. She kept smiling, but she pressed her fingernails hard into Tavio's arm until he loosened his grip. When she could get away from him, she beat it across the stage and sat with the other altos. Tavio went off to the other wing. I had the sense he was going to weep.

My aunt was down in the orchestra pit playing the overture for the final performance. She had it down pretty well after all those weeks, but it was wasted on school kids, the ones who had ridden in on the buses from the county. Fog had permanently addled a lot of them. I hadn't thought about how hard it was on Reba until I saw her playing down there, really saw her hunkered over, looking a little ancient, scowling because of all the noise coming from the seats in the dark. It must have been tough on Hansel and Gretel too. Hansel had been at her flask all through the lunch hour, and it made Gretel angry. Gretel pinched Hansel hard, grabbing that little piece of loose skin above the elbow.

"Ah," said Hansel. The top button had come undone on her shirt. I didn't want to look. "The opera," she said. "The grand fucking opera." It made Muncy turn pale. He took a step toward her, pushing his hand through his white hair. I wanted to tell him not to take it seriously; the school wasn't going to fire him if dumb old Hansel fell into the orchestra pit. But it wouldn't have mattered what I said. Somehow, during all the lunch-hour rehearsals and the after-school dance sessions, the trouble with the basses, the costumes, this opera had become Muncy's show. It didn't belong to Hansel and Gretel anymore.

I was standing next to Tavio, who had a new smell about him, as if he'd been outside burning gunny sacks. He had his eye on Teresa. The way he let his head hang against his chest, it looked to me like he'd given up.

"I'd take a little of whatever's in that flask," he whispered to Hansel. Tavio's eyes were barely open. His shoulders were stooped as if his wings weighed a ton apiece. Hansel was too drunk to hear him. When she took the stage again, she could still sing the big songs, but she couldn't be bothered with her other lines, and Gretel had to talk fast to fill in the gaps in the story. Tavio found a chair on our side of the stage and settled into it. He groaned and the chair groaned. One of the other basses laughed softly.

"He's stoned."

"He's not," I said, forgetting to whisper. I couldn't believe Tavio would do that to Muncy, who had worked so hard to keep him in the opera.

"What difference does it make?" muttered Tavio. "She's running away with that dickhead Perez. She's ruining her life."

"Don't think about it," I said. "We can deal with Perez. Think about the opera."

"Why?" said Tavio. "She isn't." He pointed to the opposite side of the stage where Teresa stood behind the curtain, out of costume in her jeans. She had folded her smock and wings neatly, and she was setting the whole works down next to Hansel's empty flask.

"Run away, little girl," said Tavio. He said it loud, right across the stage. Hansel was singing, and the woman didn't miss a beat, or she was missing them all so it didn't matter. It was Gretel who jerked her head around at the dark space where Tavio sat. Aunt Reba didn't stop playing. I could see her down there, struggling against the noise the children made, angry enough to play through an earthquake. Reba was coming up on our big scene. Muncy came out of the shadows on the boys' side of the stage. He was counting fairies.

"I need to take a leak," said Tavio. He got up out of his chair and made for the stairs to the changing rooms.

"Not now," whispered Muncy. The old man ran after Tavio, trying to keep the bass section together as the crucial moment approached, but Tavio couldn't be held back. The boy's giant head looked heavy as a buffalo's as he stood in the doorway beneath the red EXIT sign. There was a sign just like it on the other side of the stage where the door opened out to the schoolyard. As if someone had given a cue, that other door swung open, and there stood Frank Perez, his car keys in his hand, the gray light of the afternoon at his back. I made a quick calculation where the nearest fire alarm was. Tavio stopped in his tracks and looked across the stage.

"You," he shouted. "Perez. You *cabron*. You molester of girls."

Everyone in the auditorium heard him this time, even Hansel. The woman squinted into the dark to get a good look at Tavio.

"What's with the fairies?" said Hansel. But Gretel was quick.

"Oh, yon soft fairies have aroused," said Gretel. "They sing as ne'er before."

Teresa went for the door, for Perez. She looked back across the stage once—I wanted to believe it was at me—then ducked out into the gray with him. Tavio pushed Mr. Muncy aside and charged across the stage after them. Gretel had to do a graceful little spin to get out of his way.

"My," said Hansel. "I've never seen one get angry."

The girl fairies meant to stop Tavio, but they weren't able to hold him back. They trailed out the door after him. Maybe they wanted to help him save Teresa, or maybe they just wanted to watch him run across the high school campus in his tights and wings. It didn't matter. I knew what I had to do, and do it quick, before Perez and Teresa got all the way to the parking lot. Muncy was beside himself. I tell you, the man's heart was breaking as he watched the bass and tenor fairies slip up the stairs toward the changing rooms. Brian Holbert had already torn the wings from his back. We were worthless without Tavio, and Muncy knew it.

"You won't leave me, will you, Jamey?" Muncy wanted to reach out and take my hand. He was too good a man to force me to stay.

I looked where the two women stood in the footlights, Hansel and Gretel. Hansel, good and drunk now, had given up on her part altogether. As they crossed in front of the audience, Gretel gave her partner a shove off the stage and into the dark. Hansel sprawled on the floor in front of me, tried once to get up, then gave in and lay still, her head cushioned against the thick red curtain. Aunt Reba played on. Some of the kids in the audience were laughing, but I remembered that long-ago scene from *Madame Butterfly* when the two sopranos smashed into each other, how we thought it was wonderful. Children don't always know when life goes wrong.

"It's you and me, Jamey," said Muncy. "She needs us out there. Let's not let her down." I didn't know for sure who he was talking about. He was looking at Gretel out on the stage front and center, but he nodded into the pit at my aunt Reba. Then he did take me by the hand. His was trembling and warm. I looked down to where my aunt sat at the piano. Her glasses had slipped down her nose, and her hair was all broken loose, but she kept the music going. Gretel started to sing the Hansel-and-Gretel prayer.

Now I lay me down to sleep . . .

She needed someone to sing the harmony, and I heard the second voice rise up before I realized who it was, Mr. Muncy, there for her from the shadows. He knew the music backwards and forwards. When he added his voice to hers, I could see the gratitude in her eyes.

God my soul I pray to keep . . .

Their voices filled that stage. For a moment all the children in the audience hushed their foolishness. I heard the faint sound of a siren outside, and I wondered if it was Tavio's doing, or if it was something I'd done and couldn't remember. Or maybe this time it was innocent, some sixteen-year-old girl getting a traffic ticket. On the stage, they could barely hear the siren, and then my aunt played a little louder, and I don't think they could hear it at all.

Gretel and Muncy sang their beautiful duet. All they needed was a chorus to back them up. Gretel looked at me. I looked at the fire alarm. I had a choice. I was going to disappoint someone.

Good-bye, Teresa, said my heart. Good-bye, Spanish princess.

Good-bye, Mr. Perez. Good-bye, Tavio.

And if I die

Before I wake

No more false alarms, said my heart. No more hiding in lockers. I was through with all that.

God my soul I pray will take.

I was with Hansel. I was with Gretel.

I was Jamey, in the opera.

Boys from
· Poor Families ·

IF I KNEW HOW TO TELL THE TRUTH, telling this story would be easier: if I knew what part of everything I write comes from memory, what part I was told later, what part I know on a deeper level of the heart. All I know to do is to tell you the whole of it, to trust in the story as I once trusted in Jesus.

The time I'm talking about, there were still three brothers in that family. As often as not there were four boys counting me who sat down to their table for dinner, though I was no relation. Anyone looking for me knew it to be true—find those three Foster boys and you'd find me, Isaac Franklin. Their house sat alone on a dirt road halfway between Ivanhoe, where I lived with my grandmother, and Goshen, where the Greyhound stops. I did everything the Foster boys did and when they did it. I sat through the preacher's sermons in the same pew. In the orchard behind their house, I smoked the menthol cigarettes Troy stole from SavMor. Most of the clothes I wore, one or two of those boys wore before me.

Troy was the only one who was big for his age. Maybe he stayed at his mother's breast longer than Darrel, the second boy, or Johnny, who was the youngest.

"A boy of great responsibility," said the preacher of Troy. "A boy who minds."

He wanted to be a policeman. Some days Troy wavered and thought about becoming a fireman, but he always went back to his first plan, which was to get through high school and start his studies in Visalia. They had courses there on police work, and a firing range.

"God's laws need to be enforced too," said Brother Slade, who wanted to make a preacher out of Troy. Troy wasn't as interested in God's laws, though it might have been different if there had been some way a minister could carry a gun.

Where Troy was heavy and bluff, Darrel was quiet. Darrel was older than me but not much bigger, and sometimes when Mrs. Foster passed a jacket or a pair of pants down from Troy, she passed them right over Darrel to me. He didn't complain. Brother Slade called Darrel "the sweet boy." If there was a package to be carried in from the car, Darrel appeared out of nowhere, his arms ready. When Mrs. Foster was late coming in from the fields, Darrel peeled potatoes or put the chicken pies in the oven.

Johnny was youngest of those brothers, though he was the one who took up the most space. People remarked at how thin he was. He ate as much as the rest of us; he just never stopped moving long enough for the meals he ate to add up. Johnny was like the birds that tried to rest on the power lines, too easily alarmed by the ideas that came into his head. "If I could just harness his energy," the preacher would say when Johnny Foster called attention to himself, but there was no harnessing Johnny. His parents did their best to slow him down with lectures and threats, and because it was the way they were raised, and their parents before them, they whipped Johnny when all else failed.

Their house sat between two orchards a quarter mile off the highway, oranges on one side, olives on the other. During the day I could manage the loneliness there, but after dark, flanked by trees on every side, the air around that house was so full of possibilities it was all I could do to spend the night at Johnny's. Every sound he heard became the footstep of a prowler, a stranger at the window or the back door. A thief would have found little to steal from the Fosters. They spent their money on groceries.

Even so, one night as I slept in the double bed with Johnny, we heard noises out in the yard. We heard the usual noises inside the house too: Johnny's father turned over heavily in his bed upstairs, and Troy threatened someone in his sleep. "Within an inch of your life," said Troy, and then he grew quiet again. It was hot for spring, though not as hot as it would get. Come June or July, the swamp coolers would struggle to keep up with days on end of temperatures over a hundred degrees. All the windows were open as that house sought the breeze that sometimes came to the orchards at night. I pulled a thin blanket up to my chin and squeezed my eyes shut so I wouldn't hear anything else, and still, outside, over by the garage, I heard a pane of glass break and a man swear roughly under his breath.

I wanted to be dreaming that new sound, but Johnny heard him too. Johnny called out against the night, his eyes wide in terror. Mr. Foster ran downstairs with a small gun in his hand, a thing I'd never seen before. From the back steps he yelled dream words, his or mine, before he shot his pistol into the dark. I heard a man crash through the weeds and the rusted car parts behind the garage. The next morning, Johnny made me go with him to look for blood. We didn't find any.

"Of course not," said Mr. Foster, who sat at the kitchen table pouring syrup over his pancakes. He held his fork up, examining it in the light like it was evidence for the police. "I fired into the air," he said.

"We won't worry about that," said Mrs. Foster. I liked the sound of her voice better than his. We had spent the rest of the night sleeping at the foot of her bed. Sometimes she was able to settle Johnny down just by talking to him.

"If you get him all wound up," she said, "he won't sleep again tonight."

"He'll forget the whole thing by tonight," said Mr. Foster. "They both will."

And I would have tried to forget about what I heard that night, to write it off as a bad dream I'd somehow caught from Johnny Foster. Troy wouldn't have mentioned it to me again, since Troy seldom spoke to me except to threaten me. He was like a lot of boys that way, the ones who want to become policemen. Darrel wouldn't have brought it up either. Darrel was embarrassed by his father's violence. But it was different with Johnny, who was often called a liar because of the stories that formed like magic inside his head. He couldn't let me forget the night his father chased a man from their garage. Mr. Foster had actually taken a shot at someone, whoever was out there looking to rob them. More than once Johnny made me verify the story, even to the preacher's wife, who took her husband's place one Sunday evening at Bible study.

Mrs. Slade must have repeated Johnny's story at home, because the following Sunday night, Brother Slade lectured us on the wickedness of lying. The preacher said if we wanted exciting stories, we could read the Old Testament where the stories were true, unlike the tales certain boys had told his wife the week before. And he ended, as usual, by describing hell to us, a place "where the fires can never be quenched, where the wicked suffer and burn forever, where liars and drunkards are even right now begging for one drop of water to wet the tips of their tongues."

Fire was important to Johnny Foster. When we were bored, we wandered through the orchards until he found a place to gather the dry leaves in a pile and set them burning. He had an eye for what would make a good fire. It didn't matter how often his father beat him for it, for merely having a box of matches in his pocket. Johnny took too much pleasure in fire to give it up.

We had the matches one afternoon in the Fosters' garage, and the need for excitement. The building was a shed, separate from the house, with a dirt floor and a single window caked by years of grime. Outside, the sun pressed against the silent orchards, but inside, with the big sliding doors closed, the garage was dark and cool. Johnny set fire to a crumpled-up newspaper, holding it in front of him by one corner, blowing on the glowing edge when it was slow to light. He tossed it on the floor, then ran to the yard for a mouthful of water so he could spit on his fire and put it out.

"Tragedy was narrowly avoided last night," said Johnny once the smoke had cleared. He didn't mean it, though. He was pretending to speak into a microphone, the way he liked to mimic the newscasters who came to us on the television from Fresno and Bakersfield. "Firefighters from around the county were quick to respond to a blaze at the rural home of Ernie Foster," he said. He wadded up more newspaper and shook another match out of the box. I should have known better, but he made it seem like a game, what we were doing. I wasn't willing to start the fires, at least not at first, but I helped put them out.

We'd gone through half a box of matches and three or four newspapers when a shadow fell through the doorway, and I knew we were no longer alone in the garage. I choked on a mouthful of water, afraid the shadow belonged to Troy, who would turn us over to his father, or worse, exact his own punishment. More than once, Troy had chased Johnny and me around the house and into the orchards with a stick or his fists. But this shadow was Darrel's, not Troy's, and right away Darrel could see what Johnny and I were doing. Johnny had a small fire going, one I would have put out if I hadn't coughed up my water. Without a word to either of us, Darrel unzipped his pants and doused the flames in a more interesting way.

"What are we waiting for?" cried Johnny. I followed him outside to where the green hose ran in the yard. Johnny put the hose to his mouth, but instead of holding the water in his cheeks the way he did before, he drank and drank. He made me do the same, and Darrel, and then Johnny drank from the hose again himself. When we had filled our bellies to the limit, Johnny made a face so we would laugh. Johnny loved to sing. He sang part of a hymn the way one of the old men would sing it, rough and off key with the spit flying. He made his voice rise and fall like the preacher's voice, saying the word "God" over and over, drawing it out into three long syllables. I couldn't stop laughing, no matter how hard the water from the hose pressed against my bladder. Johnny didn't let up until he had tears running from our eyes, until he had me thinking

I was about to explode. When he led Darrel and me back through the garage door, I was weak, clutching at myself, sure I would wet my pants at any second.

Johnny piled the newspapers much higher than before. "The fires of hell," he said solemnly. It struck me as funny all over again. "Get ready," he said, pulling a kitchen match from his box and examining the head.

We unzipped our pants, our pumps primed and ready, and we watched Johnny strike his match against the garage wall. He held it until he was sure it wouldn't go out on its own. When he lit the newspapers, we fell back, surprised by the rush of flames and heat.

"Now," yelled Johnny. "Oh God, hurry. Put it out."

He and I pissed with all our might, and we yelled at Darrel to join us as the fire leapt up out of the oily dirt where the Fosters' pickup had been parked the night before and would be parked again as soon as Mr. Foster came in from work. A blacker smoke filled the garage. Darrel backed through the door and ran toward the house. He didn't bother to zip up. Perhaps there wasn't any real danger—who can say for sure now? All I know is Johnny didn't have enough water inside him to put out the fire. I barely made a trickle myself.

"You too?" said Johnny. He thought I meant to run away like his brother. Before I could answer, Darrel reappeared in the doorway, pulling the garden hose behind him. I was never happier to see anyone, though at first everything Darrel did with that hose made the smoke billow up thicker than before, until Troy saw it from the kitchen window, even before he heard our shouts from inside the garage. He said later he didn't recognize the voices he heard. Instead of running to put out the fire, he ran upstairs and took both of his father's guns from the dresser drawer, the short-nosed black gun and the silver one with the white handle. He carried them outside and circled through the orchard in order to slip up on us.

"Who's in here?" he shouted as he threw open the garage door. He stood away from the smoke that welled through the doorway, a gun in either hand, and he kicked at the hose that stretched past him toward the fire. Troy realized soon enough, when the three of us fell out of the garage coughing and choking, that it was just Johnny and Darrel and me, Isaac Franklin, who had been caught up in Johnny's foolishness. Darrel only paused for a breath of clean air before he ran back into the garage to finish hosing down the floor and the newspapers. But Johnny and I, we froze at the sight of the guns in Troy's hands.

"You're not supposed to have those," said Johnny. He reached a hand out toward his brother, the way a man who is cold will hold his hand out to a warm stove. "You're not supposed to lay a hand on those guns, ever," he said. I didn't say anything. I'd lost all my words. Looking at those guns, I had to piss like Noah's flood.

"I didn't know it was you," said Troy. "How could I know?" He looked in through the window of the garage before he lowered the guns and pointed them at the ground. "It could have been anybody," he said. "I had to be prepared."

I knew what Johnny was thinking. He wanted to hold one of the pistols himself, to feel the weight of it as he sighted along the barrel at a tree. He wanted to run across the grass and dive and roll to his feet and pull the trigger at least once. But he was in trouble already; it was better to let the guns be Troy's worry.

"Pa said never to touch those," said Johnny. "Now you've done as much wrong as me."

The words sank in slowly. Troy's hands trembled when he considered what he had done: he had hoped it was an emergency, or he never would have opened the box that lay in his father's top drawer. It hadn't been an emergency, at least not the kind that would have allowed him to break a rule as grave as that. Troy watched the smoke drift into the orchard, a stain against the blue sky. He tried to map out the report he would make to his father about the fire.

"Let's forget this whole thing," said Troy. He kept his voice lower than ours, but he didn't swagger as much as before. "There's no harm done here." I didn't turn my back on him until he took the pistols back upstairs.

When he had gone, Johnny and I helped Darrel cover up the signs of a fire, but that evening Ernie Foster wasn't home five minutes before he went out to the garage to sniff the air and scuff his feet through the blackened muddy floor. He came back in the house and lined us up against the kitchen wall so he could look at each of his sons and at me. I should have gone home long before then. When Mr. Foster's eyes came to rest on Johnny, he unhooked his belt and slowly drew it through the loops of his pants.

"I wasn't the only one," yelled Johnny. "It wasn't just me." He danced on one foot then the other, anticipating the belt. "Darrel and Isaac did it too."

"Darrel will get what's coming to him," said Mr. Foster. "Isaac's not my worry. He don't belong to me."

"Troy," cried Johnny. "What about Troy?"

A low noise came from the back of Troy's throat, but Johnny didn't pay attention to it. Johnny couldn't have kept quiet. He was trying to save himself.

"Troy had the guns," said Johnny.

Ernie Foster's eyes filled as he turned to look at his oldest boy. He leaned against the doorway, passing one hand over his brow. He expected nothing but trouble from Johnny. It saddened him when Troy disobeyed.

"Pa," said Troy, his mouth quivering. "I thought it was a prowler. I thought he come to burn down our house."

"You thought wrong," said Mr. Foster. He wrapped the belt once around his hand. "You knew better."

It did no good to protest. Mrs. Foster took me into the living room, where she called my grandmother to come take me home. Through the wall, I could hear what was happening in the kitchen as each of the boys took ten strokes with the belt.

"The only reason I'm not whipping you, Isaac," said Mr. Foster when he came out of the kitchen, the belt still in his hand, "is I know you'll get it at your house anyway." And when my grandmother arrived, he gave her all the details.

Without Brother Slade's church, I wouldn't have seen the Fosters again as soon as I did. They were farm boys, and I lived in Ivanhoe, which we thought was a town, and it was weeks before their parents forgave them enough to let them out of the house, before all three of them showed up on a Sunday evening for Bible class. A conspiracy of sorts was at work that night. The preacher tried not to act as if he'd been waiting for those three brothers, and for mc.

"I want to tell you something about boys who don't listen," he said. "About what could happen to boys who disappoint their parents, and disappoint God."

He was off and running. Most of the time Brother Slade led us to the Lord by gentler means. His wife baked cookies for us and served watery fruit punch. The first of every month, he managed to buy soft drinks, whatever brand SavMor had on sale. It was a hardship on a man who earned as little as a preacher did. But that night he'd given up on gentle persuasion, and he geared up his voice to a level he mostly saved for Sunday mornings and outdoor meetings.

"Let me tell you," he said, "about the last days, about the time of judgment, about *the rapture*." It was the first time I'd heard those words; I knew it must be an awful thing the way Brother Slade said it.

"In those last days," he said, his voice filling that small room, "when Jesus comes again, the trumpet will sound and the dead will rise. Your Grandpa Cy," he looked at me, "and for you boys, your Uncle Lee, and every other dead person from time immemorial, they shall rise and stand before God."

I could hardly remember my grandfather. He was an old man even before he got old. Still, I loved him for taking me in when my mother left me behind, and it wasn't fair to bring him up. As for Johnny's uncle,

Lee Foster died at sixteen when the tractor he was driving turned over on him. He was hauling sprinklers through a hillside orchard. The mention of his name could make Troy's back stiffen and put a lump in Darrel's throat. But that wasn't what made Johnny's eyes get big or his breath begin to rasp. He knew where Brother Slade was headed with this talk. He knew fire was coming.

"God will look out over the multitudes," said Brother Slade, "and to some of those people, the ones on his right, he will say, *Dearly beloved, come with me. I have prepared a place for you and you alone.*" I could see myself standing in a huge crowd, and I could see that crowd split into two parts, one part being led away through an orange grove that had just had the irrigation taps opened up, clean cold water running through the green trees. "The others on his left, all those who sinned and ignored God's word during their lifetimes, he will turn them away with these words: *Depart from me. I never knew you.*" These others passed into a grove of dry and stunted olive trees, the earth packed and dry underfoot.

Troy did his best to look straight ahead, as if he could see through the wall in front of him into the next room, where Mrs. Slade had set out the cookies and the punch. Darrel's eyes were red. He wanted nothing more than to be in that group on the right hand of God. He didn't know how he had managed to get included with the rest of us on the left.

"Those people who are still alive during the last days, those who have not died and have not been buried, will have a different experience," said Brother Slade. "The Bible tells us there will be a general calling-up of the saved to God. The rapture." He used the word again.

"There may be three boys standing under a street lamp, and suddenly two of them will be gone. You might be on an airplane, and the pilot or the copilot will be taken by the rapture, and half the passengers. The rest will be left behind."

"You might be home having supper with your family and all of a sudden you will look up and see that everyone in the room has been taken to God, except you."

Troy leaned forward, his elbows on his knees, so he could study the floor between his feet. When the preacher's wife heard Darrel start to cry, she came into the room and sat beside him. She put one arm around Darrel and one around me and nodded at her husband that he could go on. That's when I realized I was crying too. Johnny wasn't a boy to cry, but his eyes grew so wide they filled his entire face.

"And what will become of those on God's left?" asked Brother Slade. "What about those who are not transported up to be with him on that final day?"

"The fires of hell," whispered Johnny.

For a moment Brother Slade was quiet.

"That's right," he said.

"What will hell be like?" asked Johnny, his voice coming hoarse through the clenched muscles of his throat.

"It will be an everlasting fire," said the preacher. "It will be men and women screaming in pain, begging for someone to bring them water, just a drop of water. And it will never cease."

"And the beast of hell?" asked Johnny.

"The beast?" said Mrs. Slade. "Henry?"

The preacher passed his hand over his face. He didn't expect any of us to show that kind of interest. He had to look around the room once before he went on.

"There will be . . . unspeakable beasts," said the preacher. "Not just one. They will devour you, and spit you out, and devour you over again. Their skin will be sandpaper and their breath will stink of the dead . . ."

"Henry?" said Mrs. Slade again. There was a tremor in her voice I had never heard before. Brother Slade took a white handkerchief from his pocket and wiped at his mouth. Darrel had collapsed in Mrs. Slade's lap, and Troy had his face buried in his hands. Brother Slade didn't know what to make of Johnny, who sat unnaturally still and pale. In fact, nothing the preacher said was as horrible as what Johnny could imagine on his own. Johnny figured the preacher's hesitance was an

93

attempt to cover up the true worst details of hell, the ones adults didn't want to tell children.

"Oh my boys," said Brother Slade. "Let us pray."

Although we didn't often kneel, we would have knelt that evening if Darrel and I could have found the strength to do it. It was a masterful prayer on the part of the preacher. Having put the fear of God into our hearts, he was able to calm us now with his voice grown full of care, a melody. I don't know how long the prayer lasted, but when it was over, Darrel and I were no longer crying and Troy had composed himself. Johnny alone seemed less than reassured. When we left the classroom and stepped out into the night, he stayed close to the rest of us. Johnny was afraid of the dark, of whatever he couldn't see or touch. Now he had more to be afraid of.

Johnny Foster couldn't forget the fires of hell, or the rapture, or the beast. On a day late in April, the hours of sunlight lengthening toward summer, all his fears were summoned at once.

I don't remember why he got in trouble at school that day, not after all the trouble that has come since. He wouldn't back down from a fight, though he was small and seldom won. He might have got in trouble for some less ordinary reason. Johnny had his own style when it came to trouble, and a way of taking others with him down the well-traveled path. Whatever the reason was for him to be held after school, the principal's secretary, a chain-smoking woman named Purdue, later swore she called Johnny's home to let his mother know he would be staying late. Mrs. Purdue said a woman answered the phone at the Foster home and took the message, that the woman laughed and said as far as she was concerned Johnny Foster could spend the rest of his life in that school room. It was obvious afterward, to everyone except Mrs. Purdue, that she had dialed a wrong number.

"I didn't think anything of it," said Mrs. Purdue. "I knew Johnny Foster pretty well." I can see her even now, standing behind the counter in the school office, her hair swept up and frozen in place, a cigarette in the ashtray in front of her. "I knew that whole family."

On an ordinary day, the older children went home from school at three-thirty, an hour after the younger ones. Johnny's teacher meant for him to take the later bus with his brothers, but she grew angry at his stubborn refusal to sit up straight and act sorry for his crimes. She made him miss that second bus as well, then softened and offered to take him home herself, a long drive for her that took her miles out of her way at the end of the day.

Johnny wouldn't let his teacher see where he lived. He let her drive past the long lane that led to his house, let her continue on past road after identical road until she came to a white house with lots of windows that looked out onto a big front yard. That house belonged to a family much wealthier than the Fosters. A green hedgerow continued down one side of the house all the way out to the road, and there was a pool in the back. I knew the place when Johnny told me about it later. His teacher would have watched him jump out of her car and run around to the back door, never a word of thanks. What she wouldn't have seen was the way Johnny slipped into the olive grove behind the house and waited there until she drove away.

It wasn't until Johnny's parents came in from the fields that his absence caused alarm. Mrs. Foster started dinner before she took a good look around and saw that Johnny was missing. She called the school and asked to speak to Carl Speakes, the principal, but it was late on a Friday afternoon, and Mr. Speakes had already left for the day. She had to talk to Mrs. Purdue, who was on her way out the door. The conversation didn't satisfy either woman. The secretary thought Mrs. Foster was a disgrace for what she believed she'd heard the woman say earlier on the phone, and Mrs. Foster thought teachers and principals and school secretaries were conceited snobs and liars to boot, the kind of people who had it in for boys from poor families. Johnny's mother put her apron away. She told her husband to bring the pickup around so they could drive into Ivanhoe and look for their youngest son, who might at that moment be standing outside the school gate wondering how he would get home. She sent Troy and Darrel walking out to the crossroads where Johnny should have got off the bus, where she knew her son might just as likely be hiding out from his mother's anger and his father's belt.

If you did not grow up in the San Joaquin, it is hard to imagine how frightening a place the orchards can be in the late afternoon. Shadows stretch from the trees onto the road, and the silence in the afternoon is more frightening even than at night, when darkness hides everything. At night a boy can pull the blanket around him and feel secure in a room where he sleeps with his brothers. But in the last hour before nightfall, if he's supposed to be home sitting in front of the TV or pulling his chair up to the dinner table, not lingering in those shadows, the orchards can terrify a boy. Johnny had always been easy prey for fear, and lately for remorse.

Walking home, he passed no one, not a car or a truck, and the loneliness of the road made him think about the trouble he was in. He thought about how often he made his parents sad and how that must have made Jesus sad too. For Jesus wanted to be his friend. That's what the preacher had told him. It was possible to cause Jesus to lose patience with a person, just as it was possible to cause Johnny's parents and teachers to lose their patience. Johnny wondered if he had already caused Jesus to give up on him. Ideas he had barely been able to keep in check began to slip loose from his control. He thought about the things he feared, and Johnny, a boy who never cried, felt the hot tears falling onto his shirt. He argued against it, the growing certainty in his heart as to why the road was so quiet. He was almost home, the sun by then hanging just over the tops of the trees, when a strange man stepped out of the orchard to speak to him. The man's skin was dark, and he didn't speak English well. It's hard to know exactly what he said. I only know what Johnny thought he heard the man say.

"They are all gone."

The man smelled of beer and sweat, and he, too, looked terrified. "They left me here."

Johnny ran the rest of the way home through the orchards. He thought the man was chasing him at first. He didn't see anyone, but he sensed the man's presence, always a row or two of trees behind him. Johnny could hardly tell when he got close to the house, he was crying so hard. When he saw the white clapboards, he forgot about the trouble from school, and he ran into the kitchen to find his mother. The radio was on. At first he thought the announcer's voice was his father's voice, and there were potatoes on the drain board, and a pan of water had been set on the stove. Johnny called for his mother; he ran madly through the house looking for her, for his father, for either of his brothers.

Nobody was there. It was just as the preacher had warned him it would be. Jesus had come and taken all of his family. Johnny alone had refused to listen, and he alone had been left behind. It didn't surprise him. His parents were good and wise, and had trusted in Jesus for a long time, and it wasn't surprising that Darrel was gone either. Darrel had never gotten into any trouble in his life except when Johnny led him to it. Darrel was different from him, and from Troy too, but Troy was secretive about things. Troy would have made a deal with Jesus and never said a word about it to anyone.

"The rapture," said Johnny. He stopped crying, not because he'd calmed himself, but because he was past crying, lost in the deepest part of his imagination where his worst fears lived. As a last hope, he called my house. He let the phone ring twenty times, thirty times, fifty times. I couldn't answer it. I was in the car with my grandmother, who wanted to talk to Mrs. Foster about a sewing project. I had begged my grandmother to let me ride along, but Johnny couldn't know that. All he knew was how unfair it was that I had been taken to heaven. Until then, he hadn't thought he was much worse than me. He wondered if the man he had met on the road was the beast from hell. The beast could take on different shapes and disguises. Johnny didn't know where he'd learned that fact, but he was sure it was true, and he was sure, too, that the beast was after him. He thought he would lock all the doors, and looking out the back he saw a movement in the shadows across the yard. He ran up the stairs to his parents' bedroom where he hid in the closet, pulling his mother's dresses off their hangers and burrowing under them in the corner. No sooner had he done it, made a mess of his mother's closet, than he realized the beast would smell him out. It didn't matter how well he hid. He bolted out of the closet and ran to the window. He couldn't see anything outside, but he was sure he heard something, and what he heard was in the house, headed for the stairs, sniffing its way across the kitchen floor. He thought of the fires of hell, nobody left to save him.

Johnny ran to his father's dresser and took one of the guns out of the cardboard box, the first one he touched, the one with the silver barrel. He wasn't sure it was loaded, and he would have looked it over more carefully if he'd had the time, but he didn't. The beast had reached the top of the stairs. Johnny knelt to pray; he couldn't think what to say. All the words had gone to heaven too, and the beast was almost there with him in the room. As the bedroom door swung open, Johnny pointed the gun with both hands and fired it three times as rapidly as he could, sending bullets wildly into the wall and the ceiling, sending one bullet into his brother Darrel's chest.

When Johnny's parents pulled into the drive, they saw their oldest son, Troy, frozen on the back step. He had been standing in the same position, one hand on the screen door, since the moment he heard the gun go off. Johnny's father pushed past Troy and into the house. He saw Johnny at the top of the stairs and the silver barrel of the gun. Darrel lay dying on the kitchen linoleum. Darrel was his sweet son.

My grandmother pulled into the driveway next and parked behind the blue pickup. She sat in the car a moment, feeling the new loneliness, the sorrow about the house. She walked up the steps past Troy, and I followed her, thinking I had to see it. I was never so foolish.

After the first shock, the picture seemed clear to me, but of course it wasn't. It was what Brother Slade said, as if we looked through a glass darkly, as if we were all driving through the night on Highway 99 in the middle of winter, hoping against hope we would just get home. There was a lot I couldn't see. I didn't know my grandmother already had cancer, or that I would try to find where my mother had disappeared to so I could bring her home, and I would fail, and drink too much, and go to church not at all. Mrs. Foster didn't know that one autumn I would come back to this house and sit with her through her final days. Troy didn't know he would make it to the junior college where he would take his courses to become a policeman and fail all of the ones that required math. There were more things we didn't know than we did.

Only Johnny, standing on the stairs with his father's gun in his hand, could look around that kitchen and see the future clearly.

· In Dog Years ·

BEFORE CARL'S MOTHER DIED, she called him into the room where she
lay in her nightgown, her thin white hair pressed damp against the pillow. Carl had driven up from the valley thinking it would be cooler at his
mother's house, but the temperature outdoors was uncharacteristically
warm, and his mother's room smelled sour and exhausted. Carl's father
had been dead fifteen years. His mother had stayed on in the house in
Oakland, alone except for her dog, a shapeless little rag she called Jack
London. She had named the dog after the street, not the writer, and in
dog years, Jack London was as old as she was.

"After I die," she said, "I want you to take Jack London back to
Ivanhoe with you."

"You're not going to die for a long time," said Carl. His mother gave
him a look of contempt. She didn't know how to lie or how to accept a lie.

"I'll leave you the car if you'll do this for me," she said. The car was
a Buick with low mileage. "I'll leave you ten thousand dollars."

"Mother," said Carl. "Please." He hadn't realized she had that kind
of money.

"Don't tell your sister," said Carl's mother. "Let her read it in the
will."

"He's an old dog," said Carl when he spoke to his wife about it that
evening. He told her about his mother's offer, the money and the car.

They were sitting on the front steps of his mother's house in order to escape the city's heat.

"Oh, he's old," said Carl's wife, "but he's not old enough. He'll be around a long time yet." His wife hated Jack London, and the dog would have nothing to do with her.

Carl's wife's name was Jana. He had lived with her for twenty-seven years, longer than he had done anything in his life, even longer than he had been a school principal, and that seemed forever, watching over the children and their teachers at the elementary school in Ivanhoe. Jana's father had been in the olive business in Lindsay, and her family had been wealthy when she was a girl until her father lost everything in a series of foolish business deals. He had gone to prison for a year and a half, then disappeared from her life altogether. In college, when they had dinner with friends, Jana wouldn't allow anyone at the table to order a dish with olives in it, which was okay by Carl. He had fallen in love with her because she wouldn't put up with nonsense.

"It's not as if we need the money," said Carl. When he looked across the street, the cars lined up at the curb swam toward them in the heat rising from the asphalt. Hot weather didn't bother Jana the way it bothered Carl. Jana's body was lean and tough, like the way she talked. At home, she rose every morning and ran before breakfast, first to the end of their street, then on the county road that took her past the last of the walnut groves and along the dry river. She was one of those people who looked good when she ran, her face a little red as she breathed hard and deep. She looked the same way when they made love. In the early years of their marriage, those mornings when she came in from running, he could go a little crazy. She knew the effect she had on him, and depending on her mood, would let him come into the shower with her or lock the bathroom door between them.

"Take the dog," said Jana.

"You're serious?" He must have sounded surprised. Jana and his mother had never been close. They were too much alike for that, though Carl knew better than to say so to either of them.

"We'll look after her little dog," said Jana. "We'll buy that house in Visalia, the one near the freeway. We'll take down the fence, give little Jack a chance to run."

"We will not," said Carl.

"We'll take a trip to Death Valley," said Jana. "We'll drive your mother's Buick. When we get there, we'll let Jack London out to pee. He'll be gone a long time. We'll call him and call him, but eventually we'll have to leave. There are coyotes in Death Valley. Poor Jack London."

Carl knew his wife wouldn't talk that way in front of his mother. Jana tried not to come into the old woman's room, and when she did come in for a few minutes to sit by the bed, the way Jana's face turned red, Carl could tell she was holding her breath.

"Take the dog," said Jana. "Get the part about the money in writing."

His mother's final winter was the hardest time Carl had known. It was a four-hour drive to Oakland, but he went up to see her every weekend. Sometimes the highway was veiled in fog, and he would get back late on a Sunday evening, his arms and legs twitching from coffee, his eyes heavy from staring into the headlights of oncoming cars. One night on the way home he passed a horrible accident in the opposite lane of Highway 99: a long line of cars and trucks had piled into each other in the fog. There were nearly a hundred vehicles, some of the cars on fire, and he knew there were fatalities. Among the dead would be children. He tried not to stop, but it was all too much finally, and he pulled over to the side of the road and wept in the dark until he was able to go on.

Jana was usually in bed when he got home. On those nights, Carl would want her to turn to him in the dark and know how bad he felt, to ease it a little, but that wasn't the sort of thing she would do. Making love for her was a workout. He wondered if she was seeing someone. She had lots of opportunities, with him away every weekend.

"How much longer is it going to be?" she asked one Monday morning. Carl had overslept, and he was reheating day-old coffee in the microwave. "I don't mean to be cold," said Jana, "but this is no way to live."

She sat at the table in her tights, waiting for him to leave so she could make a decent pot of coffee. She could take her time getting to work. Jana sold real estate, mostly to young couples moving up from Los Angeles. They would not move to Ivanhoe, of course; few people moved *to* Ivanhoe, but she'd had success showing the newer houses that were not in the town itself, especially the houses near the river, Oak Ranch. On the job, she wore a green blazer with a skirt or slacks that showed off her figure. She had never been pregnant. They had talked about it, but Jana had looked around and discovered she wasn't interested in her friends' children, not until they got to be teenagers anyway. As for Carl, he saw enough children every day at the grade school. He looked at the ones who sat on the bench outside his office and tried to envision what it would be like to have them for his daughters, or more often, for his sons. He could imagine it sometimes, and then he would remember Jana.

"What about the dog?" said Jana. "Any signs of death there?"

"He's a nice dog," said Carl, though he didn't expect his wife to agree. "She wants me to bring him home next time. For a visit."

Jana rolled her eyes. "Did you get a look at the will? Has the dog commission been written in?"

He didn't honor that with a reply. Ignoring his wife, though, was never a good idea. Jana wasn't used to being ignored, and she refused to make love to him for days. She said he was gloomy. That winter, she ran thirty miles a week, and her body grew as lean and as hard as when she had been in college. Sometimes he wished it was a little softer.

His trips to Oakland made him realize how much the world had changed since he was a boy. Everything was different, not just the streets and buildings. When Carl was growing up, his father had driven a bus on San Pablo Avenue, and his parents had loved each other, like all the couples who rode the bus and talked about Jackie Kennedy and the Beatles or whoever was on Ed Sullivan the night before. His father didn't have to worry about guns or drugs. Sometimes he had to ask a drunk to get off the bus, and women could get their purses stolen if they weren't careful, but that was the worst of it. When he was ten years old, Carl wanted to be a bus driver.

"You're the same as every little boy," his mother had told him, "wanting to do what your father does for a living." It was hot that summer too, and Carl and his father sat at the dinner table in their undershirts, waiting for Carl's mother to put supper on the table.

"This time next year," said his mother, "you'll want to be a park ranger or join the marines, do anything but drive a bus. It's how boys are." Carl wondered how his mother knew about boys.

He hadn't become a bus driver, or a park ranger. He had taught for three years over on the coast, seventh grade social studies, before he took the job as principal in Ivanhoe. After twenty years on the job, Carl didn't know much more about boys than his mother had known. He wished he had asked her more questions, and he wished he had asked more questions of the boys who sat on the bench outside his office. Those boys knew a lot. Most men were as smart as they would get by the time they were ten years old. After that, boys, and girls too, started to get stupid.

"Don't be stupid." It was what Jana had told him the first weekend he brought Jack London home for a visit. "Your mother hasn't got that kind of money socked away. And we don't need a dog. Certainly not that little thing."

Still, Jack London was at Carl's house when Carl's mother died. The dog enjoyed Carl's house, and he liked Carl quite a lot. Jack London tried not to be in the same room with Jana. Carl was reluctant to leave them alone too. He thought Jana might frighten the dog with sudden loud noises, give Jack London a heart attack, but he knew he would never be able to catch her at it. The dog had black hair and looked as if he might be part poodle. One afternoon, Carl came home to find him covered with dust.

"I sprayed him with floor cleaner," said Jana. "What do you think?" He knew she was kidding. He also knew she had started smoking again.

"He cleans under the beds while you're at school," said Jana. "It gives him something to do."

As if there wasn't enough to do. With his mother gone, Carl had to make still more trips to Oakland. He had to arrange the funeral, then settle his mother's affairs. His sister, who lived out of state, was no help. She had three children to look after, any one of whom Carl would not have been surprised to find in his office on a Monday afternoon with a little yellow slip from the child's teacher: *June has head lice.* Or: *Kathy Rae brought these bullets to school today. Says she doesn't know how they got in her lunch box.*

His mother had remembered to write the part into her will about the ten thousand dollars. That surprised Carl. He was not surprised when his sister called, suddenly wanting the dog.

"You don't have a dog?" asked Carl.

"We have dogs," said his sister, who lived in a small town in eastern Oregon. He had never been to her home. Her husband, a mechanic, didn't care for Carl. Carl's sister referred to their home as the acreage.

"We put up a new pole barn on the acreage," she once said, and another time, "Ed's out bush-hogging the right-of-way to the acreage." Carl had no idea what she was talking about.

"We have outside dogs," said his sister. "You don't let huskies in the house."

"How many do you have?" asked Carl.

"We had four around here yesterday," said his sister. "Beau and Tripod get along, and Zeke is a dog nobody messes with. It's the little female who's missing. She probably just had enough."

Jack London, who was lying in Carl's lap, must have sensed Carl's uneasiness. He opened one eye and nudged Carl's free hand.

"We don't have a house dog," said Carl's sister. "I'm sure I can get Ed to let Mom's dog come inside."

After he talked to his sister, Carl went to bed. He had agreed to send his sister a check for half the money his mother had earmarked for the care of Jack London. In the dark, he heard one of the dogs from the neighborhood bark twice, then stop, and he wondered who that dog belonged to. Reaching out to his wife, he felt something firm. He had to move his hand up and down before he was sure he was touching her arm.

"Is your sister going to take the dog?"

Carl wondered how much Jana had heard. He wasn't a good liar, and it had always been difficult to deceive Jana, even before she started selling real estate.

"It would be a death sentence," said Carl, deciding on the truth. "If the big dogs didn't kill him, Ed would step on him with those boots he wears."

"You're going to keep that ridiculous dog," said Jana.

"I guess so," said Carl.

She got up and went to the living room to smoke. She wore a thin robe, and Carl could see the shadowy curves of her shoulders and hips as she passed through the bedroom door.

The dog lived for three years after Carl's mother passed away. Jana bought a rowing machine and won a day at a spa over on the coast by having the least amount of body fat of anyone in her aerobics class. She cut down on her smoking, and for Christmas she bought Carl a racquet and a video on racquetball. She put Carl on her membership at the health club in Visalia. But Jana and the dog never came to an agreement. When Jack London died, Carl watched his wife to see if she was pleased. Somehow the dog had dug his way under the gate that led to the neighbor's yard. The neighbor's Siamese cat chased him into the street where he was hit by a car. Carl was home when it happened; he was getting ready to mow the lawn, so he saw the whole thing. But he couldn't stop thinking his wife had a hand in it. He studied the hole under the gate before he drove to the vet and let Dr. Haggard dispose of Jack London. He didn't want to know how Dr. Haggard did it, the disposal. Carl's mother had been buried in a cemetery in Oakland, and Carl hadn't been able to visit her grave since the funeral service.

"What about us?" he asked his wife later that afternoon. He had finished the mowing, and he was sitting in a lawn chair drinking a glass of iced tea, his shirt soaked with sweat. His wife sat at her rowing machine. Carl wondered how many miles she racked up every day, and if they were nautical miles.

"What do you mean," she said, "*what about us*?" She hardly sounded out of breath, not half as winded as he sounded when he mowed the lawn. From all her training, she was stronger than he was now. If they were ever in an emergency—if, say, their car went into the river, and if the river actually had any water in it—she would have to help him to safety, not the other way around.

"Where will we be buried?" asked Carl.

"You want to be buried," said Jana, "you better outlive me. When you die, I'm not paying anybody for a hole in the ground. And don't think you're going to bury me either. I haven't kept in shape so the worms could have a meal."

"You want to be cremated?" said Carl.

"Why not?" said Jana. She got off the rowing machine and stretched in her Lycra. Her small breasts looked as if they had never known gravity. When she went in to take her shower, Carl followed her with his eyes. He could see her pull off her clothes in the doorway between the shower and the bedroom. She knew he was watching.

"Oh, all right," she said, meaning he could join her, but he got up and put the lawn mower away first. He knew she was still expecting him to come to her. He put on a clean T-shirt and drove to the Shell station, where he bought a carton of ice cream and asked for a plastic spoon. The rest of the afternoon, he drove around listening to a ball game on the radio.

That fall, Carl's longtime secretary, Mrs. Purdue, had to retire early, having ruined her health from years of cigarettes and bad coffee. When

Mrs. Purdue fell ill, Carl wanted to point out to his wife once again the dangers of smoking, but Jana told him she would rather die of emphysema than be fat.

"Smoking was the least of that woman's problems," said Jana, who had driven up to Monterey for a week of golf. "This time, get someone who knows how to answer the telephone."

With his wife out of town, Carl wasn't able to ask for Jana's advice as he interviewed the women who wanted to be his new secretary. A dozen women, far more than he had expected, had managed to get their names on the list. Mrs. Arronson came on the second day of interviews, the third candidate of the morning. Mrs. Arronson was younger than Mrs. Purdue, and Mrs. Arronson didn't smoke.

"I haven't worked since my second child was born," said Mrs. Arronson. She had a pretty face and long curly hair that tumbled down her shoulders, only occasionally needing to be tucked behind her ears. She wasn't thin, but she wore loose-fitting clothes in pale colors and appeared to be in good health.

"My typing skills are a little rusty."

"That's not so important," said Carl. He didn't want to hear about her inadequacies. He didn't want to interview any more secretaries. "We have computers. You can make mistakes now. Mrs. Purdue made mistakes."

Mrs. Arronson smiled at him. Carl supposed she thought he was being kind.

"Are your children in our school?" he asked.

She told him they were, described a girl in the eighth grade and a boy in the third. Carl couldn't picture which children she was talking about. He didn't think he had ever seen them on the bench outside his office.

"They're nice kids," said Mrs. Arronson. "They look like their father. He's supposed to pay support, but he's not very good at it."

Carl knew he was going to give her the job.

"Do you exercise?" he asked.

"Pardon me?" said Mrs. Arronson. Her full cheeks had turned red, though she kept smiling.

"I was just wondering," he said, "if you'd like to do playground duty sometimes."

He was turning red too. He wondered why he had asked about exercise. Mrs. Purdue had never set foot on the playground. She was afraid of snakes.

"Do you like pets?" he asked, and this time he had to look down at his desk. She was giving him a puzzled look, her young face framed by dark curls.

"Sometimes the teachers keep hamsters or mice in their classrooms," said Carl.

She pretended to understand what he was getting at.

"My husband always kept a dog," said Mrs. Arronson. "But I was the one who cared for it."

"Some people are just dog people," said Carl, and he was happy when Mrs. Arronson agreed with him.

He had been in the habit of taking Jack London for a walk every evening, allowing the dog to defecate on his neighbors' front lawns in Oak Ranch while they were inside watching television. Without Jack London, Carl had no good reason to be out wandering around after dark, so he stayed indoors and watched TV like everyone else on his street, a package of cookies or a bowl of ice cream in his lap. He had put on a few pounds since Jack London died, and he needed to buy some new clothes, one size larger in the waist and around the neck. He thought about asking Jana to go shopping with him in Visalia or maybe up to Fresno, but she had begun subscribing to a magazine for triathletes, and he didn't want to stand in front of a mirror while her eyes weighed him.

They were having dinner a little later in the evenings. She swam at the health club in town from six to seven. Sometimes he drove in after he left school and had a soft drink or a sandwich, sitting at a table on a little balcony above the pool and watching her swim. She had a funny hitch to her stroke. It made her human somehow, but the lifeguard was trying to help her with that. She looked up at the young lifeguard gratefully, happy, as she stood in the shallow end of the pool trying to follow his advice. After she swam, she would join Carl on the balcony. If he had already eaten, she would pass on dinner, lighting up a cigarette once they were out of the building and making their way across the parking lot.

"I thought this was a health club," he said to her once. She gave him a short dark look that made his face burn with embarrassment.

Once in a while Carl walked around the indoor track or sat in the Jacuzzi. He would have used the Jacuzzi more often if it had been for both men and women. He liked to talk to women and to hear them talk to each other. He was uncomfortable in a Jacuzzi with men. Most of the men were younger and in better shape, in off the racquetball courts or the stair-climbing machines. Their stomachs were tight and flat, and it made him stay in the water until they were gone, until he figured they would be finished using the showers too.

And once in a while the club gave each of its patrons a coupon for a free day to promote the facilities. The management hoped the coupons would be passed along to prospective new members. Carl usually forgot to give his coupon to anyone, but the fall Mrs. Arronson came to work for him he remembered to take the piece of paper to school, and he set it on her desk shyly. She was pleased to have it; at the end of the day she thought she had lost it and was nearly in tears until she found the coupon lying underneath her chair. Several days later, when he drove into Visalia to meet Jana at the club, he saw Mrs. Arronson's Subaru in the parking lot. He got out of his car, the Buick his mother had left him, and felt the hood of Mrs. Arronson's car to see how long she had been there. He had seen a detective do that in a movie. It made him feel foolish since he didn't know how warm the hood was supposed to be. He went over and felt the hood of his own car to have something to compare it to.

Carl wondered what kind of exercise she would do. He tried to picture her playing racquetball, but it was too violent an activity for Mrs. Arronson. As he passed the front desk, he saw her in a large room full of stationary bikes and mechanical stairs, and he wondered if he should wave. She wore an old pair of sweat pants, nothing as fancy as the clothes Jana wore. Her face was red and sweaty, and her hair had lost some of its curl. She pedaled one of the bikes slowly, her mouth pressed into a firm smile.

He ordered a milkshake at the bar and took it up to his usual table, wishing he could order something with gin and wondering if he was drinking too much of the real stuff these days, the way the glass of ice cream trembled in his hand. Carl could see Jana swimming, and he thought she had made progress with her stroke. She no longer fought the water. He had settled deep into his chair, forbidding himself to do more than sip at his milkshake, when he felt his heart leap in his chest: Mrs. Arronson was coming through the door from the women's locker room in a blue and red swimming suit, one he supposed she had bought just for this afternoon. Her legs, especially her thighs, were a milky white from lack of exposure to the sun. She was large without being obese, her breasts swaying a bit as she walked. The lifeguard watched her too, perhaps because she was new to the club and it was his job to watch her, but she wasn't self-conscious. She lowered herself into the pool at the ladder, pausing as the water reached the bottom of her suit. She hadn't seen Carl where he sat on the balcony, and he decided not to call out to her. Once she was accustomed to the water, she began to swim steadily toward the other end, lifting each pale arm and placing it carefully before her. She reminded him of the larger beautiful fishes he had seen at Marine World.

Carl had the uncomfortable feeling someone was staring at him. He swallowed a little of his milkshake, then looked down where his wife stood at the end of her lane. She looked up at him, then at Mrs. Arronson, then turned away in disgust.

The first time he kissed Mrs. Arronson, it was a Friday afternoon and everyone else had gone home. The school custodians who doubled as bus drivers had already come back from the late bus run and left, for good this time, in their ancient pickups and sedans. She came into his office with the forms he had to sign to order sixth grade science books. Mrs. Arronson took the signed forms from him and set them on the corner of his desk. She remained standing close to him, and when he put his arms around her, she closed her eyes and waited to be kissed.

"Carl," she whispered. It was the first time she had spoken his name. She said his name again when he locked his office door and closed the venetian blinds. He turned off the lights.

They didn't make love that first afternoon. Her milky skin glowed in the faint light that entered his office from outside the window, and he kissed her again and again. They did a slow dance around his office, without a radio or music of any kind, holding each other very tight. Afterward they sat together on the bench outside his office, and he tried to remember the report the district superintendent had sent out about sexual harassment.

"Don't worry," said Mrs. Arronson, who he felt he could call Sylvia now, especially since she was calling him Carl. She held out a hand and stroked his chest. "You didn't ask me to stay late."

The next Monday, he had the custodians move a sofa from the teachers' lounge into his office. He did it first thing in the morning when none of the teachers were in the lounge to argue. When Mrs. Arronson, Sylvia, came in to get his signature on a purchase order, she looked at the sofa and reddened.

"Carl," she whispered. "I've never even met your wife."

"You wouldn't want to," said Carl. "She's a lot different from you."

He was surprised he could keep his feelings for Sylvia a secret. Friday afternoons were the only time they could be together, and his routines with Jana didn't change. He met his wife at the health club in Visalia twice a week. He didn't want to make love to her anymore, and Jana noticed that, though at first she didn't mind. When, after three weeks, she mentioned it, he told her he was getting older and he had talked it over with his friends and they were all slowing down. One Sunday evening, Jana coaxed him into going to bed early, and he felt enormously sad afterward, as if he had cheated on Sylvia.

"I can look for another job," said Sylvia. "If this is a midlife thing for you, maybe I should go."

"I don't think it is," said Carl. It was Wednesday during the lunch hour, and he had closed the blinds and locked the door. He had his face buried in Sylvia's hair when the phone rang. He ignored the first three rings, then picked it up and said hello into it as calmly as he could.

"I know what you're up to," said the voice on the phone. It was Jana. "I'm not a fool."

"What do you mean?" said Carl. He kept his voice calm, but he had to sit down. Sylvia turned away from him.

"Tell that woman to get out of your office."

"What woman?" said Carl.

"Don't lie to me," said Jana. "Don't make yourself ridiculous."

But he made himself ridiculous all that winter and into the spring. The custodians smiled at him as they left for home on Friday afternoons. Some of the parents avoided shaking hands with him at Parent-Teacher Night. A local minister wrote him a letter saying the whole town was laughing at his foolish sin. Carl tried to ignore him; he tried to ignore them all. He tried to concentrate on his job, and he tried to enjoy being with Sylvia.

The passing of time made little impression on him until the month of June arrived, and eighth grade graduation, the twenty-third graduation Carl had presided over. He felt completely unprepared. He had not done any of the things he was supposed to do. He had not submitted the paperwork to repave the outdoor basketball courts, nor had he made the formal request to have the number two school bus replaced. He had not fired Sylvia, the way his wife had insisted. He had not prepared a speech with which to send these graduates on to high school. He had not done any productive work in more than a month, had just let the school coast along under its own dwindling momentum. Jana had given him her ultimatum a week earlier on a Friday evening when he came home after midnight, satiated by Sylvia and chocolate ice cream. Jana was sitting in the dark smoking when he came in.

"I've been patient," she said.

"Yes," said Carl. "I suppose you have."

"You have to make up your mind. It's me or that Arronson woman."

"I need time," said Carl, though he knew Jana would not want to hear him say that.

"Time's up," she said.

"It's graduation," said Carl. "I have lots on my mind."

"You have nothing on your mind but a load of tired old hormones," said Jana. "I'm not putting up with this anymore."

"Give me until the summer." Carl wished he didn't sound so much like he was pleading.

"I'll give you until Friday night," said Jana. "I'm coming to that graduation."

Carl thought about Sylvia and her fourteen-year-old daughter, who was supposed to receive an award from the American Legion. It was for good citizenship.

"You don't have to come this year."

"I wouldn't miss it for anything," said Jana. "I'll be there as the principal's wife, or I'll be there as the very angry woman. It's your choice."

"Don't come this year," said Carl.

"I'll be there," said Jana. "You can count on it."

The custodians had set the chairs up on the baseball diamond. They had built the stage against the backstop, as they had every year since he had first come to the school, except for two years when it threatened to rain and they crowded everyone into the cafeteria. The first of the parents had already arrived. It was always the same; the first parents were the ones whose kids were in the band. He had thought about asking Sylvia not to come to the graduation, but he knew that was unreasonable. She deserved to be there to see her daughter walk across the stage and receive her award from Mr. Herbert, the pharmacist who headed up the American Legion. Carl had thought about asking Mr. Herbert to give the principal's speech as well, so he wouldn't have to go. But Jana said she was coming whether Carl was there or not, and he would have been a coward to let Jana and Sylvia come face to face while he sat home alone on his patio amid the wreckage of his life. And if what the minister had written him was true, if most of the parents had heard whispered stories about him and Sylvia, his absence would only fuel the rumors.

A boy lugged a tuba in its case through the infield, knocking over several of the folding chairs. A large banner had been wired to the backstop: UP THE ROAD TO PROGRESS. Carl wondered if it was the same banner the kids had used the year before. It seemed to be the same theme. The last letter on the word PROGRESS had come unwired, and Sylvia stood on a stepladder doing what she could to reattach it. Her daughter, a plain girl who might one day have her mother's heavy beauty and might not, stood alone near one of the light poles. She was shredding a tissue, dropping the pieces on the ground, and Carl wondered, not for the first time, if the girl knew all he hoped she didn't know.

He went into his office and lay down on the same sofa he and Sylvia had made love on every Friday for months. He had a headache that gave everything a pink tinge if he looked at it straight on, so he looked at the plaques and photos on his walls out of the corner of his eye. He had never wanted to be anything more than a school principal. That was the only thing clear to him now. He called his house to tell Jana once more not to come; the phone rang several times before he heard his own voice on the answering machine. He couldn't remember making the recording. It must have been years before, when his mother was still alive. He thought he heard Jack London barking in the background.

"Be sure to wait for the beep," said his voice.

He thought about leaving himself a message.

"This is for Carl," he could say. "Take heart." Or, "The darkest hour . . . ." But he decided against it.

He waited until he heard the band warming up before he came out of his office again. At eight o'clock, it was hardly dark out, but in the distance, the lights had been turned on over the ball field, and moths had gathered high above to flutter at the lamps. He could see that most of the folding chairs had been taken already by mothers in bright dresses and fathers in unaccustomed sport coats and neckties. He knew these parents: farmers and the wives of farmers, a few mechanics, a deputy sheriff, Mr. Herbert from the drugstore. Some of them might dress up for church on Sunday. Others went months, even years at a time, without pulling their good clothes from the backs of their closets. They were not the type to have their love affairs in the open. He gave his own tie an unconscious adjustment and walked slowly out to the edge of the ball field.

He saw Sylvia in the second row and realized she had been watching for him. The band struck up "Pomp and Circumstance," one trumpet terribly off-key, and to his right, out of the library, the building nearest the baseball diamond, the graduates marched slowly across the grass toward the lights and the chairs and the banner hanging from the backstop. The boys and girls alike were dressed in white shirts and black ties, the boys wearing black slacks and the girls in skirts. He saw a car drive slowly down the street past the ball field and turn at the corner, and he imagined it was his wife's car. She was perhaps even now trying to make up her mind whether to come to the graduation. She was looking for a parking place.

He walked onto the infield, up the wooden steps to the portable stage. The band had come too soon to the end of their piece, and there were several awkward seconds of silence before the director could get them started again. The graduates entered by twos, stepping from the shadows into the lighted area of the ball field. Sylvia looked at him and smiled, and for a moment he was sure they were all looking at him, the students, the band, the parents who had trusted him with their children.

Movement rippled forward from the back rows of chairs. At first he couldn't tell what caused it. Then he saw Jana making her way down the center aisle. She was dressed in a black sheath with a light silk shawl she wouldn't need on a June evening. Her short hair was perfect, the blonde highlights dancing in the lights of the ball diamond. She smiled at everyone and no one, especially not at Carl, and took her seat across the aisle from Sylvia. Carl tried not to look at his wife. He found himself looking at Sylvia. In Sylvia lay his strength.

"Oh Carl," said Sylvia, moving her lips silently against the soft night. "I'm so sorry."

From the back rows, the whispers grew. He had heard that noise many times before. It was the noise a breeze would make, filling the trees on the playground. He read the banner again, watched the final *S* droop away from the other letters. He was sure another class had used this same theme, just as he was sure, staring out at the frowns he saw on the faces of the parents in their chairs, that this night would be his last time to stand on this stage. He had stumbled into a new part of his life.

He felt as though he were floating free above his school, unsure if he was ready for this freedom, his spirit rising from the ball field as he soared over the long line of students. They were willing to take their places on the stage, willing afterward to follow their parents from the schoolyard, on foot if necessary, as they labored up a road to a place called progress. He wondered if he had failed them. He wondered if they would understand, now or in the years to come, the reason he was leaving them. He hoped they would live contented and safe, with children of their own and dogs in their homes, celebrating one happy marriage per lifetime.

The Gospel According
· to Octavio Ruiz ·

OCTAVIO RUIZ COASTED HIS PICKUP into the alley behind the convalescent hospital and parked in the loading zone. He got out and brushed the sawdust from his pants, swearing softly when he saw he had forgotten to change his shoes. His loafers were covered with silver paint, but there wasn't time to go home and change. Visiting hours at the hospital were almost over. He took two flights of stairs, past the first floor of old men and the second floor too, mostly women who were able to walk on their own. On the third floor, he spoke to the nurses at their station.

"I'm here to see Thomas," he said, realizing again that he didn't know the boy's last name. "Brother Thomas."

They recognized him now, even the nearsighted Mexican nurse, short as a bug, who worked the three-to-eleven shift. She knew him from high school and called him Tavio. It was the name everyone had called him as long as he could remember, going back to the time he was a small boy following his mother through the vineyards, crying because the grapes his mother picked and gave to him weren't as sweet as the ones she brought home from the grocery store. The nurse couldn't keep from laughing when she saw Tavio come down the corridor, and though Tavio knew she laughed at his shoes, the way they sparkled under the fluorescent light, he worried she might also have seen the pint of Four Roses tucked inside his shirt.

"You're good," she said. "You know where to find him." He nodded to her and slipped quietly down the hall to Brother Thomas's room.

At first, when Brother Thomas had shared this room with the other boy, the shortstop, the room had been a busy place, full of nurses and aides and visitors who stared at Tavio as if he didn't belong there.

"I'm falling," the shortstop boy had said to Tavio again and again. Maybe he was out of his head. He certainly acted like he was. When the shortstop cried out at night from his side of the room, Brother Thomas would wake up and ask for another painkiller so he could go back to sleep. Brother Thomas had grown tired of his friend's complaining. He made the nurses come with their bed on wheels and take the shortstop down the hall to a room of his own. What bothered Brother Thomas most was when the boy rolled his feverish eyes at the ceiling, as if someone was up there listening to him. It was always the same talk, about the miracle.

"I had the real thing," said the shortstop. "No tricks. Like in the old days, only me. It happened to me."

And Brother Thomas hated the way the other boy ended each of these outbursts, pointing his good arm across the room.

"My God," said the shortstop, "I had a miracle, and you ruined it."

Tavio wasn't sure about miracles. They were a kind of truth though, and he was interested in truths. He knew one small truth: it was no sin to be out of steady work, even if Vera didn't agree with him.

"But a marriage is a fragile thing," Vera would say as she left for the dentist's office in the morning, her brown skin glowing in the white dress she wore to work. "Look for a real job, Tavio. You promised." He tried not to feel guilty about promises he didn't remember.

He did odd jobs, instead. He'd been doing a job on the roof of the Hotel Mooney in Visalia when he met Thomas and the shortstop. Tavio was a tall man, especially for a Ruiz, and he weighed 265 pounds, and he didn't like the way the longest ladder he had ever seen swayed beneath him. By the time he'd hauled twenty-five gallons of silvery paint onto the roof of the hotel, along with his last donut in the white paper sack, he was soaked with sweat. He felt as though he'd been through the car wash.

"The terrific thing about the Mexican people . . . ," said a voice from the sidewalk below, "they don't mind the heat. Not this dry heat. A hundred and ten somewhere else, they might think that was hot." The voice belonged to the bald *pendejo* who ran the hotel. Tavio enjoyed the way, from up on the roof, the little man looked like he'd been stepped on. He was glad he didn't have to be around that one all day, glad not to be inside the hotel putting down the new red carpet, or worse, taking up the old one. That was a filthy job. The worn carpet smelled like the men's room at the high school stadium: old socks, old cigars. The roof was better. Tavio didn't have to smell the football stadium up here. He could see it. He could see Mooney Boulevard to the west, all the way to Mooney's Grove where they had the go-carts and the rowboats you could take out on the pond. To the east, he could see the smooth brown foothills that gave him a hard-on if he stared at them long enough. He wondered for a minute who the hell Mooney was. Some white guy.

Looking north, he could see the park, the one they called the oval, where northside high school boys looked bad on Saturday nights. The oval was where he'd first set eyes on Vera. She moved down from Salinas her senior year of high school, and although he told her how he wasn't looking for a girlfriend, how he had once been in love with a girl who broke his heart to pieces, and how he wasn't in school anymore, how he had run out of time at school and they wouldn't let him come back, Vera didn't mind. She was lonely. They started riding around evenings when Tavio could get Ramon's Fairlane. Weekends they went to the drive-in on the edge of town, and Vera smiled when he pushed the front seat back as far as it could go so they could make out, Vera slowly shedding her clothes while the windows fogged up and Tavio's heart raced against feelings he couldn't hold back. Afterwards, Tavio wouldn't know what movie they'd seen, or if there had been a movie showing that night, or other cars in the lot.

He opened a can of paint and stirred it with the end of a broom handle. Vera thought she was pregnant the summer she graduated. Tavio remembered how happy he was, how drunk he got with Ramon and Billy. Then Vera decided she wasn't pregnant, but only after the wedding and the presents came and the uncles from Sonora, one of hers and one of his riding together on the Greyhound. Tavio told her not to worry. She would have children. Instead she started the course at the junior college to become a dental hygienist. Tavio went to see about a job posted at the Safeway on Mooney Boulevard, but the manager hired three white kids instead. And none of them were married. Tavio was pretty sure of that.

Using the broom, he spread the aluminum mixture over the roof's weathered tar paper, careful to get plenty into the small cracks and seams where leaks might start. He was dying for a drink of water but hated the thought of climbing down the ladder to get one. The silver paint reflected the sun, made him wish he wore dark glasses like in high school. His pant leg was silver now. So were the toes of his shoes. Those shoes looked like what a fairy would wear, and it made him stop for a moment and remember the time he was in the opera with those other boys. He still had the shirt that old piano teacher had made for him to wear in the opera. He never gave it back to her. It was funny the things you hung on to like that. Tavio wondered if there were such a thing as Mexican fairies. There had to be. There were Mexican gangsters, and ballplayers like Valenzuela, and oilfields making Mexican millionaires. He wondered if Vera would have stayed with him if he had been a millionaire, and he vowed to become one to see if she would take him back. But he knew becoming a millionaire was unrealistic. He could become a Mexican bank robber, although that could end badly too.

"A man can only be the man he is," said Tavio, wiping the sweat from his eyes, trying not to get silver on his face. He worked his way across the tar paper, slopping paint vigorously into the corners and along the edge of the roof. A little of the silver paint splashed over the edge. Down below, two young men on the sidewalk squinted up at him, and Tavio waved to let them know he hadn't meant to get paint on them. They watched him until he pretended to go back to work, when one pointed to the ladder propped against the side of the building. They were just boys, Anglos in white shirts and dark slacks, but when they started climbing to the roof, Tavio wished he had pulled the creaky ladder up after him.

"Mr. Ruiz," said the taller of the boys, the first to make it to the top rung of the ladder. He paused for a moment before raising one leg and letting himself onto the roof. He was so thin his throat stuck out on one side, as if he had half a case of the mumps. His legs were thin too. He reminded Tavio of a pigeon, except a pigeon would probably be fatter than this boy was. The one climbing behind him had darker skin, but he wasn't Mexican. Maybe Italian. Keep an eye on him, thought Tavio. He was worried that they knew his name.

"What do you want?" said Tavio. "Do I know you?" He let his accent get thicker and tried to remember who he owed money to. He owed some to Ramon, but Ramon wouldn't send Anglos after him. Ramon didn't know any Anglos.

"Your wife told us about you." The tall boy stepped gingerly onto the unpainted part of the roof and looked around. His friend followed, swinging his legs off the ladder as if that were some sort of sports event. Tavio could imagine the dark one playing baseball. He was built like a shortstop.

"Your wife's concerned about you. She thought we might visit with you here."

"Ex-wife," said Tavio. Though to tell the truth, they were only separated. "I'm kind of busy."

"We don't want to keep you from your work," said the shortstop. "My name is Steven, and this is Brother Thomas."

"You guys from the phone company?" asked Tavio.

"No," said the shortstop. When he smiled, his teeth in the sunlight were as bright as Tavio's silver paint, and as hard to look at. The after-noon pressed down onto the roof and pooled around the boy's ankles.

"What do you want?" asked Tavio.

"Your wife . . . ," began the boy, but the other one cut him off.

"We want to know if you've met a friend of ours," said this tall one with the swollen glands. "We want to know," he tapped himself on the chest, "is Jesus in your heart."

Tavio looked at the circles of sweat spreading down the tall boy's white shirt. He didn't like to think about his heart. If you thought about your heart too much, it would stop working. He poured more paint onto the roof, splashing it toward the boys' feet.

"Jésus Flores?" said Tavio. "I thought he was in jail."

He pushed his broom through the silver puddle and tried not to look angry. So it was Vera who had sent them. He considered Vera, how he could get even with her, and not just for this, not just for sending these guys to talk to him. She'd always been after him to change. Night school, the Diet Center. He cursed her under his breath, imagined accidents hap-pening to her. Let her fall off the front porch, he thought. Let her house catch fire. But immediately he took it all back. This time when he wiped the sweat from his eyes, he turned an eyebrow silver.

"Jesus Christ," said the tall missionary earnestly. He fell into step with Tavio, making large footprints on the freshly painted tar paper. This boy talked the same way as the counselor at the high school, as if he was on the radio, a classical station. There had to be someplace where people learned to talk that way.

"Do you know the Lord?"

"I know when there's a *pendejo* in my paint," said Tavio. The short-stop laughed, but the tall missionary, the boy called Thomas, looked lost, like one of those little white kids at the fair.

"Don't get that shit on your shoes," said Tavio in a softer voice. "It won't never come off." His own shoes were ruined now, covered with silver paint. They would be waterproof, though.

"Let me start over," said Brother Thomas, closing his eyes to gather his thoughts. "Mr. Ruiz . . ." The boy swept his arm to the south. "Are you on the road to salvation? Are you on the expressway to heaven?"

"How's that?" said Tavio. "Mooney Boulevard?"

The shortstop pretended to yawn into his fist. "That's good," he said. He had folded one of his religious tracts into a paper glider. As Tavio watched, the boy sailed it over the edge of the roof. "Message from God," he said.

Tavio wondered how anyone could think Mooney Boulevard was the expressway to heaven. All the angels he'd seen on Mooney were Hells Angels. The shortstop laughed again, and Tavio wondered if he'd said that thing about the Hells Angels out loud. The boy made another glider, studying the strange-looking people on the sidewalk below. Tavio saw a young woman he knew, a cocktail waitress from the bar across the street. He imagined how nice she must look, made up for the evening, ready for her shift. The shortstop scored a near miss on her as she hurried inside.

"Divine inspiration," said the shortstop.

Ignoring his partner, Brother Thomas read aloud from his Bible. He pronounced the words carefully in a soft nasal voice.

Tavio's head hurt when he stared at the silver paint. The job was only half done, but if he could get these two holy ones off the roof, he would quit for the day. He wanted a cold beer, and he wanted to sit someplace dark. There was a program on television he liked to watch at four o'clock, a country-western show out of Bakersfield with local singers who had a sweet sadness to their voices, like the men and women who lived out in Ivanhoe. He'd worked for some of those men and women, and worked alongside some others. Tavio especially liked to hear the steel guitar, the way a man played it across his lap. It sounded like someone crying with dignity. It sounded like the truth. Vera hated to come home and find him watching that show.

"That's worse than Mexican music," she would say, changing stations until she found the local news. "Is that your only ambition in life, to become an Okie?" He tried his best to understand Vera, but sometimes it was hard to know what to say.

Like the morning Tavio had gone to the Anglo dentist Vera worked for, a man who wore sky blue shirts and smelled of mouthwash. While the dentist leaned over and put his fingers in Tavio's mouth, Tavio sat with his eyes closed, not wanting to see up the man's large pale nose.

"You certainly take care of your teeth," said the dentist. Tavio could tell the man was disappointed. He probably liked to find lots of cavities, maybe a tooth so rotten he could use the pliers to pull it out.

"You must eat right." The dentist smiled across the chair at Vera, who looked efficient and beautiful in her white dress.

"I drink a lot of beer," said Tavio. Vera left the room, and Tavio didn't talk anymore after that unless the dentist asked him a direct question.

It just seemed easier not to talk. In time, Vera had less and less to say to him. She was watching the six o'clock news the day he went to collect his clothes. It was their last evening together.

"Don't forget your razor," said Vera. "And there's clean underwear in the dryer." She gave Tavio seventy-five dollars and her key to the pickup.

"Call me when you get a phone."

Tavio remembered carrying his duffel bags out the door, and he remembered how his truck, a white Ford with one black fender, wouldn't start. He had to get his wife out of the bathroom to help push it. He offered to let her steer.

"No, that's all right," she said. She wiped her face with a Kleenex where she had been crying. "I can push."

Tavio had dropped by that morning on the way to his job at the hotel so he could talk to Vera. He heard his wife's voice through the screen door before he had a chance to knock.

"He's a good man," Vera was saying. "He's got lots of good qualities. He just doesn't think about issues the same as you and me."

"Issues?" That would be Vera's sister, Felia.

"Oh, you know," said Vera. Tavio wondered why his wife's voice didn't sound Mexican. She could be Chinese, he thought, if she set her mind to it. "Fiscal issues mostly," said Vera. He couldn't remember her saying the word *fiscal* before.

"Like in bed," said Felia. "You mean he always wants you to do that thing . . ."

Vera came to the door with a copy of *Time* magazine in her hand. She wore a dress and nylons as if she was going somewhere special.

"Octavio," said Vera. She was surprised to see him, but she let him come in. "I wasn't expecting you."

"I'll make coffee," said Felia, jumping up from the couch. Vera laid the magazine down. She left it open to mark her place.

"I'll let you talk," said Felia. She disappeared into the kitchen.

"Right," said Vera.

"Pretend I'm not here," said Felia, shouting over the sound of running water.

"Sure," said Vera, as she settled onto the sofa. "Pretend we're the Rockefellers."

"What?" shouted Felia. "What about the Rockefellers?"

Tavio offered his wife a day-old doughnut from his paper sack, but he knew she wouldn't want one.

"You don't want to talk?" said Tavio.

Vera shook her head and pointed toward her sister in the kitchen.

"You were talking about me when I got here," said Tavio.

"No, we weren't."

"Who is it then with the fiscal problems?"

"Oh that," said Vera, smoothing her skirt. "We were speaking of the president."

"What president?"

"Of the United States," said Vera. She frowned at him. "It may surprise you, but we often speak of such things." She got up to water her house plants. Tavio knew what she was trying to tell him: he'd been in the house five minutes and she wanted him to leave. She moved about the room from plant to plant, murmuring to each one. He had once counted forty-seven of those plants in the living room. Viny plants, flowering plants, hanging plants, plants with thorns. He took a last look around the room before he opened Vera's front door. He suspected Vera had bought some new plants since he left. There were always new things about Vera.

Tavio blinked his eyes, burning now behind their lids. Two stories below, the bar and the sidewalk were bathed in shadows. He longed to be down there, away from the glaring paint and sun and the blue sky with its brown dirty edges. He cleared his throat so he could tell the missionaries it was Miller time. They could all knock off.

"Manna from heaven," said the shortstop, folding another of his tracts. "Get it while it's hot." He walked along the edge of the roof firing his missiles to earth, and Tavio thought he threw them a whole lot harder than he needed to. The tall missionary's voice droned on, reminding Tavio of the rosary, and Tavio wondered if Vera would stop being Catholic. It would be easier to get a divorce that way, and Vera had told him the marriage was a mistake. She could divorce him and marry a dentist. He leaned against a short brick chimney. Music drifted up from one of the hotel rooms below, Okie music. He closed his eyes to hear the steel guitar better, and swaying lightly on his feet, he imagined a long-faced man playing it at that moment in a cool television studio in Bakersfield.

When the first missionary went over the edge, it was an accident. Tavio had opened his eyes to see the boy give a violent throw to one of his tracts and slip in the wet paint, the soles of his shoes flashing in the unbearable sun.

"Wait," said the shortstop. He caught hold of the flimsy gutter at the edge of the roof, but he couldn't stop himself from falling any more than Tavio or Brother Thomas could run across the roof to his aid. When the boy dropped out of sight, he left a handful of leaflets stuck to the silver paint.

"Steven," said Brother Thomas. "Good Lord." He got to the edge of the roof and peered over, careful not to get too close. Tavio didn't need to see it. He knew how the shortstop would look, a crumpled heap on the sidewalk. A crowd of people would soon gather. The manager would come outside and put his hands to his face and run back inside to call for an ambulance, and the police.

But Tavio looked anyway, and he saw scraps of dirty red carpet lying on the ground and long ragged runners of carpet hanging from the mouth of a garbage bin. There must have been a lot of that filthy mess in the dumpster too, for there was an old man, a tramp, leaning headfirst into the dumpster, and when the tramp straightened up, he pulled the shortstop out of the garbage by his hair as if he were saving him from drowning. The boy had a cut on his forehead, and blood ran into one eye. He held his head to the side as if he was trying to clear a ringing in his ears. His right arm hung loose behind him, but he seemed unaware of it. Standing two floors below Tavio and Brother Thomas, the shortstop stared at his good arm and his legs and broke into a tearful smile.

"Praise God, it's a miracle," he said to the grinning old man who had pulled him from the bin. "I should be dead." He fell to his knees. In spite of his smile, his face turned the color of the sidewalk.

"I've been spared."

"Amen," said the tramp.

From the rooftop, Brother Thomas stared out over the broken rain gutter. His mouth tried several sentences, but he had yet to finish one.

"I can't believe it," he finally managed, barely loud enough for Tavio to hear. "I'm sorry, but I can't."

"Oh, believe it," said Tavio, and he gave Brother Thomas a gentle push that carried him awkwardly over the edge of the roof after his friend.

The shortstop was trying to get up from his knees when Brother

Thomas came flailing down on him. Tavio watched to see if there would be another miracle. The tramp, who had started into the hotel for help, came cautiously back, one hand over his head in case anything more fell from the roof. But this time there was nothing he could do.

Tavio never finished patching the roof. He told the hotel manager he was afraid to climb the ladder again, and that *pendejo* shook his head and hired someone else. Tavio worked for a week digging up the sewer line at a trailer court out by the drive-in theater. Then he started preparing a house to be painted for a widow lady who lived behind the mall. The woman had thirteen or fourteen cats, even she couldn't keep count, and one small dog who was frightened of all those cats and who wanted to go home with Tavio. He would have taken the dog, but he wasn't supposed to have pets where he lived now. For the widow, he had to go up a ladder again, a tall one, and Tavio was curious to see if he really had developed a fear of heights, but he found it didn't bother him. He would scrape paint for a while, then stop and rest where the eaves of the house came together and he could think about his missionaries lying on the sidewalk. How the cops came. How one of them climbed the fire escape to talk to Tavio and immediately slipped and fell in the wet paint. The cop was lucky he didn't go over the edge too. They didn't need to ask a lot of questions after that.

Leaning against the widow's roof, Tavio wondered why it happened. He wondered about all the people who filled his life, especially the people with good ideas, white boys in clean shirts and ties who told him what to do. He had never cared for missionaries. These boys had come to the roof of the Hotel Mooney to tell him about his heart. He remembered how hot and tired he was. Maybe that had something to do with it. He'd been upset about Vera. And he'd wanted a beer. After he'd come down off the roof of the hotel, he'd gone into the bar across the street, where he put away eight beers without getting drunk. That was strange.

It was the pain that made him do it, Tavio thought finally, his pain and Vera's pain, and his cousin's pain and the pain of the old ones, and Teresa Cruz's pain and stupid Ramon's pain and little Jameycarril's pain. The pain of Jesus. The pain of the world. It had to be. It was the jobs he couldn't get, the baby that never came. There was pain now, sleeping alone in a room over the laundromat, wanting Vera and wondering if she sometimes wanted him. He needed to share that pain. The boys needed to feel it. Like the steel guitar, a man could have dignity if he once had pain, and Tavio had wanted to give the tall boy, the one who read the Bible so carefully, a little bit of dignity.

In the convalescent hospital, the tall thin Brother Thomas swore at the shortstop and asked for a private room. He swore at everyone until his family and the people from the mission stopped coming to see him altogether.

"Did you bring it?" asked Thomas when Tavio walked through the door. The boy's dinner dishes sat on the tray beside the bed. It didn't look as though he had touched his evening meal. Outside, the afternoon was giving way to a still hot night. Tavio handed over the Four Roses he had been carrying inside his shirt.

"The smokes."

"I'll give you some before I leave," said Tavio. "You don't want to overdo it."

"Don't start," said Thomas. He poured bourbon into a cup of cold coffee. Then he took the last cigarette from a package on the table and lit it with one hand the way Tavio had taught him. His left side lay in a series of casts and bandages.

"Can I read to you now?" asked Tavio. He moved the dinner things away from the bed and opened the nearest window as far as it would go. He screwed the cap back on the bottle and hid it under the bed covers.

"Jesus," said Thomas, "why don't you lay off reading for one night?"

"I like to read," said Tavio. "I read pretty good."

"But it isn't true," said Brother Thomas. "What you're reading. I don't believe it anymore."

"Oh, it's true," said Tavio. "I mean, maybe it is. Maybe it's not the only thing that's true."

"Give me a break," said Brother Thomas.

"Listen," said Tavio. "I've been thinking. Look at it this way. If you could lose your faith, maybe you could find it again. Or a better one."

"What?" said Thomas. He turned to stare at Tavio, as much as his casts would let him.

There was a knock at the door.

"Is someone smoking in there?"

"Keep out!" said Thomas. Tavio was impressed. Thomas wasn't afraid of the nurses anymore. He wasn't even afraid of the housekeepers.

"You could be a missionary again," said Tavio.

"I'm not a missionary. I told you."

"Well," said Tavio, "maybe you're going to be. A man has to be what he's going to be." He was thinking of Vera then, and he knew in his heart what he said was true. "There's all kinds of faith," said Tavio. "All kinds of missionaries too."

"I'm not a missionary," said the boy again.

"Anyway," said Tavio, "after all this," and he waved one hand at the gauze and plaster wrapped around Thomas's body, "maybe you'd be good at it."

Thomas took a long drag on his cigarette, the kind that burned deep and hurt. There was an ache in the back of the boy's eyes, a look Tavio didn't remember from before. Tavio got up and waved at the smoke that hung over the boy's bed, hoping somehow to send it toward the open window. He picked up the Gideon's Bible and let the pages fall to where the red string marked his place.

"This is from Corinthians again," said Tavio. "Unless you want something else."

Slowly, quietly, holding himself as straight in the bed as he could, Thomas surrendered to the evening. And Tavio began to read.

• Union Wages •

Milk and Iron

I knew the time had come for me to leave the state of my birth. I had my reasons. Try looking at your middle brother laid out for good on the kitchen floor. Try knowing you were the one who put him there. What I wanted, moving out to Montana, was a different life, call it a better life. People say California is a beautiful place, but one thing I've noticed, a lot of those people don't live in California. California was my old man's life. Ernie Foster was a farmworker mostly, but when he was fifty-three years old, he took a job driving a milk truck, when hardly anyone in the whole San Joaquin Valley had milk delivered anymore. My father thought he'd found the greatest job in the world, getting up early as hell and heading into town where his truck was waiting for him at the creamery. He would tell you about that job like it was his calling. My older brother Troy, the one who lived the longest, he and I used to eat our dinner as fast as we could so we could get out of the house before the old man started talking milk.

Once he began driving for the creamery, Ernie used one expression in every story he ever told. "I'd stopped the truck," he would say, "*to juggle my load . . .*" He never bothered to explain what he meant by it. As we got older, my brother and I used that expression for practically anything. "I got to go out back for a few minutes to juggle my load," Troy would say. One night, the summer Troy graduated from high school, we watched a lady from down the road named Mrs. Guiniere drive by in a new Plymouth, and my brother said, "I'll bet she could juggle your load all right." Ernie got mad and went indoors. He wouldn't come back out on the porch all evening, though he knew my brother was leaving the next day for Camp Pendleton.

It was after Troy left the marines, after he found the motel in San Diego where he holed up for as long as he could stand it, that I got where I couldn't feel right around my old man anymore. It wasn't just the one thing. It was a lot of things. (Try 115 degrees outside and no air to breathe, anywhere you turn. Try eighteen months in a group home. Try thinking there's two guns in a cardboard box, one you've fired and one you haven't yet.) It was a heavy feeling. It was a feeling my mother did everything she knew how to alleviate, but it was a feeling I couldn't shake, the only son left. So I drove north out of the San Joaquin, up through Oregon and part of Washington, across the narrow part of Idaho, and I didn't stop until I got to Montana. I liked the sound of the place, and I was thinking I'd see if I could go to some kind of college out there. I never liked school, growing up. I don't know why I thought college in Montana would be different for me. I guess, finally, my heart wasn't in it. When I married this Missoula girl named Alice, I quit taking classes and started looking for a job in construction, where nobody cares if you went to college or not. In fact, Troy once told me a college degree might hold me back. I thought about roofing, but when I saw those guys pouring tar on the roofs of apartment buildings in the summer, it could make me sick. I used to watch the ads on TV late at night about learning to run heavy equipment. Heavy equipment training seemed an awful lot like college. Tell me the difference.

I might have warmed up to a better vocation. I might have seen a rodeo and gone out and bought some boots, or I might have read about a plane crash and decided to join the air force. But one night, in a bar I used to go to in Lolo, I met Sid. When he came in, he was already drunk from the waist down.

"Marry me," he said to the bartender, this sandy-haired girl who used to sing a little on Saturday nights with some old boys from Lolo. That girl ignored him. Maybe she knew him in better days. Maybe she just didn't want to listen to one more man in a ball cap.

Sid sat down next to me. "An ironworker," he said, like I'd asked him some question. I don't think I ever did. He showed me his tattoos. My brother Troy had tattoos, but not as many as Sid. Inside one elbow, Sid had the name *Dixie* written in green with red highlights. That was neatly crossed out, and *Louise* was tattooed beneath it in the same style. Maybe he had a friend in the tattoo business. I asked him where he worked and if they were hiring.

"The Fence-Me-In," he said. "Ask for Max. Me and him are related."

I wrote the name of his company on the palm of my hand.

"Come with me to North Dakota," he told that bartender, but she turned on the TV instead, and later turned the volume up so she wouldn't have to listen to the noises he made out on the steps.

Max

I worked for Max for three years. He liked to call them seasons, like we were a ball team. The Fence-Me-In was a family company. Sid and Donnie were brothers, and their sister was Max's wife, a woman with a pale complexion and a scared smile on her face. No matter what time you went over to Max's house, you were sure to find her at home drinking coffee in her bathrobe. She might have just liked the robe, but I thought she was depressed.

Max was never depressed, not really. He was a worrier. He was from New Jersey, where maybe there's plenty of half-Italian, half-Jewish fence contractors, but he was the only one I ever heard about in Montana. He had four boys and he planned to put them to work as soon as they grew big enough. They thought it was better not to grow. The oldest shaved every day (he was twelve), though he couldn't have weighed more than ninety pounds. My last season with Max, the boy was rolling cigarettes and taking money from Sid, his uncle, on Monday night football. I thought the kid might have shrunk from the year before. It's why Max hired me. I'm only medium size, but I'm strong enough, and I don't bet on football.

Max bid on all the commercial jobs, fences around grade schools and wrecking yards, but there were other companies in Missoula and not as many fences to build as twenty years ago. Missoula is a beautiful valley. It's surrounded by the whole Rocky Mountains, and if that doesn't mean anything to you, it's because you never made a living digging postholes. I didn't mind. Most of the work turned out to be backyard stuff. People loved the guy who came to build their fence. He made the yard safe for their kids, or better yet, for the dog, kept them all out of the street. It didn't matter to me what a man's dog looked like, though I never did care for Dobermans. But yard jobs didn't pay, and I was staying up late, wondering if I'd ruined my life again, watching the ads for heavy equipment when Max walked into the office one afternoon with a smile on his face. His wife was there too. She had a party dress on with earrings and green makeup.

"It's union wages without the union," said Max, and he pulled a six-pack of Schmidt out of a paper bag.

I'm not supposed to drink, but I had one or two before I called Alice at the hospital where she worked and told her we had a government job paying union wages in Anaconda, a six-foot fence around the post office with barbed wire and razor ribbon and drive-through gates. I wanted to hear the excitement in her voice, but she had to hang up and respond to a code red or code blue—not the one where the guy is going to die but the next worse one. I tried not to worry about that guy. I was tired of three-year-old kids and their yellow Labradors. This job Max was talking about, it was a break.

SID

Sid and I came in early so we could load the flatbed Jimmy with sand and gravel and six sacks of cement. When we finished tying down forty fence posts with a come-along, we had less than a two-inch clearance between the tires and the bed of the truck, and we knew the tires were going to rub, and the truck hadn't been registered in three years, and still we didn't care. It was union wages. To get to Anaconda, we had to drive east on the interstate that follows the Clark Fork River. I enjoyed the drive. Another thing I used to do is fish, and I liked to look down and guess where the brown trout were laid up. Once we left the Missoula Valley, the radio cut out the way it always does, and Sid pulled his hat over his face and went to sleep. I thought about trout, and I thought about bald tires and my future with Max, which looked better now. I remembered how they said it in the group home in Fresno, how sometimes you will get another chance. Max looked out for his men. There was a time my paycheck bounced, but he'd made that up to me a long time ago, most of it.

We drove past a place named Tony's at the top of the divide, and I was glad I was driving. Sid would have stopped. Tony's had a big statue of a black bear next to the road. For some people, a rotating bear statue is reason enough to stop and have a drink. I didn't like it. I always thought the people who stopped at that bar must be tourists or people who lived in mobile homes. Maybe the part of California where I grew up was the original boondocks, but even out in the middle of all those orange trees, we never lived in a mobile home.

Alice and I lived in a brick duplex off Rattlesnake Drive. We were looking for a house. Alice was a nurse with small breasts, and her bottom teeth were crooked. It didn't matter. She smiled with her eyes, and I don't care much about breasts. I heard a Japanese guy in the Visalia bus station talk about breasts one time. "Fatty glands," he said, and there was no way to argue with him. I guess I liked breasts as much as anybody before that. It's about all me and Troy ever talked about. I told Alice, with another season as good as this one, we'd go to the bank and sign for a loan, buy our house.

"Think so?" she said.

"Hell, Alice," I said. "Keep it in mind." It seemed like a sure thing.

When Sid and I got to Anaconda, it wasn't hard to find the post office, a typical piece of governmental confusion, a square building with seven sides. I pulled into the parking lot, and Sid leaned over and pressed on the horn until a custodian came out to show us where the fence would go. It made Sid mad to find out we had to dig postholes through a concrete slab.

"It ain't in the plans," said Sid. "I'm not digging through any kind of pavement." That old custodian laughed at us, which didn't help. Sid shoved his hands into his pockets and walked off to where a sign across the street advertised a keno game, and I figured, hello keno, good-bye Sid. "I'm calling Max," he said, but he never did. He made a small bet while he waited for the pay phone, and he ordered a beer so the bartender wouldn't think he was cheap. He was still sitting at the bar when I went to get him at six o'clock.

I was the one who called Max. Max sounded surprised by the concrete too, although not as surprised as I would have liked. I left Sid in the tavern and drove down to the local equipment rental, where I got a quick lesson in jackhammers and the names to call them when they screw up. But I liked working that jackhammer better than anything I'd done up until then, better than welding gates or running the augur or yelling directions to the guys who drove the cement trucks. You get respect with a jackhammer. I had the postholes ready by the end of the day, took the hammer back to the shop, and went for Sid at the keno place. The bartender knew a deadbeat when he saw one. He was pushing Sid toward the door.

"Lend me some money, Johnny," said Sid, before I got all the way in the room. "I'm getting lucky."

"Let's get out of here." I could see Sid was losing the war, and I didn't even know what war he was fighting.

"I have to win some back," said Sid. "Max will kill me."

"I got the holes ready," I said. "He'll be happy."

"I lost too much," said Sid.

It was the bartender who settled it. "Go the hell home," he said. He shut off the keno board, and whatever it was that held Sid together went slack.

"It's union wages," I told him. "You'll get it back."

Sid let me push him toward the exit, but I had to keep telling him about the money we'd get when we finished the job, the big fat paycheck with Max's name signed at the bottom. Four men sat at a table by the door. They didn't look like nice men or mean men. They just didn't look happy.

"You were at the post office," one of them said, a man with close red hair and a wandering eye.

"That's right." I gave him my jackhammer smile and guided Sid to the door ahead of me.

"When are you coming back?"

"We'll set the posts tomorrow."

"He thinks they'll set the posts tomorrow," said the man with the wayward eye. He spoke into the pitcher of beer on his table, so his words came to me as an echo. I was trying to get Sid into the truck, and the bartender wanted to turn the keno game on again. I didn't have time to talk.

On the drive home, Sid moaned about the money he'd lost, but I didn't listen. Coming into Missoula at the end of the day you're headed into the sunset, and it's a wonderful sight unless you're blinded by the sun and go off the road. I liked the little wisps of cloud turning red. Even the bugs that died on the windshield had a different look to them. It was still daylight when I crossed the Russell Street Bridge and parked the Jimmy in the yard of the Fence-Me-In. I considered waking Sid up, but I was tired of Sid. I locked his door to keep him from falling out into the gravel and I left him there. The air was full of the smell of the river, and I knew Alice wouldn't be home yet, so I drove out through East Missoula to a place where I could get in a few casts before dark.

Fishing is best when you don't care if you catch anything. The sunset turned the water the color of roses, and a man stood on a long spit in the middle of the river working a fly rod. It was hypnotism to watch him bring his line up off the water, shoot it back behind him, then let it sail out in front again so the fly settled gently on an eddy. I put my spinning rod away and sat on a rock and watched until the sun went down and the other guy waded ashore and climbed up the bank. His headlights shone out over the river as he turned and drove back to town, and still I sat there, listening to the splashes the big fish make, the ones who feed in the dark.

I hadn't felt that positive since the day I quit school. I was making good. I could see teenage kids in my life. If I closed my eyes, I could make out their faces. We would be joking, sitting at the kitchen table, and I would send one of them to the refrigerator to get me a beer, and he wouldn't mind because he would respect me, not like me and Troy making cracks about our old man and milk. And another thing: when my kids got older, I wasn't going to stay in bed the morning one of them went off and joined the marines. We were going to understand each other. I was making good for them.

PSYCHOLOGY

When I was a boy, I played Little League for two summers before the accident, and then another summer after they let me out of the group home. I played a little better, the older I got. When I was little, I was afraid of the ball, but after I came back home, I didn't care if I got hit anymore. Sometimes I just let the ball hit me anywhere, even the face. That was better, I guess, but getting hit by the ball isn't the same as catching the ball. I had a coach who worked as the sheriff's deputy for our part of the county. Some of the parents didn't think we should have Corky Rollins for a coach, although he was supposed to be a hotshot ballplayer when he was younger. Some of those same parents didn't think I should be on the team at all, and it was Mr. Rollins who stood up for me. He didn't have to do it. The highlight of our season was the morning Mr. Rollins, because he was a sheriff's deputy, took the whole team to the county jail.

"This could happen to you," he said, meaning all of us, meaning me most of all. He was desperate too. We were losing every game.

"When you think of baseball, remember this place," he said, looking around at the gray walls and the bars and the men and women in uniform. It all looked too familiar to me. I got out of baseball. I should have gotten out sooner.

I couldn't tell you why, but the next morning at work, the scene in Max's office made me remember that tour of the jail. Sid sat hunched over in the back where customers never went. He wore the clothes he had on the day before, and he smelled like Sunday morning's garbage. His neck was stiff. I pictured how I left him, his ear pressed up against the window of the Jimmy.

"You could have woke me up," he said. At least, that's part of what he said. The rest was unrepeatable, the way a lot of what Sid used to say to me was unrepeatable. Troy was that way too. It was part of being a brother. As I learned in a psychology class before I left college and entered the world of ironwork, the big chicken pecks the little chicken and the littler chicken pecks one even smaller than him. I was glad when Max told me to take Donnie to Anaconda, leaving Sid behind to mind the office. Something hard hit the door as I shut it behind me, and I heard Max tear into Sid about being a dumb s.o.b., and keno.

"What's that about?" asked Donnie.

"That's the biggest chicken," I said.

Donnie was different from Sid. He had black hair and black eyes, the same slim upper body that didn't tell you how strong he was. You could tell they were brothers, but Donnie was only sixteen, and unlike Sid, he didn't have a mean side or much experience of the world. On the way to Anaconda, I asked what he thought about jackhammers and the men who run them. "I wish you watched more TV," he said. "We could have better conversations."

Another thing about Donnie, he had a funny skin condition, patches on his arms and hands and some on his face where he didn't have pigment. Those pale places burned in the summer, but five minutes after meeting him, you forgot about his patches. Women didn't think those patches were funny looking. When Donnie and I did yard jobs together, teenage rodeo princesses drove by the truck two or three times a day. They couldn't remember me and usually asked if I worked for *Donnie's company*. I told them I did. Even grown women got a moist look in their eyes when they talked to Donnie. They used a gentle voice they ought to have saved for their husbands.

Once, we built a fence on Marshall Street around a woman's patio. She wanted redwood slats in her fence so she could sunbathe, and she gave hints she liked to do her sunbathing in the altogether. It annoyed me about those redwood slats. We didn't have them on the truck, and it meant we'd have to come back again to finish up. Every time the woman came out of her house, she wore less clothes and she looked at me as if I was a nuisance. Twice she brought us out a cold beer, and she remembered each time to bring one for herself. Since Donnie was underage, I didn't let him have any. She was a hard-looking woman, not unlike one of Sid's girls off Front Street.

"Ever met Donnie's older brother?" I asked her.

"I'm not interested in anybody's brother," she said, and she leveled a pair of unnaturally purple eyes at me. She wanted Donnie to come back after work to finish the job. She promised to pay him extra.

"It won't take the both of you," she said. By then she had on a bikini with a broken strap, and she was going through Donnie's toolbox, asking him what he used all that stuff for. I had a hunch her strap could have been fixed easy enough, and she didn't need Donnie's tools to do it. When she came out with the Sea & Ski and that lonesome look on her face, I decided to head her off. I sent Donnie to the truck for another roll of wire.

"Lady," I said, "I know what you're thinking." It was hot, and all those beers made me tired. I settled into one of her broken-down lawn chairs and prepared to reason with her.

"He's a handsome kid. But you can't."

She wanted to pretend she didn't know what I was talking about. She was out of beer—I can count to six—and I saw no reason to play that game.

"Those patches," I said, "the ones on his face and arms."

She had grease on her hands from digging through Donnie's tools. She must have been rubbing her nose because she had grease there too.

"Those patches are not what you think," I said.

Her eyes got small. Her eyes were purple lasers cutting into me to see if I was telling her the truth.

"Those patches are the secondary manifestations of a terminal and chronic contagious disease," I said. I knew I might not get the medical words exactly right, but I was close. I used to hear Alice talk to her friends on the phone.

The sun was behind the woman now, and I had to squint so I could follow the look on her face. This woman was a hard case. She had been lied to before.

"He got it in South America," I said. "Down in the jungle."

"He's too young to go to South America," she said.

"Tierra del Fuego," I said. "He was there with his parents." I could see she wanted to ignore me, but sex and diseases are what people can't ignore. "On mission work," I told her. Still, she had the dreamy look in her eye. That's the awful truth about women. You don't really ever convince them of anything.

"Lady," I said. I let my voice get low, which makes people think I'm sincere. "His heart is weak from it." Her hand flew up to cover her own heart and left a greasy smudge in the fine hairs between her breasts. "The doctors told him it's dangerous," I said. "They told him he can't do it."

She shook her head. She was going to fight me all the way.

"Ever," I told her. "They told him, find something else you can do. Be a priest or something."

It's funny when you say a thing like that. If it's one of those days and you just put away all that beer, you can believe yourself. I was getting choked up.

"You could kill him, lady."

There were tears in her eyes over that. "He can't do it?" she said. "Ever?"

Donnie came around the corner with a fifty-foot roll of chain link on his shoulder. The way he threw it onto the grass made the woman bore her eyes into me again.

"Lifting wire isn't the same," I told her. "You know that."

She looked at Donnie. It was hot, and he wasn't wearing any shirt. She looked at me. She couldn't make up her mind. Donnie had jammed his tape measure deep into the pocket of his jeans, and the sweat ran down his stomach. The woman tried not to look at his pocket. She didn't know that was a tape measure.

"You all right?" she said to Donnie. She couldn't stop fidgeting with the broken strap on her bikini.

Donnie stared at the greasy spot over her heart. "I don't feel so good," he said. "I feel like I could faint."

"Oh God," she said. "I hate South America." Tears spilled out of her purple eyes. The tears were purple too, at first. Then they turned into regular tears. She ducked into her house and slammed the screen door behind her.

"What's the matter with her?" said Donnie. "She got something in the oven?"

"Worse," I said. I wished I hadn't sat down in that woman's lawn chair. It was one of those chairs where sitting down is simple but getting up is hard. Donnie had to give me a hand. "A lot worse than that," I told him. "She has to take it easy. She told me all about it. She's got a bad heart."

He felt sorry for her then. He was a good boy that way. And it wasn't hard to talk him out of going back there after work. I told him Max wouldn't like it. That part was true.

ANACONDA

Donnie and I put in twelve hours in Anaconda mixing cement and setting fence posts. Most of the afternoon, that white-haired janitor stood on the loading dock and watched us. He was betting the light would fail before we finished.

"You don't know this town," he said. I figured he had to be close to retirement, the way he leaned on his push broom. He leaned a lot but seldom pushed. Anaconda looked normal to me. Clean streets, a few bars with pickups in front. A Safeway store. The houses in the old part of town were fifty or sixty years old, but they were kept up. There are towns just like it in every state, except a lot of your other states are flat.

"They shut the plant down," said the janitor. "Things ain't the same." I didn't let on, but I knew what he was talking about from reading the newspaper. Anaconda was a one-horse town, an aluminum refinery. The horse was dying, or maybe dead already. "Everybody's out of work," he said.

"You got a job."

"Hell, this ain't a job." He spit towards the door, a strange thing to do since he'd have to clean it up later. Maybe he liked to keep busy.

"Try to raise a family, what I get paid," he said.

I tried not to laugh. "You starting a family?"

"You're not from here," he said.

I hosed out the wheelbarrows we used to mix cement, and Donnie threw them on the back of the Jimmy, which was empty now. The fence posts stood in a line as straight as soldiers, three a little higher than the rest. I wished I'd cut down the tall ones before we set them in concrete. They spoiled a perfect effect. The way the old man waited, I knew he had more to say. My father could do that, look at a person as if he had a telegram from God, and what he had to say was going to be painful.

"It isn't none of my business," said the janitor.

Donnie jumped into the truck and hit the horn. He hadn't planned to get in on this job. To him, it was gravy. We waved at the old guy as we pulled out of the parking lot, but our custodian friend didn't wave back.

"Gee," said Donnie. "What's with him?"

"Nothing," I said. "He needs to juggle his load."

"Do what?" said Donnie.

I told him it was medical talk. I told him never mind. We drove past the bar where Sid had lost his money. The neon sign was lit up and the place was doing business.

Max didn't operate the same as other businessmen, so it didn't surprise me when he said we would all go back to Anaconda bright and early Sunday morning to finish the job.

"We'll leave at four," he said, which meant we'd get there by six when the town was still asleep. I expected Sid to complain since he rarely went home on a Saturday night before the taverns closed. But Sid just nodded and winced. His neck was still stiff. Then I thought I would complain about it. I didn't see the need for an early start.

"We'll be finished and on our way home by noon," said Max. "Nice and quiet."

"It's a quiet town," I said.

"Let's leave it that way," said Max. Max was the first person I'd met from New Jersey, and nothing he did or said quite made sense to me.

We left Missoula Sunday morning in the dark, four of us jammed into one truck to save gas. Donnie fell asleep before we got out of the yard, and Sid looked as if he needed sleep too, but he was tense from being up so early. As Max drove, his dark eyes shone in the dash lights. We had the back of the Jimmy filled with rolls of chain link and gunny sacks of fittings. Long sections of top rail arced over the cab of the truck, taut as a bow. There was a gun rack in the cab, though I'd never seen a gun in it before. I don't know much about guns, not really. Maybe I know too much about guns. This one smelled like three-in-one oil.

"We're going hunting?"

"Shut up," said Sid. "I want to listen to the radio."

"I'm not supposed to be around guns," I said.

"Neither am I," said Sid.

"I'm sort of a felon," I said.

"So am I," said Sid.

"Don't be rude," said Max. He had the headlights on, and he drove with both hands tight on the wheel as if he feared an animal might jump out of the dark onto the road. It happens. That winter an elk came over the freeway fence outside of Bonner and totaled a Volkswagen van. The elk died. I never heard about the people. We were still waiting for the sun to come up when we passed the hot spring a few miles beyond the Rock Creek exit. I wished it was later in the day. At dawn, the steam would come off the pond near the road, and I liked to see that. I couldn't see a thing in the dark, so I leaned my head against the stock of Max's gun and slept.

When I woke up, we were driving down the main street of Anaconda. We had the town pretty much to ourselves at that hour. In a downtown café, we ordered hash browns and eggs. A sign over the till said we were in a union restaurant, and Max read it and grinned, but Sid didn't think it was funny.

"You ought to tell him," said Sid.

"Eat your breakfast," said Max.

I thought it was something they were keeping from Donnie, a way they had figured out not to give him all his wages. He was over by the revolving pastry shelf, and he didn't hear them. I figured it could wait.

At the P.O., we set about the tasks we knew by heart. I liked that, working quietly, helping unload the bulky rolls of chain link, getting a tool Max wanted before he asked for it. When Sid cut the top rail, the tattoos jumped up and down along the muscles of his arm. Donnie hummed a few notes that wanted to become a song, only to take off in a new direction every time I thought I had it figured out. We rolled the chain link flat along the outside of the fence line. It took three of us to get an end up off the ground and tied into the corner. I was the only one who noticed the white Impala drive by, but when you're on a job, it's not unusual for people to drive by slow and stare. I might not have noticed when it came back except this time it wasn't just the Impala. Three cars stopped at the curb on the other side of the street, and a truck pulled up behind them, one of those pickups that sits high off the ground and has tires too big to fit into the wheel wells. Another car stopped in the middle of the street, pumping thick blue exhaust from the tailpipe. Five men got out before the driver left in a hurry.

"Wonder where he's going," said Max.

"After more of his friends," said Sid.

I kept working. I thought if I ignored those men, they would go away. One of them opened the trunk of the Impala and pulled out a bundle of signs nailed to sticks. As he passed them around, I could see the words "Ironworkers Local" and some numbers. The signs didn't look so great. They made me think maybe they'd been used before.

The last car to drive up was an El Camino, low and slick with the biggest trailer hitch I'd ever seen. The car was painted the color of dark beer and it sparkled in the sunlight.

"The big guy," said Max, although the man who got out of the El Camino wasn't big in any usual sense. He had a black mustache that reminded me of Mr. Rollins, my old Little League coach. He wore Levi's and a sport shirt, what you would expect a sheriff's deputy like Corky Rollins to wear on his day off. This man didn't look as if he'd just gotten out of bed. He looked like he'd had his jog and his shower and a light breakfast before he came down to see about us.

Max pounded on the door of the loading dock, and when the janitor came out, Max got his foot in the door before the old man could shut it.

"I want to use that phone," I heard Max say, and the old man shrugged and led Max on into the building, leaving the rest of us staring at the metal door that shut behind them.

"Come here, Donnie," said Sid. Donnie was still trying to look busy, but at least he'd stopped humming.

"What's going on?"

The morning was cool, and Donnie had his jacket on. Sid took him by the arm and slid a short piece of top rail up his sleeve. Outside the parking lot, thirty men were trying not to look at us directly. Some carried their signs over their shoulders. Watching them, the way they hunched down into their coats, I was full of the tense feeling you can get in a waiting room or a strange city after dark. The deputy sheriff lookalike walked up to Sid. You could tell he was the one in charge, but he didn't call attention to it. He might have come to the post office that morning just to mail a letter.

"You don't run this outfit," he said to Sid.

Sid pointed toward the door, then took out a cigarette. We stared at him, like we'd never seen anyone smoke a cigarette before. We watched him smoke until Max came out.

"This is your scab outfit," said the man with the mustache, the one who reminded me of baseball and the county jail. This time he spoke to Max. Nothing he said was a question.

"This is my company," said Max, correcting him. I could have told Max it's no use trying to correct someone who thinks he's a sheriff's deputy. They're the big potatoes. They've got authority they've never used.

"We know you," said the man. "You scab us over in Missoula all the time. You scabbed a job from us in Helena last summer." I didn't like the word *scab*. Nobody could like that word. He didn't care. He meant to use it as much as possible. "You're not going to do it here," he said. "Shit," he said. "I hate scabs."

"I made a call," said Max. "The police are on the way." But he said it to Sid, not to anyone from Anaconda.

"They won't stay," said Sid. "They won't stay long enough to be remembered."

The man from Anaconda got up close to Max, and Max made a sour look as if he smelled something bad. The other man ignored that look.

"We're shutting you down," he said. "And listen to me."

We listened. We'd been listening.

"We don't fuck around," he said.

It felt to me as if the air in the parking lot had gone thin and useless. I couldn't breathe deep enough. I was fourteen years old, walking through the creamery where my father worked. It was his day off, and we were there to pick up his check. One of the men he worked with saw us. He stopped my father and wanted money.

"I can't give you any," said Ernie. "I got kids at home."

"For their future then," said the man from the creamery. "You don't want them on the wrong side of the union."

"Piss on the union," said Ernie. When we walked away, I wanted to take hold of his hand, even though I was too old for that. I was scared by the way the sweat came to the back of my father's shirt. Now it looked as though that creamery man from a long time ago was right. I was on the wrong side of the union again, but I couldn't help it. I grew up that way.

Two cops drove up slow and got out of a patrol car, adjusting their belts and nightsticks, all that stuff they have to wear. They looked at the post office as if they'd just discovered it in the middle of their town, some ancient ruin. The way they approached Max and the rest, it made me think of cats walking through a puddle.

"Someone call in a disturbance?" asked a tall silver-haired cop. The younger man with him looked as if he didn't feel well.

"We'd like to finish this job," said Max, "and go home."

Noise came over the police radio, but I couldn't make it out. It could have been astronauts from the moon. One of the cops cocked his head as if he could hear better that way, and then both of them headed back through the pickets toward their patrol car. They hadn't shut the engine off.

"We'd like you to stay," said Max, the way you might ask a burglar to leave the small change.

"No sir," said the older cop. "Post office is federal property. We don't have jurisdiction here."

He spoke quietly to the men on the sidewalk.

"No problem, Henry," said a pot-bellied man, leaning on his sign. He grinned and made his sign take a slow breezy swing, as if he was about to step into the batter's box.

"I hear you got a boy this time," said the silver-haired cop. The man with the sign grinned a little harder. He reached into his pocket for two cigars.

"We should call the FBI," said Donnie.

Maybe I would have laughed if Donnie hadn't looked so bad. His face had turned white so you could hardly see his patches. And maybe we really should have called the FBI office in Butte, but I read somewhere that they keep their worst agents over there. You have to be some kind of FBI misfit to end up in Butte. I heard the dead bolt slide home in the post office door, and the pipe fell out of Donnie's jacket onto the ground. Nobody else noticed it. Everyone else was watching the cops drive away, the younger one bent over trying to light his cigar.

I think about that morning. Probably not a week goes by that I don't think about it. I see the pickets step away from their cars and trucks. I see a man throw his cigarette down and another man spit in the street. They walk toward us, toward Max, who stands in front of the Jimmy, still loaded down with wire and fittings. Max's neck is too thin, and his Levi's have shrunk an inch too high. Sid opens the door of the truck. He rests an arm, the one with all the names on it, along the back of the seat. And the man who is in charge of the rest of them, the man I know now has never been a sheriff's deputy but would have made a good one, comes a little nearer.

"You can't win," he says.

It's funny when you get in trouble. Sometimes you don't believe it's going to happen, and you don't get scared at all. Other times, especially if you're a little kid, you get so scared you can hardly move your arms or legs to save yourself. I pull my hands away from my pockets and try taking steps in place. I want to know how it will be this time. I see the red-headed man from the keno place, a crooked-nose man whose one eye catches mine while the other one looks off at the mountains in the distance. The closest man to me, he looks hung over, and I think, *I have to try to knock him down.* I wish I had more practice knocking people down. I was in a lot of scrapes when I was younger, but it's hard to actually knock someone down. Some nights I stand in front of the mirror and pretend the person who looks out at me in a T-shirt with a towel around his neck is after Alice, and I shadowbox a little. It must be the same with the man I am looking at. Maybe his wife isn't named Alice, but that doesn't matter. He shadowboxes too. He has to.

"I want this job," says Sid.

As hard as I stare at the man from Anaconda, it doesn't seem like I'm looking at someone else. I'm at the bathroom mirror, watching myself with the towel around my neck and a half-crazy look on my face.

Sid's voice has gone dry. "I need the money," he says.

Sid doesn't look at Max. He doesn't look at me either. Sid is seeing pictures in his mind's eye of people I don't know. He is seeing green felt card tables and lit-up keno boards and thinking his number will never be called. He has forgotten all about Donnie, and Donnie is his brother. Sid reaches into the truck and takes the gun from its rack. He bumps the barrel against the door, but other than that he is quick and smooth. You might think he has been practicing that move. He points the gun at the ground halfway between us and the men from Anaconda.

"It ain't loaded," says the man who's in charge of that crowd. But there is movement among the others. They know what I know. Every gun is always loaded. They grab pot-belly with the cigars and push him to the back. Still, they don't leave. They don't go get in their cars the way they're supposed to.

Donnie picks the pipe up from the ground and holds it in his fist, awkward but tight so the blood leaves his knuckles. He watches Sid for some clue what to do next. When I look at Sid, I realize I don't care about him at all, and at the moment I don't care about the Fence-Me-In either. And I sure don't care about Anaconda. I only find it hard not to care about Donnie.

"This isn't right, Max," I say.

"What?" says Max. "What?" His eyes are so glassy he can't see the boy, who is shaking, or Sid, shaking too, but willing to gamble.

"It's union wages," says Max. He turns his face to me. He's a blind man. I can hear Sid's breathing, shallow from cigarettes and fear. That's the only sound. The men from Anaconda don't even clear their throats.

"This isn't right," I say again, as if those are all the words I know. And finally Max looks not at me, but at Donnie. What he sees is family, I guess, the brother of his wife. Maybe he sees one of those family get-togethers, a picnic or Christmas Eve, where Donnie is always the star, or he thinks about how Donnie will still clown around with the little kids in the backyard. Maybe Max sees himself on the phone calling Donnie's mother with some kind of awful news. Or maybe all he sees for that one single moment is how Donnie is sixteen years old and scared, and how he's going to get hurt. I hold my breath ten seconds that seems like an hour.

"Christ," says Max. He's wheezing lightly, the way he does during hay fever season. He looks at the truck, at the Fence-Me-In sign on the door, then at Donnie's face, white as a cottonwood.

"Forget it," he says at last, and the glassy look fades a little from his eyes. What replaces it is dull and as far away as New Jersey. "This is not the only fence in Montana," says Max.

There is a moment, quiet as a prayer, then Max is moving again. He takes the pipe away from Donnie and throws it into the back of the Jimmy. I get Donnie to sit down in the truck, and I don't watch while he wipes his eyes with his sleeve. The lights go out in Sid when he gives up the gun. He slumps over, and his hand pulls another cigarette to his lips, as if that hand has a mind of its own.

"I got to take a leak," says one of those Anaconda men. "Before I do another thing."

Half a dozen of them stand in a line and piss against the post office wall. They know we are beat. Max puts the gun away, so casual you might think he had Sid take it out so he could show us the inscription on the stock. The shadowboxer from Anaconda catches my eye again, then looks away as if he is ashamed.

Max agrees to take us home. He says he will come back later in the week and hire Anaconda ironworkers to finish the job, union men.

"I can't pay both crews," he says, loud enough for everyone to hear.

"You'll make it up to them," says the guy in charge. To me, he looks relieved.

"Thanks for digging all them holes," says an ugly man standing in the back of the crowd. I'm glad when nobody laughs.

HOT SPRING

It was ten o'clock in the morning when we started back to Missoula, a corny song on the radio that kept repeating this line: "Our hearts were young and free." It was true though. I felt the way I felt that afternoon Mr. Rollins took us to see the jail, or just after he took us to jail, when our baseball team was piling back on the bus that brought us into town. Because even if we were little kids, it felt good to know we weren't in jail, or going to jail. I'd spent a year and a half away from home after my middle brother died. It's always a good feeling to leave a place like that. This time, I was just glad to have Anaconda behind me, although I didn't look forward to telling Alice the union wages were gone. I wanted to sing along with the truck radio.

Donnie didn't stop shaking until we got out onto the highway where fresh air could blow through the cab. Max was twitching too, from adrenaline, but he didn't need to feel bad. He still owned the company. He would make his money. We stopped for gas at the Circle K, and Sid went in and bought a grocery bag full of beer. It was a good thing I bought beer too, because Sid wasn't going to share any of his. When he paid, I got a good look in his wallet. There wasn't anything left in there to speak of.

Max drove the lake road home. The road drops down through the canyon following an old wooden flue from Georgetown Lake to Philipsburg. The flue is rotten, and in the winter the leaks form giant icefalls. College boys come from Missoula to practice climbing the ice. They must fall sometimes, but I don't remember reading about it. Seeing the water leak down the mountain, we had to stop and relieve ourselves off the side of the road. I needed to go since before we left the post office, but I couldn't have stood and pissed next to those men from Anaconda. It wouldn't have been right. From where we stood at the edge of the canyon, the water we made would have fallen five hundred feet if the wind hadn't blown it sideways until it disappeared. I felt I was standing on the edge of my life.

"Go ahead," said Sid. "Jump."

I laughed, but I stepped back away from the drop-off, scared by the hurt in his voice. Donnie went to sit on a rock. He looked confused, as if he thought Anaconda was his fault.

"I know what you're thinking," said Sid. He spoke softly so only I could hear. "You saved Donnie. It makes you better than me."

"Don't say that," I told him. I wasn't going to admit to anything like it. Still, we could have sat there and talked it out. We had no reason to rush home.

But the next minute, we were back in the truck and roaring down the road, nobody making a sound. There was only the radio and the whine of the Jimmy's rear end. We drove on that way, fifty miles or more. Max was careful with his trucks, and he would have given us hell if anyone else had driven that fast. An old flatbed starts to come apart at ninety. Donnie and I had identical red toolboxes in the back, and one was sliding around as if it would pitch off at any moment. Maybe it was his, and maybe it was mine. I wondered how many times in one morning I could almost die.

"Let's stop," I said.

"Stop?" said Max. He threw an empty can out the window at the back of a blue pickup, an old farmer taking his wife to town. As we shot past the pickup, the can skittered across the pavement and into the weeds.

"Let's go swimming," I said. What else could I suggest? If I'd seen a deer or an elk, even a crow, I'd have suggested hunting. If there had been one of those petting zoos beside the road, I'd have said let's stop and pet the animals. The no-name hot spring with its green pond was there on the horizon. There were cars parked on a gravel road that ran alongside the freeway. I wanted out of the truck.

"Hell, why not?" said Max. He let up on the gas, and the truck back-fired twice. My heart wanted to backfire.

"I think we lost the muffler on this thing," said Max. He reached across Donnie and me and hit Sid on the leg. "Don't worry so much," he said. "You're only broke." I guess he meant it as a joke.

Sid wouldn't get out of the truck, so we left him with the rest of the beer and headed down to the water where a dozen people were picnicking in their underwear. It was Sunday afternoon and we were going to swim naked, which seemed like an okay thing to do, but walking on the gravel Max sobered up and said we should keep our shorts on.

"Can you swim?" I asked Donnie. The pond was colder than it looked of a morning when the steam had been rising off it. Donnie was way ahead of us, into the water up to his knees before I could get my pants off. One of his patches started on his stomach and ran down to where it disappeared beneath the elastic of his shorts. Two women sat on a blanket talking quietly to each other the way women do, like they were sharing secrets. They weren't young anymore, but they looked good to me. I was tired of the company of men. I could tell they were wondering where that pale patch ended up on Donnie, what color he was under his shorts.

"I don't remember," said Donnie.

"That boy's drunk," said one of the women.

I felt tired myself. Donnie sat down in the pond without meaning to, and the other woman laughed. She had a beautiful laugh, like music.

It wasn't a big pond. It wasn't really hot water either. I'd been there twice before, and I was thinking how the only thing special about it was that it didn't quite freeze over in the winter, when I realized with a start all those picnickers were women. While I eased my way into the water, letting it creep up my legs an inch at a time, Max swam across the pond and found himself a friend. She'd been drinking too, or she was high on something. They held hands, and she stuck her tongue out at Max before they ducked under water. The water was too cold for much to happen. I wondered how they would proceed.

The laughing woman rescued Donnie. She took him to her blanket and dried him off with a big towel. He had one tiny patch of white hair on the back of his head that she rubbed carefully and showed to her friend. I was cold and sober and making up my mind to ask if I could borrow the towel after they finished with Donnie. Max and his new girlfriend came up for air. She had her arms around his neck as if she was saving him from drowning, and he was choking and laughing and treading water when we heard the shot.

Nobody moved at first. Nobody could think. We kept doing what we were doing before while the sound of a gun repeated off the mountains on either side of the highway. I couldn't say what that sound was, or if I'd heard a sound just like it only some other place, some other time, or if I'd heard that sound a thousand times in my memory. I couldn't say where I was, or who I was with. I had a burning in my hands, despite the cold water. Sadness rose up as if it would cover me. I didn't know if I could keep the sadness at bay.

Donnie was the one to say it.

"Sid. Oh Christ, Sid," he said.

He got up too fast and fell down on one of the women whose blanket he was sharing. Max was trying to find a place to stand when he heard it. He pushed the girl's arms away and pulled himself onto the rocks, running barefoot across the gravel without a thought about his feet. That girl ran after him. I did my best to follow him to the truck, but I couldn't keep up.

Sid was sitting up in the truck when I got there. He held the rifle across his lap, and there were tears mixed with the dust on his face. There was a hole in the roof of the truck where there hadn't been any holes before. Max reached in through the open window and took the gun away from him. I was sick from running so hard, and Donnie started crying. The girl who had been swimming with Max sat down hard in the gravel. My mind refused to work properly for a while. I knew I was riding towards Missoula in the back of the truck with Donnie. Sid was up front with Max, and they were yelling at each other, only it was Max who was doing all the yelling, and Sid was sitting lower and lower in the seat. I knew Max was driving too fast. But all I could think about was what it was like to have brothers, how I had two a long time ago and later only one, my brother Troy who went out to San Diego, which I had always thought would be hot and full of Mexicans, but which I now knew must be very similar to Montana.

BROTHERS

Sid left town within a few days, and nobody knew where he went. The season was almost over. On payday, two men I didn't know came to the office to see Max. They said Sid owed them money. Max took them into the shop and told the rest of us to stay out. When the men left, they carried away the portable welder, but they looked grim and said they'd be back. I thought I'd wait on my check.

Donnie missed his brother, and he needed some time off. Three weeks after our last trip to Anaconda, I took him down to the bus station so he could get the Greyhound to New Jersey. I told him to take it easy back there and not go to work for the Mafia. I told him, don't join any unions.

"We should have fought those guys," said Donnie. He wasn't his old self. "Sid needed the money."

I wanted to tell him he was wrong. Sid could have lived without the money. What Sid couldn't handle was the way he turned his back on his brother.

"It wasn't that way," said Donnie.

I wanted to tell him about brothers. I wanted to tell about Troy joining the marines and getting kicked out and living in that motel in San Diego. I wanted to tell him that much anyway. But a woman started talking nonsense on the P.A., and the bus driver asked everyone to get on the bus, and Donnie wouldn't listen to me. I wanted to tell him he was like a brother to me. He found his seat on the bus, and when he saw me standing outside, he opened his window.

"I was there," he said. "The money was everything to Sid. We should have fought for it. You let us down."

He looked around the station as if he wanted to remember the place. Then he laid his head back against the seat. When he closed his eyes, I could see the pale patches on his eyelids. Maybe he was trying to imagine Anaconda, the way it should have happened. Maybe he was just tired. He didn't say, though I stayed until the bus pulled out.

So I worked by myself, which isn't bad except when you have a lot on your mind. I started a backyard job up the canyon not far from where Alice and I lived. I didn't like working close to home. I kept thinking Alice might see me and think I didn't work hard enough. She might come by when I was taking a breather in the truck, having coffee. Alice wanted to understand about Anaconda, but she didn't know Sid or Donnie, so she couldn't feel bad about them. When you're a nurse, you see it all the time. People get hurt.

Max gave me the plans to build a dog run on the hill. The neighborhood had a real name, but I only know what Donnie called it, Snob Knob. It should have been simple, eight posts to quick-set between the house and the garage. People up there, they want you in and out in a hurry. There were kids' toys scattered around the yard, yellow plastic trucks and a naked Barbie doll, a wading pool full of leaves. I piled them all up in the driveway and dug my holes. I mixed the special cement in a wheelbarrow according to the instructions, mixed it light and made ready to use it right away. It hardens in no time.

When I leaned my shovel against the garage, the aluminum door made a hollow bang and a terrific barking started up, loud as the animal shelter on River Road at feeding time. I wondered how many dogs were inside. I should have gone about my business, but I had to see for myself, so I went around the side of the garage and looked in the window. There was only one dog, a slick black Doberman, as mean an animal as I ever saw, trying to chew his way through the garage door. I tapped on the window to make him stop. The garage door was new, but it wasn't built to hold a Doberman. He barked and snapped and bounced off the walls. Here was a violent dog, a dog with mental problems.

My cement was setting up in the wheelbarrow, and I had to get down to business. I'd positioned the first post, slopped some mud into the hole and leveled the post up, when I heard the sound of the Doberman throwing himself against the window. That sound, dog against glass, made me pick up my shovel and head straight for the truck. Before I took three steps, I heard the crash of a window pane falling to the ground. There was a woodpile in the yard wedged in between the garage and a big maple tree. I didn't think I could make it to the truck, so I climbed the woodpile as the Dobie came around the corner of the garage looking for me. He'd cut his nose coming through the glass, and the smell of his own blood made him crazier than ever. When he found me, I realized right away the woodpile wasn't high enough. He was up on it in one leap, though he fell back when I hit him with a stick of larch. That was temporary. He was going to keep coming until he got me. I tossed another chunk of wood at his head and I went up on the roof.

A kid's shoe was up on the roof, wedged into the gutter. I wondered how it got there, but I know a lot of stuff can end up on a roof, given time. I pulled myself up away from the edge and took a look out over the neighborhood.

"Hey," I said, but I didn't say it loud. I felt too foolish, and there was nobody there to hear me. Rich people are the same everywhere. They keep a distance between themselves and their neighbors. I hoped I might see a man out mowing his lawn or a woman hanging up the wash. Of course, nobody would hang up the wash in that neighborhood, but somebody could have been waxing the car. There wasn't anyone. The Doberman stopped barking and settled down to watch. His growling sounded like the Jimmy idling on a cold morning.

When you're an adult, there's not a lot to do up on a roof. Troy and I used to have this spot we could get to, a tree house Ernie built for us when we were younger, where the shade of the tree kept us cool even in the middle of summer. We could get away from the world, all those damn orange groves, my mother's sadness, my father's milk dreams. It was our one safe place. Troy practiced smoking cigarettes there, but he wouldn't give me any. He was afraid they would stunt my growth and the parents would look at me funny and know why I was smaller than the others, that he was to blame.

That tree house, Troy wrote me from the marines. *There's no place like it here. Maybe I need a place like that, Johnny. Maybe I get wasted too much.*

I had a view of the Missoula Valley and the Clark Fork River worming its way through town. I sent a mental message to Max at the Fence-Me-In. "Help. Am being held hostage." But from where I was I couldn't see the Fence-Me-In, and who knows, I could have been sending mental messages to a barbershop or a dry cleaners. All I could do was sit and think about myself, about being an ironworker and before that a college student for a little while, and before that all the memories I didn't want to remember. I wondered if a Doberman had ever chased my old man up on a roof when he was doing his milk route. I thought about my middle brother, Darrel, but then I made myself stop thinking about him. I thought about Troy and the night we sat on the porch when Mrs. Guiniere drove by and Troy said, "She could juggle your load." The next morning he went to San Diego, where the marines were looking for a few good men. *Maybe I get wasted too much.* He wrote that in a letter. Maybe he wasn't good enough.

The hands of my watch moved toward three o'clock, when Alice would head to the hospital. There was nothing wrong with Alice. She would never get stranded on a roof or be chased out of town by men in pickups or die in a hotel bed, ashamed to call home. I wondered what Alice would do that evening if she got home and I wasn't there. Those people who owned the Doberman might be out of town for days. Alice would think I'd run out on her. She would guess that I'd fallen in with a religious cult, or all along been a secret bigamist.

"My first husband?" I could hear her say. "Johnny Foster? He was an ironworker."

At five, the Doberman's lady came home. She had her car full of groceries, and she looked tired. Her kids stared at their toys piled in the driveway, the way people stare at hurricane wreckage. She offered to make it up to me, to pay me a day's wages out of her own pocket.

"Union wages?" I asked. She didn't understand.

"It's not your fault," I told her, not meaning the dog so much as Anaconda, Donnie, Troy, Darrel, the works. I came down off the roof and got right into the truck. She had put the dog in the house, and he was up on the couch looking out the picture window. It looked to be a strong window.

"What about your wheelbarrow?" she asked. I pretended not to hear her. I saw her in my rearview mirror when I pulled away, standing next to that load of hardened cement. It must have weighed two hundred pounds. It could be in her driveway today.

MONTANA

Sitting on that roof, it occurred to me that with Donnie gone to New Jersey, I could get along without the Fence-Me-In. I thought I'd give it a try. I went fishing for a month, first in Montana's Big Hole, then over to Idaho, to the Snake River. I fished my heart out. When I got sick of trout, I went to Washington to stay with friends. Somebody said I should look for work while I was there, but I didn't. I knew they were hiring in Missoula too, at one of the smaller lumber mills. A hardwood mill, and it wasn't union. But I wasn't ready to go back to work. I thought work was overrated. I thought I might go back to work, and I might not. I called Alice from Bellingham. She knew what was up.

"No hard feelings," she said. It was over the phone, and I couldn't tell if she was lying. "I'm not storing your stuff, though," she said.

I might yet go pick up that stuff. I don't say I am planning to. I don't make plans that way. Sometimes a guy has to juggle his load. That is what I plan to do, keep on the move until the money runs out. On the highway, I meet people. Some of them are like me, and they ask where I'm going or where I've been. If we come to an understanding, they ask for directions. I don't mean how to get somewhere. I mean where to go. I give them advice. Some I send to Utah, which is a place where I have not been and don't plan to visit anytime soon, but I know it's there. Others I send east. In New Jersey, they can work in fast food and make enough money to get by. Or to California, to the San Joaquin Valley, where there's farmwork and they won't freeze.

Two things I always tell them. You are not your brother's keeper. And don't go to Montana. Montana will break your heart.

· Mediators ·

THAT MORNING WHEN THE DOORBELL RANG, Isaac Franklin was alone in the apartment on Azalea Street. If he had been upstairs in bed, he wouldn't have answered the bell, but he was downstairs on the sofa, and he knew if they looked in through the window, whoever was out there could see him: a tall man in jeans and a flannel shirt, trying to sleep with a child's quilt over his legs. When he opened the door, he was relieved to find two young girls on his front steps. It could have been religious people or the teenagers who showed up every three months with their memorized speeches and tubs of candy. He had just come in from the night shift at Morgan's Station, and it made him lightheaded to stand in the doorway. He could see he wasn't what the girls had in mind either. His stomach turned over from the package of sweet rolls he had eaten for breakfast and from the glare of the sun off the street.

"Did you need something?" he asked. The look on their faces made him check his fly.

One of the girls held a piece of paper in front of her like a treasure map. It was folded into three parts and stained, as if it had been buried in her backyard for years. She had pale hair and a square face that wasn't going to be pretty when she grew up; she knew how it would turn out for her already. Her eyes gave it away. The station wagon at the curb belonged to her mother, who kept the car close to give the girls courage.

"Your turn," whispered the girl with the map. She elbowed a second girl who stood beside her. Isaac thought this one might be part Japanese or Filipino. She had dusky brown skin with freckles across the bridge of her nose, and her dark hair fell over one eye. The other eye, the one staring past him into his apartment, was a surprising and delicate shade of green. She couldn't have been older than ten.

"We go to the Henry Martin School," said this darker girl, "in Visalia." She said it as though the name of the school should mean something to Isaac. "There was this fight," she said. "At the Henry Martin School."

"Don't say fight," whispered the first girl, the one with blonde hair. "Nobody got hurt."

"There was this disturbance," said the dark-skinned girl. "It wasn't no riot or anything. Now they want us to start a club." She talked as though she were in a trance, as though she took some kind of drugs for kids.

"We're the madiators," she said.

"*Mediators*," whispered the blonde girl.

"Whatever," said the other. "You want to buy a T-shirt, or what?"

If he had been fully awake, Isaac would have said no, or if the girls had been more polished, or if the one who had stared into his apartment hadn't turned her eyes on him. Her eyes were like something he'd seen once in a magazine, like Japanese lanterns, green and glowing. He tried not to give money to people at the door. He didn't have anything extra to give away. His wife, Lynette, was a student, and they had a five-year-old daughter, Marcie, thin and never quiet, who would one day go door-to-door in Ivanhoe with her friends the same way this green-eyed girl was going around, trying to raise money. Marcie would never be the leader of a group. She was timid around other children, though with her parents it was different. She was a tyrant in the apartment. Isaac wanted to lean on her a little, but Lynette wouldn't have it. Lynette said they should build Marcie's confidence.

He didn't think to ask the girls why their new club needed money. He wanted to know about the riot, probably nothing more than a food fight in the cafeteria. It was good for kids to let off steam. Soon enough a girl grew up and all those hormones came to life. Isaac could picture it. This girl would want to date some boy, and that boy would pressure her to ride his motorcycle and watch his football games and stay out later than her parents wanted her to. The next thing, she would be married and pregnant, maybe in that order, and living in a two-bedroom apartment while she went to school in business or nursing to get a decent job. Her husband would work at a gas station or a transmission shop, or simply drive around all day with his tattooed arm out the window of some piece of junk car, the kind he swore back in high school he would never own.

Isaac ordered a purple shirt for his daughter with green frogs on it and a logo: *Even Frogs Need Friends.* He guessed his daughter liked frogs. She liked the shows on TV with puppets. He wrote out the check for fifteen dollars, and he should have looked at the balance first, but he saw the station wagon inch up the street, and the blonde girl was impatient. She took his check and showed him where to sign his name. The other names were already unreadable where she had twisted up the paper.

"Thank you for helping the Henry Martin School," said the one with the pretty eyes.

"How long do I have to wait?" he asked. His question made the girls look at each other blankly. "For the T-shirt?" said Isaac.

"We don't know," said the blonde girl. The other girl grabbed the check and ran for the idling car.

"We got another one," she called to the woman. "We can quit."

He saw his check slip out of the girl's hands and flutter into the street. She darted behind the station wagon after it, and Isaac closed his eyes, waiting for the sound of brakes, of a car hitting a body, a mother's cry. But that part was his imagination. He hadn't slept and he was on edge, and the green-eyed girl retrieved his check from the street and climbed into the station wagon after her friend. They were happy, the two of them, freed from their obligations to the Henry Martin School. Isaac lay down again on the couch, pulling Marcie's quilt over his head.

He couldn't remember what it felt like to get enough sleep. Waking up of an afternoon he had a bitter taste in his mouth from coffee and cigarettes, and his feet felt wooden, as though he had slept standing up. He had asked Marcie a hundred times not to slam the door when she came in from school, or maybe he only thought about asking her as he lay on the couch with the sound echoing in his head. Every day now, he woke up with that hungover feeling in his legs and a worse feeling, one that came to him when he imagined what it would be like to work nights for the rest of his life at Morgan's Station.

The clock above the television said it was after five, later than he usually slept. Lynette was cooking; she had the radio on low so it wouldn't wake him, but that was just for show. She could make the pots and pans sound as if they were falling from the sky. Through the doorway to the kitchen, Isaac saw his little girl at the table with her markers. Marcie had written on a piece of paper, random letters and strange private symbols, and now she read what she had written out loud, as if it were a book.

"Then," said Marcie to her mother, "all the dinosaurs died." She had the tone of authority she used when she had just come in from the library. "Ask any paleontologist," said Marcie. Isaac didn't know what a paleontologist was. He was sure his daughter didn't either. "They will tell you," she said, "those paleontologists. All of these dinosaurs certainly are dead."

His daughter saw him in the doorway. Her eyes focused above his head, and she gave her mouth a small sideways motion like she did when she was trying to put something over on him.

"These dinosaurs," said Marcie, "are dead as poop."

Lynette turned from the stove. "Marcie," she said.

The girl laughed out loud. "Deader than poop. These are poop dinosaurs."

"Marcie Franklin," said Lynette, but she looked at Isaac. "Good morning." That was the thing she always said when he slept too long. "You were going to make dinner."

He remembered his promise. Lynette was frying onions and garlic in the cast-iron skillet. She had chopped up other vegetables and pushed them into little piles on the counter, and when she dumped a pile of cabbage onto the hot oil, Isaac's stomach tightened.

"What are we eating?" he asked. "Glop?" It was one of their old jokes, but she wasn't in the mood. She dropped a lid on the skillet.

"We could eat whatever you want to eat if you brought it home and got it on the stove."

"I don't want to hear this," said Marcie. The girl had been holding one of her markers up like a pointer. She dropped it and put both of her hands over her ears. "I don't want to hear this kind of talk."

"Sorry," said Isaac. He didn't know if he was saying it to his wife or to his daughter. It wasn't what he wanted to say. "Some of us aren't perfect."

"Dinosaurs were not perfect," said Marcie, her hands still over her ears. "Dinosaurs pooped large green eggs." She was practically shouting now. "Actually, they were tremendous. Dinosaurs ate cabbages and lived in nuclear families and long ago they pooped themselves until they all died."

"That's some theory, Miss Know-it-all," he said.

"Don't start in on her," said Lynette.

"I thought you didn't want her to talk that way at the dinner table."

"Dinner isn't ready," said Lynette. "You didn't notice."

"Sometimes dinosaurs pooped on their own heads," said Marcie.

Isaac got a beer out of the refrigerator, though he knew it was the last thing to settle his stomach.

"We're going to her recital," said Lynette.

"I'm just having one beer."

"Daddy," said Marcie. "How do you draw a dinosaur?"

"Ask your father to set the table," said Lynette.

"As soon as you're finished drawing me a dinosaur," said Marcie, "you have to set the table."

He took the marker and drew the kind of thing she liked, a big belly and scales everywhere. He gave the dinosaur long straight hair like her mother had, and bug eyes.

"Are there any dinosaurs left?" asked the girl. She knew what he was up to.

"Just a few," he said.

"It starts at six," said Lynette, "the recital."

"I heard you."

"You might want to take a shower."

"I don't know if I can eat anything," he said.

"Suit yourself."

"Don't worry, Daddy," said his daughter. "We're not eating glop." She was trying not to laugh. She leaned toward him as though she were sharing a secret.

"It's poop," she said. "We found it in the backyard. It's from dinosaurs."

He wanted a cigarette in the car, but Lynette didn't know he was smoking again, so he drove in silence into Visalia, to the college where his wife took classes, where he'd always thought one day he would sign up for something himself. The car made a complaining noise every time he pulled up to a stop sign. It was Lynette's car, one she'd had since before they were married. He wondered how she hadn't noticed a sound like that. She would drive the car back and forth to Visalia week after week until the brakes froze up some morning in the middle of the road. He found a parking place, and his wife hurried them into a large hall with heavy oak doors and worn chairs that creaked when he sat down. Isaac looked through the program a young woman had thrust at him. His daughter was in the beginner class. Hers was the biggest group of dancers, and when they came out on the stage, all in red leotards and fluffy red skirts, there were chubby ones and thin ones and tall ones, and girls with their hair up in fancy arrangements, and girls who were shy the way Marcie was shy. Before and after their performance, they huddled together in the wings as if they were doing something incredibly important, but when they danced he was disappointed. They waved their arms like the crowd at a football game. He wished he'd left the beer alone. When Marcie's group was done, he had to go find the men's room.

There was a line. Waiting, he wanted the old days to come back when it was okay to smoke in the men's room. He could hardly remember those days. He remembered being a boy and going into a men's room with his grandfather, his grandfather tossing a cigarette into the toilet and laughing as Isaac flushed it again and again, watching it swirl around the bowl. He looked at the other men in this restroom, and he wondered what they were thinking about, away from the women and their daughters in leotards. The man in front of him had a bad leg, and his right shoe, heavy and brown, had a sole three inches thick. He steadied himself ahead of Isaac, leaning on a cane. Isaac found himself relaxing for the first time since Lynette had woken him up with the sounds she made in the kitchen.

"What do you make of this recital thing?" Isaac asked the man. "Pretty lame, huh?"

Staring at the man's thick shoe, he realized what he had said, and he wanted to take the words back. It was the sort of mistake he usually made in front of Lynette. But the man with the bad leg must have been lost in thought. He hadn't heard Isaac clearly.

"Yes," said the man. "Isn't it something?"

"Great costumes too," said Isaac, watching the other man disappear into a stall. Isaac wondered what the man did with his cane while he was in there. He waited his turn at the urinal. It took a long time. None of the men seemed to be in a hurry.

Leaving the men's room, Isaac didn't want to go back to the recital, so he looked for a drinking fountain. It was more comfortable in the hallway than in the auditorium itself, where everything smelled musty, like the church basements he'd been in as a kid. Maybe they had another auditorium somewhere else that got used more than this one. Maybe this was just the auditorium for dancing little girls. He heard the recorded music begin, trumpets and a drum set, and then a man's heavy shoe as it came along the hardwood floor toward him. Isaac stepped away from the fountain to let the other man drink. They looked at the floor and for a moment they listened to the music together.

"It's interesting," said the man with the game leg.

"Yes," said Isaac. "Great show."

"It's ordinary enough," said the other man. "No, I was thinking about how all this makes a father feel. Like a changing of the guard."

Isaac didn't have an answer for that. He didn't have a problem talking to strangers, but if he talked much longer to this one, the man wouldn't be a stranger anymore, and Isaac wasn't ready for that.

"When I'm here with the girls," said the man, "I feel relieved of my duty in a funny way." He was older than Isaac, pushing sixty, and he spoke with an accent, the same as on those TV shows from England.

"I no longer have to think about whether I'm going to amount to anything," said the man. "Now the focus is on them. They've taken over."

"Like mediators," said Isaac. "That's how I see them."

The man looked at him, one eye closed, his face a gray question mark. "How do you mean exactly?"

"Just a thought," said Isaac, laughing. He shoved his hands into his pockets and started back down the hall. He walked slowly and let the other man go into the auditorium ahead of him.

He was supposed to clock in at Morgan's at midnight, and he wouldn't have been late again if he hadn't gone upstairs to read stories to Marcie. They had driven home in silence, taking the road back to Ivanhoe that ran past one of the last walnut groves, where the air cooled off a little in the evening. Even Marcie was quiet. She sat in the backseat in her dance outfit, upset because she had forgotten the steps to her final number.

"You did fine," said Lynette.

"Sure," said Isaac. "You were great. What do you call that dance?"

"You don't call it anything," said Marcie. "It's a dance. It's dumb. I hate it." She cried the rest of the way home. Lynette tried to comfort her, then gave up and stared out the window at the lit-up farmhouses.

Half an hour later, he had fallen asleep next to Marcie in the middle of one of her storybooks, the one about barnyard animals who wore clothes and cooked their dinner in a regular kitchen. He'd thought Lynette would call him, and maybe she had called, but he wasn't able to get up from the bed and get dressed in time. There was an accident on Mooney that slowed him down, and it was a quarter to two when he got to the station. Derek, the night manager, wouldn't listen to him.

"Don't even sign in," said Derek. He was stocking the ice cream coolers, and Isaac saw that he was breathing hard. The back of Derek's shirt was damp with sweat.

"You're kidding," said Isaac. There were people waiting at the counter to pay for their gas and beer.

"I'm not kidding," said Derek. He stopped fooling with the ice cream. The thin gray lines in the cloth of his shirt had turned a deeper shade, an inky black. "Just go on home. You can come by for your check next week."

Isaac closed his eyes against the lights of the store. He went outside and stood next to the pay phone to think what he could do. He would have gone back in and tried to apologize. He saw himself doing just that, humbling himself in front of Derek, then losing his temper and tearing the store apart, throwing food off the shelves, smashing jars of mustard and instant coffee against the cinder block walls. None of it really happened. He only saw it happening. He wondered if he could take Derek, and he wasn't sure, and he wondered if the only reason he didn't hit Derek was because he was afraid Derek would hit him back. He got into his car and wanted to sit for a moment, but he didn't want Derek to know how upset he was, so he turned the key and pulled out of the lot as quickly as he could.

When he got home, he opened the door to the living room and let himself in, trying not to wake Marcie or Lynette. The apartment looked different to him now. He remembered how he felt when they moved into the place, new and clean, part of a short street of identical living rooms the government had built in Ivanhoe. It was the best place in town to live with a baby on the paycheck he brought in from Morgan's Station. He hadn't expected they would live here as long as they had. As he closed the door behind him and hung up his keys and jacket, he decided he would sleep on the couch and explain everything to his wife in the morning. She might be angry, or she might surprise him the way she used to and take his side. He saw that the kitchen light was on.

"Isaac?" she said. He heard her chair scrape. Lynette came into the front room, holding a pair of scissors. She was uneasy in the apartment at night, and he had scared her. She was in her bathrobe, which meant she had been asleep for a while. She had gotten up to work on a dress for Marcie.

"What happened?" she said. Lynette slipped the scissors into the pocket of her robe. He could tell she was relieved to find it was only him standing in the doorway, but her relief wouldn't last. He stared at the wallpaper of the apartment, at the place near the sofa where the cornflowers had turned brown from one of Marcie's spills. He didn't have to say anything. Lynette could see how it was.

"Oh, Isaac," she said.

He walked past her through the kitchen and out onto the back steps for a cigarette.

Through the kitchen window, he watched his wife put away her sewing and pour a glass of wine. She began to leaf through a stack of bills, sorting them into two piles. He knew what she was doing: she was deciding which bills would have to be paid, which ones she could put off. She wrote a check and entered the amount in the ledger, then flipped through the checkbook with a frown on her face.

When she opened the back door, she had the small blue book in her hand.

"There's a check missing."

She watched him smoke without saying anything, watched as he looked out at the other apartments that curved away down the street. The whole lot of them had gone up in one summer, and the rents were subsidized. He and Lynette had been lucky to get one of them. In the distance, there were lights on in one or two windows, but most of the apartments were dark. As much as he hated getting up and driving to work at midnight, he would miss how it felt to be awake when the rest of the town was asleep. That part, and getting to know the voices of the all-night disc jockeys, made him feel special.

"Do you have any idea about this check?"

He remembered the way his grandparents had lived, the old ones who had raised him. Their house was still there across town, over near the elementary school, though they were long gone. A Mexican family lived there now, had been in the house for years. His grandparents never had any money either. *There's a dollar missing from the jar*, his grandmother had said one night, and his grandfather had got so angry he came apart. *A dollar*, Cy Franklin had cried, letting a dish fall to the floor. *A whole dollar?* His grandfather had thrown the kitchen fan against the wall, thrown it at a piece of needlepoint his grandmother had put up long before Isaac was born. The fan was broken already, but it could have been fixed.

"I didn't write any checks," said Isaac. "How could I? You keep the checkbook in your purse all the time like you're afraid I might spend your last penny."

"Like what?" she said. She came closer to him on the deck. The scissors fell from the pocket of her robe, and she stooped to pick them up.

"Never mind," said Isaac.

"Why do you start something, then pretend you haven't?" said Lynette.

"I'm not starting anything. Why are you accusing me of wasting money?"

"I just need to know who you wrote this check to."

"I'm telling you, I didn't write any damn check."

A light came on in the apartment next door. Isaac had never been in that apartment, but he knew how it looked inside. It would be laid out exactly the same as the one he rented, with the same sort of yard-sale lamps and sofas. His neighbor, a thin woman who worked in Visalia at the bank, had the place to herself. All she did was clean the bank after they locked the doors, but she thought that made her better than everybody else on the street. She stood in her kitchen now, hidden behind the little bit of curtain she had hung at the window.

"Great," he said. "Let's entertain the neighbors."

"The neighbors," said Lynette. "I don't care about these stupid neighbors. Just tell me who you wrote the check to."

"I'm telling you, I didn't write any checks. Count them again. You must have written it. Or maybe your genius fucking daughter wrote one."

Lynette came toward him then with the scissors in her hand. He had seen her angry before, had made her so angry she couldn't speak, but her face was different in this anger. There were no tears this time, just a white hot look that robbed her lips of softness and of color. He took a step away. The stairs were behind him and he didn't want to step down off the deck and out of the circle of light. Isaac heard a soft cry from an upstairs window, and he swore again, this time under his breath.

She meant to stab him. When he told the story later, he wouldn't be making that up, though she would deny it. She would say she only meant to poke him with the scissors, but it was more than that. He fended her away with his arm; he dropped his cigarette at the same time and jostled her harder than he meant to. It knocked her to her knees, and when she got up her hands were empty, but she clenched her small red fists and went for his groin. Isaac managed to turn away so that she hit him on the hip and sent him falling down the stairs onto the concrete slab below.

He could see her on the deck above him, unwilling to follow him down to the darkness. She knelt and waited for him, unafraid. In the weak light that came through the kitchen window, her hand groped for the scissors she had dropped on the deck. Isaac heard the voice again, a small chest wracked with coughing. He didn't place it at first as he readied himself to lunge at his wife. He couldn't let her knock him down. He didn't intend to hit her, but he could see himself holding Lynette's arms, squeezing them until the tears came to her eyes. He would make her see reason.

"Mama," said the voice, breaking against the night. "Where are you?"

He moved halfway up the stairs to the deck, trying to hold off recognizing that voice until he dealt with Lynette. His wife took a step toward the door, her head tilted to one side as Marcie called once more from the upstairs bedroom. Before Isaac could move again, his wife was inside the house, shutting the door against him. He heard her turn the lock and slide the chain into place. She would try to calm herself, try not to appear before the child with tears on her face.

Isaac heard his own breath coming rough and quick through his mouth. He sat down on the deck and leaned his back against the wall of the apartment. The wall felt cool against his damp shirt. When he got hold of himself, he could hear the crickets from under the deck, and down along the fence he could hear the frogs that were misplaced from the orchard when the last apartments were built. They made a high-pitched sound he always associated with tree frogs. He wondered if frogs really lived in trees. He wondered if they lived in nuclear families and fought with their wives. He wondered if his own mother, a woman he had never known, would have been willing to fight someone in order to defend him.

He got to his feet and stood close to the door.

"Lynette," he whispered, not wanting his voice to carry across the yard.

He had a vision of himself, and in his vision he wasn't standing there on the deck. He sat alone on a wooden chair in a third-floor apartment in town, eating dinner in front of a television. He saw himself leave the apartment in a car whose backseat was littered with old newspapers and food wrappers. Then he saw himself in winter light, on a park bench in Visalia with other fathers, watching Marcie ride the swing with a grim look on her face. In his vision, he was afraid to look at his watch and see how little of his time was left.

"Lynette," he said, "open the door." But he wasn't begging. He felt the cold sweat on his back, smelled his own smell of cigarettes and fear.

"I remember now," he said. "About the check." In his mind, the scene had changed: he was parked in his car here on Azalea Street at sunset. He was drinking coffee from a Styrofoam cup, watching Lynette through the front window as she read a storybook to his daughter.

"I remember who I wrote it to."

Above him, he saw Lynette at the upstairs window, the real Lynette, not the one in his vision. She looked out, but she looked over his head. She held Marcie in her arms, and the girl coughed again before lowering her head onto her mother's neck.

"Lynette," he said, a bit louder. His hip hurt where he had fallen on the concrete, and he rubbed at it gently. "I'm sorry. Let me in now." His wife drew the blinds against the night so that all he could see upstairs was the silhouette the two of them made together. She stepped away from the window, which caused him to smile. She was going to come down and open the door now. He was glad he had only imagined the other things, the park and the strange apartment. She was going to let him in. She made her shadow do a dance against the drawn blinds as she put Marcie into bed, and he heard the frogs call to each other in the yard, and he heard the hum of the refrigerator inside the apartment. He imagined each footstep as she came down the flight of stairs from the bedroom into the kitchen. He moved to the door, listening for the sound of the bolt and the chain. He was still listening, waiting, hardly breathing at all, when she turned off the porch light and left him outside, alone, already accustomed to the dark.

· Rivers of Wood ·

THERE ARE NIGHTS I LIE AWAKE and can't remember my life before I started at the mill. The farthest back I can go is the day Gary Wright caught a sliver in his eye and a man named Chatten came to the mill to work in Gary's place. I had a life before then, sure, but anymore it seems like it was somebody else's life, a life I was told about one afternoon by some old woman who had a lot of photographs she wanted to show me, and some of them were photographs of me. I grew up in a different state around hardworking people. My folks were decent. I once had two brothers. Certain events happened to me, some good and some bad. I was married for a time to a Missoula girl. All of that is history, and history can be hard to bring into focus. A sliver in the eye is not history. We didn't see why Gary Wright had to lose his job over it. It wasn't like he cut anything off.

Missoula Lumber hires three winos for every hard worker, and we figured this Chatten would not be one of the hard workers. He was over six feet tall and looked strong enough, but it was obvious he hadn't worked in a mill before. He didn't have any gloves, and I'm pretty sure there was an extra pair in the washroom, but I'm also pretty sure nobody offered them to him. The first morning he came over from the Job Service, I watched him pull four-quarter oak off the planer and pile it in a loose heap on a cart. In no time at all he'd made himself a terrible mess. I knew Duffy wouldn't put up with it. Duffy was our foreman.

"You," shouted Duffy, "new guy." Duffy always shouted. He'd been too long around all the machinery. "You know what the hell you're doing?"

He made a big production of turning off the planer and waiting for the knives to stop spinning. They said Grant Duffy was a pretty fair football player once, how he tried to go to college on football a couple of times but had trouble keeping his weight down. Now he meant to tell the world how tough it was working with a new man like Chatten. I hated Grant Duffy, but so what? Everybody hated him.

"Why didn't you show me how you wanted it done in the first place?" said Chatten. This new man was soft-spoken, his voice so deep it sounded as if it came all the way up from his shoes. I could see Duffy's neck swell. If the owner of the mill, a college type named Henries, hadn't come onto the floor just then, ranting and raving about a shipment of doorstop that got sent halfway to Moscow in Russia instead of the Moscow that's in Idaho, Chatten might have wished he'd kept his mouth buttoned. Christ, it would have been simpler if he had.

It didn't take long to discover how much we were going to miss Gary Wright. At noon Chatten sat against the wall next to his bicycle while he built his lunch. It was strange food he brought from home. He didn't eat lunchmeat, and I don't know if he even ate bread. He brought a bag of crackers made from rice and a jar of brown spread that looked like peanut butter, only it wasn't peanut butter, and he made a kind of a sandwich out of that, topping the whole mess off with alfalfa and honey. Half of it never got past his beard.

Gary Wright on the other hand used to have normal habits, and what we missed the most, he had the best jokes to tell at lunch. He didn't go in for the real nasty ones. Mostly he told ethnic jokes, but he wasn't prejudiced either. He would tell a joke about Mexicans, then one about blacks, then Indians. We had some Hmong boys working in the mill, and Gary was getting up a few Hmong jokes. He didn't have it out for any one group. The rest of us wanted to tell jokes the way Gary did, but none of us were as good at it. Chatten's first day, I told the one about putting Velcro on the ceiling so little black kids won't jump on the bed. And Vernon Waddy told the one about what happens when a North Dakota boy marries a Puerto Rican girl, but Vernon got it screwed up.

I started to tell the one about why there were only ten thousand Indians at Custer's last stand. I never got to the punch line.

"My wife's Indian," said Chatten.

I couldn't remember the rest. A couple of guys laughed as if the joke was on me, and Duffy came into the lunchroom with that ugly glare on his face, like glaring was his true vocation, like maybe it was something he practiced every day. He told us all to get back to work. He glared twice at Chatten. I didn't see Chatten again until five o'clock when I went to the lunchroom after my thermos and found him standing next to his bike, an old-fashioned Schwinn with fat tires. He was pulling splinters out of his hands with his teeth.

"Is this a joke too?" he said. He spoke to me in that same voice he used on the foreman, sort of a no laughing matter, no shit voice. I could see from across the room someone had let the air out of his tires, and it looked like they'd buggered up one of the valve stems too. I figured if I didn't want an enemy for life, I'd better offer the man a ride home. It had been snowing all day, so lucky for Chatten somebody *had* let the air out of his tires, but you couldn't make him admit he was thankful for the ride. He hardly said a word all the time he was in my truck, even when we slid through an intersection on account of the snow and almost hit a station wagon.

We took the underpass to the other side of the Burlington Northern tracks where I suspected Chatten and his old lady had some kind of mobile home. I don't care for mobile homes, but that's more history, and we're not after history here. A mobile home is about the cheapest way to live. I was looking for his trailer when he said, "Right here," and had me pull up in front of a big white tepee. There was a painting of a blue buffalo on one side, or maybe it was an ox. He caught me staring at it.

"There aren't any blue buffalo," I said. I skipped over the ox part.

"You're right," said Chatten, and he stood there on the sidewalk until I drove away.

February was bitter. Night after night the pilot light went out on my furnace, and I woke up shivering. If I get too cold, the muscles in the small of my back ache, sometimes for days.

One morning about five, I couldn't get back to sleep even after I relit the furnace, so I got up and sat in a chair. While I was waiting for the paper boy, I could hear the woman downstairs arguing with her boyfriend about how often he wanted to have sex. Pretty often. That sort of thing can put me in a bad mood.

When I got to work, I found Duffy already in the lunchroom, peeling an orange and telling an Indian joke to the Hmongs. He can't tell jokes, but he's so big and awful most of the younger guys will wait around until the end to laugh.

"Talk about Indian jokes," I said, "you should see where this guy Chatten lives."

"Screw Chatten," said Duffy. Like it was something he thought I should do.

"No thank you," I said right back, and I could see Duffy didn't appreciate me for it. "He lives in a damn tepee," I said.

The room got quiet for a minute. The only sound I heard was someone in the washroom fighting with the towel dispenser. I thought maybe the Hmongs didn't know what a tepee was.

"You know, like the old-time wild Indians lived in," I said. "Like in the movies." I heard the can flush, and it was Chatten who came out of the washroom. He went over to study the different lists of rules pinned on the bulletin board, as if there was something there he needed to know. He didn't look at me.

"What kind of Indians?" said Duffy. He stuck half his orange in his mouth and smiled real big at me.

"Never mind," I said. That thing Duffy did with the orange, that was no pretty thing to see.

"Johnny Foster," said Duffy, "you help Chatten on the planer." He spit a half dozen seeds onto the floor, still smiling. "You guys will make a good team."

I smiled back, my sad smile. I wasn't going to fight with Duffy. I wasn't even going to get angry. Duffy couldn't touch me. It's a long time since I got close enough to anyone for that. It's like the old song says, "You can't please anyone, so don't even try to please yourself." It's what the song should say. I just kept my head down mostly, and did a day's work, and once in a while I got a kick out of the wood that passed between my hands.

The funny thing was, we did make a good team. We made a great team. We ran the planer together for two weeks, both of us determined we weren't going to screw it up. Chatten didn't take our working together as any reason he had to talk to me, and I didn't have anything to say to him either. I fed the boards in at one end, and Chatten caught them at the other. That first morning when we stopped for a minute so Duffy could bring up a new bunk of rough lumber, I showed Chatten a couple of tricks I'd seen guys use to stack the boards easier. After that he didn't have any trouble.

We planed oak, ash, cherry, maple, birch. Hardwoods mostly. Working on the planer is like holding rocks under running water and watching what happens. Beautiful patterns come out, like the plowed fields you see from an airplane. Like rivers of wood, the way a creek will wind around and double back on itself in flat country. One afternoon, we surfaced a small bunk of cedar, and for a day the mill smelled sweet as a hope chest. It made me remember one of my cousins had a hope chest once. I don't know what she put in it, except towels. She had a lot of bath towels in there. Planing was hard work, but Chatten and I learned to get along. Sometimes an oversize board would jam up on me and Chatten would come around and help push until the knives could clean up a big knot. I didn't have to ask him. If my back was bothering me, we would switch off for a while so I could tail. I noticed from time to time Chatten's hands were bleeding, but he didn't complain. He wouldn't give in to wearing gloves.

It was only normal somebody eventually took exception to Chatten's lunch. The most unusual thing any of the guys was likely to bring to work was a slice of banana bread his old lady had baked for the kids, and he'd eat that on the sly. A couple of streets over from the mill lived a crippled lady with her dachshund, Pete, who made a habit of doing his morning chores just outside the mill door. One morning while we were planing eight-quarter walnut, somebody went out in the snow and gathered up four of those frozen dog turds Pete had left behind. They were just the size of Vienna sausages. Then whoever it was used some of those rice crackers Chatten was so crazy about to make the man a sandwich. When twelve o'clock came, Chatten took one look in his lunchbox and left the room, not giving anybody the satisfaction of seeing him pissed off. Everybody laughed too hard, which is how I knew Duffy was behind it.

I ate most of my lunch before I went out to where Chatten was sitting on the bunk of cherry we were going to plane next. "You want a decent sandwich?" I said to him. "This is baloney, but it's good baloney. It's real mayonnaise."

"No thanks," he said. He was wearing an old jacket with *49ers* written on the back in faded blue letters. He turned the pockets inside out, and we watched two handfuls of sawdust fall to the floor. "Any reason," he said, "why we can't get back to work a little early?"

It had never been done, but I couldn't think of the reason why. When we fired up the planer, Duffy came out to stare at us, then stare up at the clock, then back at us, but he couldn't think of any company rules we were breaking either. Except for the unwritten rule that says do as little as possible when the boss isn't around.

Going back to work a half hour early wasn't too good an idea. The others meant to ignore us. They just couldn't ignore the planer for long. It sounds like a 747 revving up for takeoff inside your hall closet. It's not a sound you want to eat lunch to. Duffy turned the light off on us, but it doesn't get that dark in the middle of the afternoon, even if the mill is as cold and damp as a cave in winter. I glanced toward the lunchroom to see who was playing with the lights. Two guys pulled their pants down and stuck their butts through the lunchroom door at me. I hadn't seen anyone do that in a while, and it made me laugh.

Duffy dug up an orange Frisbee and threw it clean across the mill at us, bouncing it off the ripsaw and one of the molders. There's something funny about a man as big as Duffy and a Frisbee. Some other wise guys grabbed a length of board and thought they'd use the dog turds from Chatten's lunch for baseballs. At least those things were still frozen, pretty much. Everybody got in on the act. The Hmongs, who were practicing driving the forklift in little circles, started honking the horn at us, shave-and-a-haircut. Times like that, somebody's always got to carry things too far, like Duffy deciding the Frisbee wasn't enough. He came tearing out of the lunchroom and onto the mill floor on Chatten's bicycle, trying to ride without any hands and juggle the Frisbee and two cans of soda. When he started to lose his balance, in a desperate act he flung the Frisbee at us again, this time sending it straight into the knives of the planer. Little bits of orange plastic came spitting out the other side, and I thought I better turn it off. That's what they always say you should do when something goes wrong: first, turn off your machine. Chatten was staring at Duffy with a look of his own, one that said, *I don't believe this for a minute.*

"It's just a Frisbee," I told him. But I saw what Chatten was upset about. The foreman had crashed into a pile of scrap lumber with Chatten's bike, and the Hmong boy who was driving the forklift speared the rear wheel before he could remember how to raise the fork or even how to step on the brakes. He'd torn the chain completely off the hub and broke six or eight spokes as well. Even then, everyone's feelings could have been smoothed over probably if Duffy had said he was sorry. He could have offered to pay for a new wheel. Instead he took a swing at the kid on the forklift. Of course, he wanted to take a swing at Chatten.

"I guess you'll wait until everyone goes back to work from now on, chief," said Duffy. "You'll quit trying to be so damn different." He walked back to the lunchroom, pretending not to limp. Chatten picked up the pieces of his bicycle. He was holding himself in so hard his eyes were going bloodshot.

"We'll see about being different," he said.

I gave him a ride home again. This time he wouldn't speak to me, even to give me directions to his house, although that's no big thing. I've lived in Missoula off and on for years. I know my way around.

"Come on in," he said, when I pulled up in front of the tepee.

"Well," I said, and I was stalling, trying to think of a way I could stay in the truck. "What do you do in there? I mean, can you sit down?" I was tired, and I didn't really want to stand all stooped over in any kind of tepee just to watch Chatten's woman grind little seeds into peanut butter. That's how it always starts.

"Oh come on," said Chatten. He walked up to a small brick house in the next lot and waited on the porch for me.

"This is your house?" I said. I looked at that little house with its picture window and its sagging front porch, then at the tepee and the blue buffalo next door, then at the house again. I felt cold out there on the sidewalk. I felt like an idiot. I climbed the steps onto the porch after Chatten.

"We're just renting," he said. He unlaced his boots and left them on the porch, and I did the same. He didn't have to tell me. I grew up in farm country. I could figure that much out.

The house they lived in was a normal house. They had chairs and a TV and refrigerator and everything. His wife was sitting at the kitchen table with some books spread out in front of her. She had long dark hair, and it looked like she'd just run her comb through it when she heard us pull up in my truck. Her hair shone in the kitchen light.

"How did it go today?" she asked. The way she said it, I knew Chatten had told her all about the mill and the bastards he had to work with.

"Better," he said, and he kissed her. She was a pretty girl, though not so young. I thought she might be pregnant. She moved careful, the way pregnant women sometimes do. I've not been around many pregnant women. I always thought it would be nice to talk to a woman who was carrying a baby, to find out what it's like.

"Want a cup of coffee?" asked Chatten.

"I can't stay," I told him, but I took the cup he had already poured. I felt as though I wasn't supposed to be there. They had a good home for a rental. The floors were polished quarter-sawn oak, the kind you can't buy anymore, and I could see a big oriental rug in the living room with white horses on it. A pot simmered on the stove. The whole kitchen smelled sweet and warm, like someone had been cooking onions in a frying pan. The coffee was good too, the blackest coffee I ever drank but not bitter.

"I better run," I said, trying to finish what was in my cup.

"You married?" said Chatten's wife. "You could stay for dinner." I could tell she meant it, and Chatten looked as if he was starting to relax now that he was out of the mill. I wasn't sure he would understand why I didn't stay. I had reason enough. I liked their house a lot. I liked their kitchen. It reminded me of my mother's kitchen and I still liked my mother, even if she wasn't so crazy about me. I guess I felt myself starting to like Chatten and his wife, and I wasn't ready to do that.

"Who owns that tepee?" I had to know.

"I'm not sure," said Chatten. "A bunch of leftover hippies hang around over there in the summer." That's what he called them. Leftovers.

"Isn't it awful?" said his wife.

"I kind of like it," said Chatten, the hard look coming back to his face. I gave him his empty coffee cup and stepped out onto the porch to slip into my boots.

"Tomorrow," he said, instead of saying good-bye.

I went home. I found the woman downstairs crying in her living room, her front door open. She had some old sweatpants on and a T-shirt that said something in Spanish, but I couldn't read it. She didn't care if I stared in or not. Her boyfriend was leaving with a suitcase that wouldn't close right and a big ivy plant in a fancy pot.

"You keep the rest," he said. "You keep it all." She didn't answer him.

Upstairs the furnace had gone out again in my place, and the front room smelled of gas. I propped the window open and waited for enough of the smell to go away so I could relight the pilot. It seemed like my apartment was quieter than usual. Nobody sat at my kitchen table with her books spread out in front of her. There wasn't any pot of onions cooking on my stove, and no coffee made either. There was only someone slamming the front door downstairs. I got out a baseball bat some other tenant left behind in my apartment, and I worked over the furnace a little bit. I felt better after that.

The next morning when Chatten's wife dropped him off for work, I waved to her, and she called me over to the car.

"Don't let him be stupid," she said. She lit a cigarette and took a hit off it, watching Chatten's back go through the mill door. It surprised me to see her smoke, a pregnant lady.

"Don't worry," I told her.

She took another drag on her cigarette and threw it into the snow, and I went into the lunchroom, where the boys were gathered around the coffee pot. They were watching Chatten out of the corners of their eyes, and I couldn't tell if they were still laughing at him, or if they were getting embarrassed about riding him so hard. I figured things would start to get easier for him pretty soon. Chatten took off his coat and hung it on one of the many nails pounded into the wall of the lunchroom for our convenience. Then he took off his cap and hung it up too, and I heard someone grunt.

Chatten had shaved his head. He hadn't shaved the whole thing, which wouldn't have been so bad. He shaved the sides, but he left the middle long the way that black giant on television used to wear his hair long in the middle. Only of course, Chatten wasn't any black giant. He looked like the last Mohican Indian, and he looked a little bit like the drummer in some punk rock band.

"What do you think?" he asked.

"I think you better keep your cap on," I told him.

"I could do that for a while." Chatten took his cap, a blue wool thing, down off the wall and pulled it on so it all but covered his ears. He looked normal again, for Chatten. "I want Duffy to get the full effect," he said.

"Oh, Duffy," said one of the Hmong boys, nodding his head like he understood it all. Like he understood everything.

That morning, Duffy gave us three bunks of barn wood and put us back on the planer. He knew my back was killing me after all that time on the planer, but he was too big a prick to let me switch to a molder or tally lumber for a bit. Used wood is a pain in the butt too. The boards get warped and twisted from all those years on the side of some old barn. But to look at Chatten, you'd have thought somebody just gave him a raise.

"I'll feed," said Chatten. It was all the same to me. I stuck plugs in my ears, then pulled a headset on over them. That way when Chatten started up the planer, it only sounded like one jet in the closet and not a whole squadron of jets.

Chatten looked his boards over carefully, butting them up against each other as he fed them into the knives. He had learned quick enough. The boards he planed were as clean and free of snipe as anybody's boards. He fed a dozen through without any hang-ups, and I stopped paying attention. I thought about the woman in the apartment below me. I'd never talked to her, not really. The night before, I was just getting into the spirit of things, giving the furnace a few good licks, when I looked up and saw her in the doorway.

"You're Johnny Foster," she said. "I know you." She'd changed into her nightgown, and even with her hair a mess and her eyes kind of runny, she surprised me how good she looked standing in my doorway. "What are you doing?" she said.

I guess I'd been making a lot of noise. The cover of the furnace was completely caved in, and I'd broke the little door to the pilot light off its hinges. The thermostat dial was rolling around on the floor.

"Fixing the furnace," I told her.

"Mine could use some work," she said, and we both broke up. It felt good to laugh, until I saw she wasn't exactly laughing. She was crying and not just sniffling either, but really crying from her heart, standing there with her arms at her side, her palms turned half towards me as if there was something she wanted.

This is what I could have done. I could have set down my baseball bat and put my arms around her, pulled her head against my shoulder and let her cry all she wanted. I might have stroked her hair and undone some of the tangles with my fingers, and sort of rocked her there until she stopped. Then I could have kissed her softly on her forehead, and if she liked that, I could have pulled her into the room and shut the door behind us, turned out the light so she would have been more comfortable. I could have straightened that nightgown so it was nice and snug around her shoulders and told her I was sorry for smelling like a lumber mill. It was my job and all. I didn't do any of it. I stood there watching her bawl. It must have seemed like a long time to her. Finally she ran down the stairs, and the door slammed again. I got my warm sleeping bag out of the closet and went to bed.

Chatten kept feeding the planer, and the wood kept coming out my side, cleaned up rivers of wood, the grain wandering here and there but not getting anywhere, ever. He picked up another board and looked at it closely. I saw the nail in the middle of the board, the way I know Chatten must have seen it, and I saw the smile on his face as he eased the wood into the planer.

If a planer sounds like a jet, then a planer ruining its knives on a sixteen-penny nail sounds like a jet tearing apart at the seams. I ran around the board coming through my side to shut the machine off. Chatten was supposedly doing the same thing, but somehow his hands got in the way of mine and neither one of us managed to shut the planer down before the nail did its damage. Then Chatten pushed the reverse button and backed the board, nail and all, into the knives again. I heard the same horrible noise, had the same crashing feeling in my stomach. Chatten shifted the planer into high, grinding the gears like a fifteen-year-old girl in her first driver's training class. That was too much. One of the knives broke, and small steel scraps flew like buckshot across the mill floor. I finally outmaneuvered Chatten and hit the kill switch.

With the planer down, the mill was quiet. I looked around to see if anybody got hurt, but all I saw was Duffy jumping off the forklift, running towards us, his face already twisted into his ugly look.

"God, God, God," he yelled.

"Now, look at that," said Chatten, sort of soft and sweet.

"Damn, damn, damn it to hell," said Duffy.

And then the door opened to the lunchroom, and out came the boss himself, Mr. Andrew T. Henries, all five feet five inches of him, walking in the peculiar way he has as if he's constipated, as if something is stuck down there where it counts.

That's when Chatten took off his hat.

He stopped Duffy cold in his tracks. Henries walked sideways up to the planer and asked through his nose, "What happened here?" But all the time he kept his eyes on Chatten's Mohican, like the blame was there in that patch of hair. Chatten stepped back from the planer and scratched his scalp, making us think he was puzzled by the whole thing too. Me, I picked up a crescent wrench, a big one.

"Only a fool could let this happen," said Henries to Duffy, though he obviously wasn't sure exactly what had happened. "A fool or worse." He looked from the foreman to Chatten, who was grinning a crazy grin and leaning on an oak four-by-four, a board about the length of the baseball bat I found in my apartment, but twice as thick. And Chatten was grinning right up into Duffy's face when Duffy went and said it.

"A fool squaw man."

Chatten started to swing that four-by-four, but I was quicker than he was. I beat him to the punch. I caught Duffy across the forehead with the crescent wrench. I hit him hard. I knew I'd have to if I didn't want him getting up. The foreman sat right down, but he stayed down, a pretty magnificent cut opening up over one eye, and Henries started screaming at me, grabbing hold of my arm.

Try as I would, I couldn't shake Henries loose. I shook him this way and I shook him that way. He was stronger than I would have guessed. Chatten looked confused. He'd wanted to hit Duffy, but Duffy was cold on the floor. People came running from all over the mill. The Hmongs were shouting Hmong words and sentences, whole Hmong paragraphs nobody could understand, and Vernon Waddy, for some reason, grabbed the night watchman's flashlight and shined it into my eyes. Henries stomped on my foot and got the wrench away from me. Then this guy Turner, thinking he had to be cute, wanted to wrestle me to the ground. Chatten caught him good with the four-by-four, which had everyone ganging up on us. The last thing I saw before they got the best of me was Chatten taking a swing at Henries and Henries backing through the lunchroom door.

The reporter down at the newspaper called it *an afternoon of senseless violence*, but it wasn't anything like he said. Duffy was the only one who got hurt. He already had two concussions from football, and those things will get worse the more you have of them. He was in St. Pat's for a week. Nobody visited any violence on Chatten that afternoon at the mill, and I take credit for that. But in spite of all I did, Chatten still ended up in trouble. He was on probation for beating the hell out of some guy up on the reservation. How was I supposed to know? Maybe they didn't want him up there. Maybe someone didn't like seeing him with an Indian woman and they fought over it. He never told me anything about it.

There's always been an honorable way for men to settle their differences. This is according to Mr. Andrew T. Henries, the owner of Missoula Lumber. He said it in front of this one judge who I already knew a little bit from things I did before, when I was drinking. Henries said hitting a man with a wrench was dishonorable. I didn't say anything when it was my turn. I could have said, I've seen worse. I could have said it isn't hardly worth sticking up for anyone anymore. There wasn't time to say half of it. I never wanted to be Chatten's friend, but my life didn't start with Chatten. It goes back a long ways. The only thing I wanted from Montana was work.

But if I'd been able to say it in so many words, why I did what I did, I'd have talked about Chatten's wife, how she studied her books at their kitchen table, her hair lying against her shoulders. I would have tried to tell how onions smelled in a kitchen, how that smell is nice to walk in on from the snow. And if anyone looked like he understood, I might have told about the white horses on their living room rug, how they reminded me of my mother, how it was the exact same white horses as in a picture book she once had, full of horses and mermaids and men who were goats from the waist down.

· The Window ·

HE HADN'T BEEN RAISED CATHOLIC, but after what happened that fall, Paul Hubbard thought about driving over to the Catholic church to see the priest. He had grown up in the San Joaquin among no-nonsense Baptists and Presbyterians who wouldn't have had time for anything as fanciful as what he had seen one afternoon in a high window. He had moved to the coast for college, and had lived in Chesterton for twelve years off and on, interrupted by his graduate program at UCLA. For five of those years in Chesterton he had taught American Studies at the same small college where he once had been a student himself. His wife, the less serious student when they first met, was the one who taught now. She taught German, the introductory courses, and she managed to avoid the unhappiness he had found as a professor.

They had been married a year when he quit teaching, and their circle of friends and family, including his two sisters who still lived in the valley, weren't sure their marriage would survive. Leslie had fallen in love with a man who was going to become a college professor, not with the man Paul became, a housepainter and a handyman. He had learned to do simple wiring and dry wall, to make the other repairs people needed if they wanted to live so close to the sea, and he brought in more money than he spent, which wasn't true of everyone who taught at Chesterton. Leslie had respect for the building trades. Her father put up suburban homes outside of Stockton. Still, she was careful not to compare her father's business—his line of trucks and the men who worked for him—with what Paul did out of the back of the station wagon.

Although they had talked about children, it wasn't until the day he drove home from class and told her how he had quit that they became serious about starting a family. They weren't big on tradition, and when it came to children, they saw no reason to follow any prescribed blueprint. Maybe he didn't have a job, but Leslie did. Once he convinced her that he was willing to look after a child, she told him she wanted to take as little time off for the birth as possible, just a summer she hoped. Paul would watch the baby. He could do a little painting or carpentry, build someone a deck or put a solar panel up on a roof, but he wouldn't let it eat up his life. They wouldn't have to explain to their friends why he gave up teaching. They could tell everyone it was all part of their child-rearing plan.

If it hadn't been for the pool, he might never have set foot on campus again. He had been a swimmer all his life, in high school and for a year on the college team before he realized he would never be Olympic material or anything close to it. He quit swimming for several years, until he started graduate school and began to put on weight. He tried dieting and new ways of exercising. He tried meditation, and a three-month stint with a beautiful hypnotist, before he gave up and went back to the pool.

It was different when he went back. He swam only as much as he wanted to, without a coach keeping track of every lap from the deck. And his place in the order of things had changed. He had been a good high school swimmer, an average, at best, college athlete. He had no illusions he could keep up in the pool with the same eighteen-year-olds who had made his life miserable in the classroom. But if he swam during the hours when the pool was reserved for grad students and faculty, he was as fast as anybody. Once in a while, a graduate student, some young woman still strong from her days as a college swimmer, would come to the pool. For a day or two, she would humble him. Then invariably she would disappear again. Swimming didn't mean the same thing to her as it did to him. She had to give it up first and come back to it.

It was Leslie's day off, and they had been sitting at the kitchen table arguing, or almost arguing, a state in which married people, it seemed to Paul, spent a lot of their time. His swimsuit lay on the table, and more than once he had nearly given in to the urge to grab it and leave the house. They were both frustrated that Leslie wasn't pregnant. She felt the fact that they seldom made love except during the safe times was his doing, while he thought she was the one who counted the days.

"What about Tuesday night?" he said. "Tuesday night I was interested."

She got up from the table and poured herself another cup of coffee. He knew she would take that cup with her to the back room she used as a study.

"Tuesday I had the flu," said Leslie.

"How about now?" he said. He raised his hand and looked at his watch. "Got a minute?" The low clouds that had moved in to surround the house looked as if they had no intention of leaving for the rest of the day. He was tired of clouds. He felt better when he heard her laugh.

"Go on." She handed him his suit and goggles. "Go swim." She kissed him on the forehead before she slipped down the hall to her German quizzes.

He drove the station wagon across town and parked it a block from the college gym. Carvell Pool sat inside a massive gray-columned building. The pool was twenty-five yards long, and there was talk of tearing it down and building a new one twice as big, if one of the school's more generous donors would come up with the money. The fact that Carvell was outdated made the pool feel right somehow to Paul, especially on days he felt outdated too. In the locker room, he changed to his suit and walked past the showers onto the deck. There was a rule that said every swimmer had to take a shower before getting in the water, a rule he conscientiously broke every day.

He felt strong in the water that afternoon as he swam a thousand yards, then kicked five hundred. Afterward he did repeats on the clock for another thousand yards. He had the lane to himself, so he finished his workout with ten fifties of butterfly, pacing himself so he could get a good rest in between each fifty. He knew there were people watching him, and he didn't want to look as bad as he felt. If he took it easy, he could still look like the kid who used to swim the butterfly all afternoon.

A boy he didn't know came onto the deck, a tall boy, lean, with a dark tan. Paul didn't look directly at him, but he knew the boy was watching him, waiting for him to finish his swim. The boy wasn't in any hurry to get in the pool. Paul knew the feeling. Some days he needed someone to push him in to get him started. Paul swam an easy fifty of backstroke to warm down, lifting his arms and stretching them, trying to work the bad stuff out of his muscles. He watched the boy, who was no older than twenty and who wasn't supposed to use the pool at noon. If Paul had been on the faculty still, he might have asked the lifeguard to speak to the boy.

It was while he was swimming backstroke, trying to figure out the little smile on the boy's face, that Paul looked up and saw the window for the first time. Carvell was an indoor pool, but because of the large windows on three sides, it wasn't gloomy. At one end, there were six of those high windows. That afternoon, the second window from the left let in less sunlight than the others. It looked as if someone had splashed something dirty on the glass from the outside, a water balloon or an egg. It would have taken a strong arm, for the windows were a good three stories above ground level, and there wasn't any ledge.

Paul stood up in the shallow end and took off his goggles to see better. There was a face in the window. The stain on the glass had formed into eyes and cheeks, a long straight nose, a beard. At first he thought it was a trick of his imagination, that if he tried he could make the thing take on another shape—a tree, or a map of North America. But no matter how hard he tried, he couldn't see the stain on that window as anything other than a man's face. He wanted to dismiss what he saw as chance, a Rorschach. He thought of the Shroud of Turin and other miracles he had read about in the newspaper.

He stopped one of the swimmers in the next lane, an older man named Evans who taught biology.

"Can you see that?" said Paul, once he'd pulled Evans to his feet. Paul pointed to the window.

"Am I blind?" said Evans. He was out of breath. He wanted Paul to think he was annoyed to have his swim interrupted. Paul knew the man welcomed any chance to stop.

"So the window's a little dirty," said Evans. "So what?"

"It's not just dirty." Paul wondered if he was making a fool of himself. The dark boy watched him from the deck, listening, though he pretended not to.

"It's a face, Evans. Don't you see it?"

Evans studied the window harder, until a look of slow recognition came to his own heavy features. He was blocking the lane, and the other swimmers were piling up behind him.

"Everybody okay?" This came from a skinny economist named Ashe, who leaned on the lane line next to Evans. Ashe was one of those men with no body hair who spent all his time in the pool doing the sidestroke. It occurred to Paul that Ashe might be religious. Paul had never heard him get angry.

"I wonder how long that's been there," said Evans.

"What?" said Ashe. He didn't wear his glasses in the pool.

"That window. There's a face in the window."

"There's a window up there?" said Ashe.

"Whose face is it?" said the lifeguard. A muscular girl in baggy shorts, she had only recently come to work at Carvell. From her chair, Paul knew she couldn't see what they were looking at, but her question annoyed him just the same. Whose face did she think it would be?

"No question about it," said Evans. There were half a dozen swimmers looking at the window now, all willing to deny what they were seeing as long as they could say later they had been in the pool when the face first appeared. "It's plain as day who *that* is," said Evans. He looked at each swimmer in turn, as if he were in his lab waiting for his students to figure out an idea he'd come to terms with thirty years earlier. He took off his goggles and rubbed the bridge of his nose. "It's Che Guevara."

The others laughed, Ashe and a woman from Evans's department named Eleanor Bunch. Only the lifeguard didn't laugh. She didn't know who Che Guevara was.

"I don't think so," said Jim Killy. Killy taught sculpture, and he was unusually serious for an artist. Paul had known him a long time. If Killy saw the face of God, Paul didn't think he would make a joke about it.

"I think it's Van Gogh," said Killy. It was hard to tell if he meant it. "See how the ears are kind of indistinct."

"No, no," said Eleanor Bunch. "It's Charlie Manson."

"It's Jimmy Hoffa," said Ashe, but nobody listened to him. Evans and Eleanor Bunch set off toward the other end of the pool, Evans doing his crooked freestyle and Bunch laughing so hard at her own joke she had to switch to the breaststroke. Paul wanted to let it go, the way the others had, but he couldn't laugh at what he saw. He thought about those children in Portugal who saw the Virgin Mary, and he wondered what they thought the first time it happened. What he saw wasn't Mary. It was the face of a man. When he closed his eyes, he could still see it.

When he had first come back to Chesterton, he thought he would like being part of the town itself, along with the other people who were no longer students, who had jobs and homes. Chesterton was a quaint place where he saw the same people in the shops every week. High Street was paved with brick, like a street frozen in time from the last century. Whether those bricks had been in place for years or were a more recent innovation, he didn't know. When he had come up to the college for his interview, Dr. Stone, an elderly linguist with the look of a drinker, seemed not to realize that Paul had been a student at the same college where he was interviewing for a job.

"It's a quiet town, Chesterton," said Dr. Stone. "Very little crime. No X-rated movies. No bathhouses. A good place to raise a family."

Paul knew Stone was overlooking a great deal. The heritage of the town was more complicated than those eight blocks paved in red brick. Names of institutions like Standard Oil and Bank of America resonated with the town fathers in ways the names of ordinary people never would. In the nineteenth century, Chesterton had not been an easy place to be Chinese, and later it had not been an easy place to be Irish or Italian. Nowadays, although most of the hard labor was done by newly arrived Mexicans and Guatemalans, older families with last names like Sanchez and Reyes seemed to have forgotten how their own grandfathers and great-grandfathers made the same trip across the desert these new people were making. There were stories about what took place on campus too, about the fraternity boys, and about an abundance of drugs, stories the college took pains to keep out of the newspaper. Even in Chesterton, the world was an imperfect place. Knowing it was, Paul had chosen to stay. At least here he knew who his enemies were. And in the end, it was not the townspeople who proved too much for him. It was the students.

When he was in college, and he didn't like to think how long ago that was, he had been troublesome enough. He had driven an old Volkswagen and insulted his parents at the dinner table, had gone out of his way to anger the people in neckties who had made a mess of things. Life had gone on that way at Chesterton too, during those years of the draft and weak marijuana and assassinations. But the mood had changed. Students had grown cautious. They had learned to take pride in each new brick building, each added measure of heritage. The botany department had developed a fast-growing strain of ivy. Boys and girls came from all over the state, from other states too, their parents willing to pay extra for four years of maple and oak, the duck ponds, a football team untouched by scandal.

He used to ask students on the first day of class to write a short essay telling him what they would most like to get from the years they would spend at Chesterton. When they wrote about Porsches and Corvettes, and one semester a misspelled Maserati, he quit giving that assignment. He asked them to read Thoreau. He asked them to read about South Africa and Palestine. About Harlem. They resisted. One day shortly before final exams, he discovered one of his students was only pretending to follow along in the class discussion of a Vonnegut novel. Secretly, she was reading from her accounting text. He asked her to leave the room, then reconsidered.

"Wait," he told her. He noticed she wasn't embarrassed. "You stay. I'll go." He gathered up his books and left as quickly as he could. He couldn't bear to see if there was even one look of disappointment to go with the looks of relief.

He was content to have quit. Now he built decks and installed ceiling fans, and he didn't mind the work. He scraped paint from the sides of apartment buildings, inside of which for a few short years people had planned revolution. Afternoons, he could hear the TV sets going— Gilligan, Mr. Ed.

And he swam every day, more yards than he had since he was twenty. On a cold afternoon in January, when he was the first person to come out of the locker room and get into the water, one of the lifeguards asked him what he was training for. He pretended he didn't understand the question. He was training for the life he lived.

Each month, he knew as soon as Leslie did that she hadn't conceived. She had always been irritable during her time: her feelings came to the surface more easily; his slowness was a trial to her. He felt the tension build, and without looking at the calendar, he knew she wasn't pregnant. On those days, he went back to the pool and swam his disappointment away rather than let her see it in his face. He put in thousands of yards, trying to reassure himself that they were just unlucky, though he became more and more convinced the problem was his. When he swam backstroke, he studied the face in the window. Sometimes he said a small prayer, and felt foolish afterward.

Nobody else mentioned the window. He would point the face out to another swimmer who would say what he saw made him think of Abraham Lincoln or Ho Chi Minh. He never spoke about it to the dark boy, who was there at the pool every day. The boy stood on the deck and stretched as he waited for Paul to finish his swim.

Paul took pictures of the window and sent one to each of his sisters.

"It looks like Walt Whitman, if Whitman would trim his beard," said his sister Lettie, the one married to a minister.

"It looks like Lassie's last breakfast," said Coral Ann. She had never been married. Paul tried not to pay any attention to her, to either of them.

"See a doctor," said Killy, when Paul told him Leslie wasn't pregnant yet. Killy gave him the name of a proctologist. He said it quietly, but Paul was pretty sure the dark boy overheard him. Each day the boy came to the pool, he glanced up at the window. Some days he got in the water and did his warm-up while Paul swam his sprints. The boy was a powerful swimmer, but he hadn't challenged Paul for the lane.

Chesterton wasn't far from Santa Barbara, where the doctor Killy recommended had his office. Paul drove down on a Wednesday morning without telling Leslie where he was going. It was a problem he thought a man should check into on his own. Dr. Thomas's office was in one of those modern complexes that drew ten or twelve doctors of different specialties into one location, the way bees would be drawn to a hive filled with honey. It seemed to Paul he could have sought help for any disability there.

"Paul Hubbard to see Dr. Thomas," he told the receptionist, a young woman who looked a lot like the students he once taught.

"Hubbard," she said, running her finger down her appointment book. He could see the name plainly. She had misspelled it as Cubbard, which reminded him even more of his students.

"You're sure it was Wednesday?" said the receptionist. Her voice had that piercing quality he associated with women who play basketball. He glanced around the waiting room and saw that everyone else was carefully not paying attention. The room was filled with men sitting in plush chairs reading back copies of *Sports Illustrated*.

The woman leaned across the counter so she could whisper to Paul through her little window.

"Are you thinking about a vasectomy?" she asked.

"What?" said Paul.

"A vasectomy," she repeated, somewhat louder.

"Lord no," said Paul.

She was still scanning her list, so he pointed to the name that should have been his.

"Oh," she said. "*Cubbard.*"

A dozen magazine pages turned at once, but he didn't look behind him. Instead, he did what he often did when he felt anxious: he envisioned himself doing a perfect flip turn, his feet touching the wall of his imaginary pool in a flawless synchronicity, his legs driving him ten yards or more back up his lane in the direction he had just come. He accepted the paperwork the receptionist shoved through the window and filled it out quickly, then sat down in a corner with a magazine of his own. It was an old swimsuit edition, and he didn't want to read it, but he didn't want to call more attention to himself either. He pretended to read about the models, their lives and their interests. They, too, reminded him of his students.

He didn't have to wait long. Dr. Thomas ushered him into a room where two large anatomical charts hung from the wall. He heard the doctor confer with his receptionist in the hallway, heard him say the word "vasectomy" too, and "prostatitis," before the receptionist got through to him. Paul studied the charts, thinking he might be able to figure out what was wrong for himself. He was amazed as always by the intricacies of the body, male or female. A man's plumbing seemed simpler than a woman's until he saw it laid out neatly on a wall chart.

"So," said Dr. Thomas, stepping in the door backwards as he read from the papers on his clipboard. "You and your wife are having a little trouble getting pregnant, is that it?"

"I've been studying this chart on your wall," said Paul. "Maybe there's some kind of blockage."

The doctor looked up at the chart too. He looked at it closely, as if seeing it for the first time.

"Drop your trousers," he said. "We'll have a look."

The doctor put on a pair of surgical gloves and bent low to look him over, the way Paul had seen little children bend carefully over a large bug or a dead bird in the dirt. He had Paul lie on the table while he examined him gently, and from every angle. Paul wasn't used to having another man touch him there, but the doctor was quick. He put lubricant on his finger in order to check the prostate. That part was unpleasant, made worse by the fact that Paul suddenly heard the receptionist's voice as if she were in the room with them.

"If you'll stay on the line, Mrs. Ramos," said the receptionist, "Dr. Thomas will be right with you." There must have been a telephone out in the hall.

"I don't see anything irregular," said the doctor, stripping off his rubber gloves so he could wash his hands. Paul quickly got back into his pants. He wondered if the receptionist and the doctor were both slightly deaf. They spoke very loudly to each other, and to him.

"We need a sperm sample," said the doctor. He handed Paul a small container that looked as if it could have been a film canister or a pill jar. "Take this home and . . . you know . . . fill it up. You can keep it in the refrigerator a couple of days, but bring it back as soon as you can. We'll put it under the microscope and see how many we can count."

The doctor spoke to him as though he were a small boy opening his first bank account. The man meant to be reassuring, but Paul's thoughts were with Leslie, and how he had avoided telling her where he was going that morning. If she saw that little receptacle, she would want to know more. He didn't want to put the idea into her head that he was failing her in some way, at least until he knew whether he was or not. And he wasn't at all sure, once he left Dr. Thomas's office, that he would come back.

"Do you think," said Paul, trying not to sound tentative, "I could take care of that here?" Dr. Thomas looked at him as if he didn't understand.

"It's a bit of a drive," said Paul, which was true, "and I can't often get away from my work." He made that part up.

"Okay," said the doctor, "I guess." He looked around the room as if there might be something he should lock up first.

"I won't be long," said Paul.

Dr. Thomas shut the door softly behind him, and Paul waited to hear his footsteps recede before he undid his pants again. He heard more footsteps in the hall, the quick sharp steps of the receptionist followed by the slow shuffle of one of the old men from the waiting room.

"Come right along in here," said the receptionist to whoever was following her down the hall. Paul froze, his back to the door.

"Not that one," Dr. Thomas called out to her. A hand, he was pretty sure it was her hand, was on the doorknob to Paul's room.

"That room's occupied," said the doctor. "Mr. Cubbard will be with us for a while." Paul heard the doorknob twist once more before the receptionist relented and led her patient farther down the hall.

He closed his eyes to shut out that cold room from his mind. He let his thoughts wander to other places. Thinking about the models in the magazine he had been looking at provided a bit of excitement, and excitement was what he wanted. But then he happened to look up at the anatomical chart on the wall, and the enormity of what he was trying to accomplish overwhelmed him.

He thought about the pretty young women who each spring used to emerge from their winter coats and sweaters and bloom in his classroom. He thought of them in ways he hadn't let himself think of them before.

"Mrs. Ramos," he heard Dr. Thomas say heartily into the telephone. Paul lost some of his enthusiasm.

"We have your father's results back," said the doctor. "I'm sorry to say, they're malignant. Yes. Both of them."

Paul tried hard not to listen. He concentrated on the memory of a girl he had dated in high school, one who was never intimate with him, but who had figured in his dreams in this same way many times when he was seventeen.

"There's a couple of things we can do," said Dr. Thomas. "The simplest thing is just to remove them."

Paul had to stop. He decided to give himself a rest.

"Look at it this way, Mrs. Ramos." Dr. Thomas sounded reasonable. "We're talking about his life."

Paul heard the receptionist lead another patient past the door. He thought about her for a moment. It was better than thinking about Dr. Thomas. Paul thought he might be able to go on, until the receptionist spoke to the patient in her overloud voice.

"Oh," she said. "I can't put you in there."

He was about to give it up, though that would have been embarrassing too, when he realized the solution had been with him all the time. He closed his eyes and thought of the most beautiful woman he had ever known, the soft secret places he had shared. He imagined it was her, his own sweet Leslie, who was touching him now, and with his eyes closed, rocking steadily in that bare sterile room, he managed to accomplish what the doctor had ordered.

He swam fifteen hundred yards that day without stopping, not hard but steady, working his arms and shoulders until the pain began to build, and then he kept on until the first pain went away and his stroke smoothed out. He wanted to wash the doctor-office smell from his skin, to forget about poor Mrs. Ramos's father, and the other men in that waiting room, about how hard it was for all of them to live up to the charts on a doctor's wall. The water was warmer than he liked. He thought about doing three or even four thousand yards before he stopped, but he had already forced himself to do one difficult task that morning, and he decided it was okay to take a breather after the first fifteen hundred.

As he rested at the end of his lane, letting his pulse slow and his breathing return to normal, the lifeguard climbed down from her chair and walked along the side of the pool until she could look at the high window and the face that watched over them. She stared up for a moment, then came back thoughtfully to stand beside her chair.

"Do you see it?" he asked.

She smiled and nodded her head. The dark boy came out of the locker room and walked self-consciously toward Paul's lane. He leaned against the tiled wall to stretch his calf muscles.

"You know who I think it is?" said the lifeguard. She spoke softly so the boy wouldn't hear her. "When I was a kid, I saw a face like that in Yuba City. We used to buy these cough drops—they were called Smith Brothers. And there was this picture of both of the Smith Brothers on the package."

Paul felt a great weariness in his shoulders.

"He looks just like one of the Smith Brothers," said the lifeguard.

The dark boy dove into the water and began his smooth perfect stroke. He moved through the pool, a dolphin, gracefully, as though he had been born to the water. Paul watched him do four laps, his turns slow and easy. The boy's goggles were tinted gray, and Paul couldn't see what it was the boy looked at when he turned his head to breathe.

He had only put in half his usual workout, but Paul had no heart for the rest of it. He got out and went to the showers, where he stayed a long time, studying the old men who were there rinsing off arms and legs that had seen lifetimes of service, letting the hot spray do what it could to make them limber again. One man nodded to him, and Paul nodded back. It wasn't until he was in the car and driving home that he recognized the man as one of Dr. Thomas's patients.

Weeks passed, and he neglected to call the doctor's office and ask for his results. He wasn't sure he wanted to know anymore whose fault the whole thing was. He thought maybe he needed to save up longer in between the times they made love. Leslie was tired a lot. He didn't think they had the money to go further with the medical route. They couldn't afford the in vitro process, and he had to face it, his ego couldn't afford artificial insemination. One afternoon he went through the phone book looking for adoption agencies, but he didn't make any calls.

Thinking about adoption, lawyer's fees and the like, made him seriously consider Nettie Rigby's offer when she called later that week. Nettie was the new chair of American Studies and she wanted to know if he would teach a course in the spring. Nothing permanent, she said, an adjunct position. He liked Nettie, and he was tempted. He had taken a false step two days before and fallen off the chair he was standing on, straining the muscles across his stomach. She was calling at a bad moment. But he couldn't imagine being in a classroom again. When Leslie came home, she told him Nettie had spoken to her too, which seemed unfair. Leslie didn't argue, but she thought the money would come in handy if they had a child.

He worried about the child they might have. Could he steer a son past fraternities and football teams? And if he had a daughter? Would she think further than boys and clothes and a sports car of her own? He thought about those questions, and he swam, and he watched the high window as a farmer studies the sky for rain.

The fall had turned unusually cold, had turned to winter everywhere but on the calendar. The rain became ice as it hit the ground, something Paul had only seen twice before on the road between his house and the college, and the ice held to the blacktop in a thin layer until the road was unsafe. He was cleaning up an apartment that had been trashed by four sophomores when they learned they were flunking out. The sophomores were gone, and the apartment was almost back in shape, though it would sit empty until the next great migration called semester break. He saw a telephone lying on the floor where it had fallen off a small broken table. Paul left it there as long as he could. He did everything else to that apartment, he cleaned his paintbrushes and mopped the kitchen floor, until finally he had to pick up the phone to vacuum the carpet. Out of habit, he put the receiver to his ear, and there was a dial tone.

Like a sleepwalker, Paul pulled his wallet from his pocket and took out the piece of paper, the one with the Santa Barbara phone number on it. He dialed what was written there. He didn't give himself time to think.

"Dr. Thomas's office," said a woman's voice. "Please hold." She made a popular song from twenty years before come over the phone, a song once considered a little bit raunchy. Now it was a song he heard in the grocery store, the sort of thing that could make him feel old.

"Sorry to make you wait," she said again. It sounded like the same receptionist as before. She shouted on the phone too. "How may I help you?"

"This is Paul Hubbard," he said. "I'm calling to check on a test you ran for me."

"Spell that," she said. "Spell Cubbard."

He spelled the name his way. Then he spelled it her way. He was wishing he hadn't called.

"Doctor wants to speak to you," she said.

"What for?" said Paul. But instead of answering, she dropped the phone on the counter. There was a rustling of papers.

"Hello, Cubbard?" It was Dr. Thomas. "Good news."

"What's good news?"

"You," said the doctor. "You're fine."

"You're sure?" said Paul.

"There weren't so many of them as you might think," said the doctor. "But the main thing is, the ones you have are healthy."

Paul could picture the doctor's office. He wondered if there were men sitting in those plush chairs listening to what Dr. Thomas was telling him.

"When was the last time," said the doctor, "you and your wife got away for a little vacation?"

"Pardon me?" said Paul. "What did you say?"

"I said," said the doctor, and he was impatient now, his voice reaching its upper limits, "you just keep trying!"

Paul thanked him and hung up the phone.

He drove carefully across town to the pool, caught up in thought about whether to take the course Nettie Rigby had offered him, and about Dr. Thomas's advice. He wasn't careful enough. Luckily, when the station wagon went into a skid, he was moving slowly, and there were no other cars on the street. He hit a tree and crumpled a front fender. He was glad it was a big tree. It would survive the accident. He was able to pull the fender clear of the tire, and he drove on to the pool, feeling discouraged but knowing if he didn't work out, he would end up downtown in one of Chesterton's grimy taverns drinking beer all afternoon.

He had stroked through a mile of his swim, trying not to think about the station wagon, when the dark boy got in his lane. Because of the foul weather, the pool was relatively empty. Paul couldn't complain that the boy didn't wait for him to finish like he usually did. But as he stood at the end of the pool and watched the other swimmer's smooth and powerful freestyle, Paul felt himself get angry. When he began swimming again, he picked up his speed so that the boy wouldn't pass him. Paul's arms hurt from three days of sanding and painting, and he had been swimming every day without a break for weeks. He was swimming against someone who was rested. Paul felt the unfairness of it all.

He lengthened his stroke until he pulled up behind the dark boy and swam in his slipstream, matching him lap after lap until the boy stopped to clear his goggles. It was an innocent move, thought Paul, but it took away Paul's advantage. The boy was behind him then, drafting off him as Paul began his third mile. He was younger than Paul, and less tired, and he had Paul to go first, to break the water's tension with each stroke.

They did another thirty laps that way. Paul stopped counting. The dark boy grew stronger as Paul weakened, but now that Paul had the lead, he refused to give it up. The boy made as if to pull alongside him, and at each turn, Paul cut him off. He did it without being openly rude. If he felt the swimmer behind him speed up, so did Paul. Paul knew he was pushing himself past his limit, but he refused to let this dark boy, all the dark boys and blonde girls of Chesterton College, pass him by.

He could refuse his body and its truths only so long. Paul felt the acid in his throat, the quick spasm in his stomach, and he stopped and grabbed the side. He did what he hadn't done since high school: he surrendered what was left of his breakfast, careful to get it all in the gutter. For the most part, he heaved nothing but air.

"Here," said a voice he hadn't heard before, but one that he recognized anyway. The boy knelt on the pool deck, water running from his chest into a puddle at his feet, and he held out his towel to Paul. At first Paul refused the boy's kindness, until the thought of wiping away the water and sickness with a soft dry towel overwhelmed him.

"It's the flu," said the boy. "It's going around."

Paul nodded. He was as grateful for the lie as for the towel. The lifeguard climbed down out of her chair and came to where they rested, one swimmer in the water, the other crouched on the deck. The dark boy spoke to her, and she went away.

"I'm okay," said Paul. He gave back the towel. It was no longer clean, but the boy didn't seem to mind. He tossed it onto a chair near the wall and eased himself into the pool.

"You go ahead," said Paul. "I'll warm down."

Neither of them moved, and neither spoke. They stood in the middle of the lane and looked up at the window, where the gray sky outside made the features distinct, made the face's great sadness clear as never before. Paul was tempted to ask the boy what he thought, as he had asked all the others. He didn't think the boy wanted him to because the boy didn't say anything at first, and when he did speak he didn't talk about the window.

"You know," he said, "your right hand comes over a little too far."

"My right hand?" said Paul.

An uncertain look crossed the young man's face. He wasn't sure how Paul would take the advice. Paul wasn't sure either. He looked at the window again, the beard, the world-weary eyes.

"Like this?" said Paul. He placed his arms in the water as he usually did, then made a small adjustment following the boy's advice.

"That's right." His voice was soft but sure. "Hold your stroke out a little. Don't try to grab so much water all at once."

They swam slowly then, a lap at a time, stopping to stretch each time they returned to the shallow end. There were questions Paul wanted to ask. *Have you read Thoreau? Do you know who Che Guevara was?*

"Do you teach here?" asked the boy.

"No," said Paul. He didn't know why he said what he did next. Maybe it was the look of disappointment on the dark and glistening face. Maybe it was the other face, the one in the window.

"Actually," said Paul, "I might do a course in the spring." The way the boy smiled, it felt like the right answer. Paul checked the window again when he was sure nobody was watching him. He wondered if maybe the face up there would be changed somehow, less grim. He wondered if there was anything he had missed.

The lifeguard stood on the pool deck, one hand on her hip, absently scratching her bare shoulder. She blew her whistle, but the dark boy acted as if he didn't hear her, and he pushed off the wall to swim another lap. Paul pulled himself out of the water and sat, his legs dangling from the edge of the pool. The lifeguard was going to blow her whistle again, but he hoped the boy wouldn't stop yet. He hoped the boy would go on and on.

· Wedding Day ·

IN THE LAST LIGHT OF THE AFTERNOON, Gerald Michaels lay on his bed in his slacks and his white shirt and thought about the wedding he would perform that evening. The girl's name was Grace; she was plain and her brown hair was oily, and she spoke with a lisp. But she had a sweet smile. She reminded him of the girls he had seen in the sixties, hundreds of them, who had run away from farm towns in the valley to wander through the parks of San Francisco. He had been a student then at the Bible college in Anaheim, and he had taken a long weekend one October to drive north, thinking about what it would be like to witness to those girls, or to sleep with them, too confused finally to do either one.

Because he was Grace's pastor, he had been to the girl's house on three occasions for heavy dinners of pork and mashed potatoes, always wishing there was a man present to talk to. The house belonged to Esther, Grace's grandmother, an immense olive-skinned woman with hard dark eyes. Grace's mother had died when Grace was eight years old, leaving the girl and her younger sister in Esther's care. Now, late in the afternoon on her wedding day, Grace would be dressing in the back room of Esther's house. Michaels could picture Grace in the church just before seven o'clock when the guests would arrive. It was the only church the girl had attended. The weddings he had performed there were all she would have to go on as she imagined what her wedding should be like. He tried to remember his own wedding but could only vaguely recall standing with his wife in a wet field, shivering while a minister he hardly knew stumbled over a passage from Ecclesiastes.

In the seven years he had pastored this church, he had never canceled a worship service, but he had been glad to cancel this evening's service for the sake of the wedding. He had nothing new to say from the pulpit, and most weeks he knew he was rambling, telling pointless stories about his grown daughters or about baseball, which he had once loved. It was difficult enough on a Sunday morning. By Sunday evening, the words he hoped to use felt as heavy as the air in the church, burdened with the scent of floor wax and old hymnals. A few outspoken members of the congregation wanted him to leave. Some days he thought about his future with sadness and uncertainty. Other days, like a middle-aged pitcher sent to the showers, he felt the sweet anticipation of release.

When Pastor Michaels had first moved to Ivanhoe, Grace had been thirteen. She'd reminded him of a quiet young girl he had known at his first church in Salinas, a girl who had a smile for everyone and who was certainly smiling, if only for herself, on the day she was struck by a car while riding her bicycle. The accident happened in February, and Michaels went to see the mother and father of that other girl, who was dead, on a rainy morning when the roadside puddles were swelling onto the highway. The father of the girl from Salinas had turned to him, hoping for words a father could make sense of, and Pastor Michaels had shared his thoughts about God and his mercy. But standing in the man's living room, Gerald Michaels felt doubt open up inside of him, a door that led down to a basement. Within a month, he had resigned his position in Salinas, and he and Lettie had taken a long break, a sabbatical. Eventually though, he had come back to the ministry, and the ministry had brought him back to his wife's hometown, to Ivanhoe.

The Ivanhoe church was small. He hoped enough people would come to Grace's wedding to fill the place. The girl's family hadn't sent out invitations, though Grace would have loved those small white cards wrapped in tissue paper, the words written in gold: *Grace Marshall and Orland Newberry . . .*

There was no money for anything so fancy as that. On such short notice, he hadn't taken any special steps to prepare the church. When other girls had their weddings, the girls or their mothers, someone, taped up a thick piece of yarn, a rope, to reserve the first two pews for family. Grace didn't have much family. He wondered if he should tape up the yarn anyway, slip his shoes on and walk to the sanctuary. It would only take a moment, but alone in his room, he felt as if he couldn't leave his bed, as though a large liquid weight was pressing the back of his head into his mattress. He couldn't remember where some yarn would be, some tape. He thought about calling Grace's grandmother to do it. It was too easy to imagine that house, Grace in her bedroom, Esther rocking silently beside the ancient television set. And Michaels didn't want to talk to Esther Marshall. The old woman would tell him, proud of her poverty, how they all planned to walk to the church a little before seven. She would say there wasn't time for her to do anything about the pews.

When Esther had stood up that morning, filling the aisle and clutching an enormous black purse, Michaels had seen the smile playing at the corner of her mouth. With her announcement she was settling an ancient feud with some other old woman, or starting a new one.

"My granddaughter Grace will be married this evening," said Esther.

"Dear God," said one of the others, and it hardly sounded like a prayer. A hymnal fell to the floor.

"We know it's sudden," said Esther, "but with Orland in the military, there isn't time to wait." She sat down, then stood again before the others could catch their breath.

"You're all invited," she said.

• • •

For the third time that afternoon, Grace took the long white dress out of her closet and held it in front of her at her bedroom mirror. She didn't know whether it was time to put the dress on, or if she should carry it on a hanger to the church. If she dressed now, she would have to walk carefully on the edge of the road, holding the hem of the dress off the ground so it would stay clean. It had not rained in months, and the dirt beside the road would make a thick fine powder. The dress belonged to her cousin Vivian. Grace wasn't as tall as her cousin, and her breasts and hips were larger than Vivian's, but it was a forgiving kind of dress. Vivian had picked it out for her own first wedding.

Grace wished she had one of those long plastic bags from the dry cleaner. She didn't want to walk down the road with the dress on a hanger for everyone to see, walk past someone like Miss Whitefield, who would choose that very moment to be out watering the dried-up grass in her front yard. The woman wouldn't be able to keep quiet: "Where are you going, Grace? What's that you're carrying, some kind of parachute?" Grace didn't think she could stand it. She found a large brown bag from SavMor and folded the dress into it as neatly as she could.

She wondered what Orland would wear. The part about him and the military wasn't true exactly. Orland planned to join the army in a few months. He had looked everywhere for work, but he couldn't find anything in Visalia or Tulare, or even up in Three Rivers, and he was pretty sure he could still get in the army. It was too bad he wasn't already in the army. He could wear his uniform, the way Terri Beasley's husband wore a uniform when Terri got married. It looked nice that way, though Terri Beasley's husband died in a car accident later. A uniform looked good at a funeral too.

Esther had offered to lend Grace a pair of shoes, black pumps with a medium heel. Her grandmother was in the bath, or Grace would not have gone through Esther's closet without asking first. When she found the shoes, Grace carried them to her own room to try them on. They pinched her toes, a feeling Grace knew she would never forget. She would remember every detail of this day. When she walked across the room, the shoes were awkward, but Grace knew she would get better at it the more she practiced. She gathered up her hairbrush and lipstick and the bag with the dress in it, and she called out to let Esther know she was going.

"I'll meet you there," said Grace. "I'll be in the Sunday school rooms." Grace heard the water shift in the tub as her grandmother sat up.

"Don't be late," called Grace, and she ran out the door, watching her feet cautiously, as though they were small dogs running loose ahead of her.

By the time she got to the church, Grace was ready to throw her grandmother's shoes into the weeds of the vacant lot next door. The shoes refused to make allowances for the shape of her feet, and Grace knew she had blisters forming. When she found the front door of the church locked, she took off Esther's shoes and her white socks and ran barefoot like a schoolgirl through the dirt and across the thin grass to the parsonage where the pastor's wife let her in, smiling uncertainly. Grace hurried past Lettie Michaels, down the familiar hallway to the back of the church.

In the children's Sunday school room, she shut the door and pushed a chair against it. She looked at the watch she carried in her pocket and saw she was an hour early. It was Orland's watch. He had given it to her one night and told her as long as she had the watch in her pocket, she couldn't kiss anyone else. Grace draped her dress across two folding chairs and sat down on a third to compose herself.

"Today, I'm getting married," she said. It didn't have the same force as when her grandmother had stood up in the church.

"My granddaughter Grace will be married this evening."

Grace had been thrilled to hear the coughs, the gasps really, of the other women who sat big as mountains in their pews. Esther Marshall might be slow and quarrelsome, but she could move mountains. She was a mountain herself.

But she was slow. Oh my God, everything in life was slow. Grace thought the watch Orland had given her must need a new battery. The hands quivered, but when she looked at them again, they hadn't moved. It made her wish she had someone to talk to, a maid of honor. She hadn't mentioned a maid of honor to Orland. They should have planned better.

The way it happened seemed sudden to her now. Of course, she had known Orland a long time, two years at least. He was younger than she was in high school, but then he stopped going, so it didn't matter. Before he quit, he belonged to the FFA, and when he got his jacket, blue corduroy with a single patch, that was the time Grace noticed him. The jacket brought out the blue in his eyes. He didn't pay attention to her in high school, which was why it surprised her so, early that summer when she had been out of school for a year, to have Orland come around in the evenings. He wanted to take her for a ride, but his car had broken down. He was looking for another car, the same make and model, so he could buy it for the engine. Orland was smart that way.

They walked to the Jolly Kone one night for a milkshake, and Orland kissed her and slipped his hand in her blouse. She wouldn't have minded the thing with his hand if he had moved a little slower. When she pushed him away, she did it by instinct, the way a few years earlier she might have knocked a boy down on the playground, some boy who had tumbled into her, dizzy off the merry-go-round. She thought she had chased Orland off, but two nights later he came back. They kissed behind a tree in the front yard so her grandmother wouldn't know where she was. This time she kept hold of both his hands. He pressed her against the smooth bark of the tree, and that part felt nice. Then her grandmother turned on the porch light, and Orland slipped out of the yard, leaving Grace with a weakness in her legs and the feeling she had misplaced something.

"What were you doing out here?" her grandmother asked.

It had been hot all day, over a hundred by noon, and Grace's arms were sunburned from standing too long in the yard, staring up the road. The evening had brought a faint breeze, and the smell of the orchards.

"Nothing," said Grace. "We weren't doing nothing."

"What did he say to you?"

"Nothing," said Grace, and she ran around the tree and into the house.

In the Sunday school room, she decided to get dressed. Grace turned her back to the portrait of Jesus over the piano and wished her sister, Lisa, had come along to help. She wanted to be nicer to her sister, who was four years younger than Grace and prettier. Lisa did better in school too. Grace knew she and Lisa didn't have the same father, although nobody talked about it. Grace couldn't remember her father. She remembered a time when she lived with her mother in an apartment over the barbershop on Main Street, and she could remember the day they loaded everything they owned into the back of a man's green pickup and drove the few blocks to her grandmother's house. It took two trips. When Lisa was born, her mother married the man with the pickup, Brady, and he moved in with them. But Brady fought with Grace's grandmother, fought every day until he finally left. He said he was going to Texas, and he was going to send for his family. Grace never knew if he meant to include her or not. She waited for years, afraid she would have to go with her mother and Lisa to Texas, afraid they would leave her behind. She couldn't relax about Texas until her mother died.

Grace thought about running home to get her sister, but she had the white dress on now and the clasp earrings, and she had combed her hair, wetting down her bangs so they would stay in place. She looked at Esther's shoes again and hated them. Maybe no one would notice if she got married in her socks. They were white socks. She wondered if Orland would notice, and she thought about how he had come to see her night after night since the beginning of summer, how her grandmother started bringing her rocking chair onto the porch so the woman could rock and complain and ask Orland questions. Sometimes he barely stayed half an hour before he went away.

"What does that boy want?" Esther said one night. "As if I had to ask."

"What he wants is for nosy old women to mind their own business," said Grace, knowing she would be slapped for it later. She ran out into the road after Orland, who was gone.

That was the night he came back. She loved the memory of it, waking up afraid, not knowing who it was at first, someone throwing pennies at her window. When she looked out, she saw him kneeling near the house, out of the moonlight. She could see the board fence at the back of her grandmother's yard, and beyond that, darkness to the very edge of town. He wanted her to come out to him.

"Go away," she whispered. "They'll wake up."

"Then let me in," he said.

"I can't," she said. She wanted more than anything to raise the window and let him come into her room. "My sister," said Grace. She pointed at the sleeping figure in the other bed.

"Where's that old woman?" said Orland. "She's a damn terror."

A light came on in the front of the house. As quick as Orland had appeared, he moved away through the bushes, walking funny, all bent over so he could keep in the shadows. Grace got back into bed in a rush. When her grandmother looked in a moment later, Grace pretended to be sleeping.

Esther moved to the window and looked out into the night. Grace held her breath, trying to imagine what her grandmother saw out that window: the mulberry tree, the alley, the long black car that had not moved in years. "I know how to deal with this," said Esther. She grasped the window on either side and shut it hard, as if she didn't care if Grace were awake or asleep. She did not look at Grace in her bed, but left the room, closing the door behind her.

The church parking lot slowly began to fill with cars. Grace watched the people arrive from behind a long dusty curtain, more women than men, but that didn't surprise her. Everyone was dressed up. All these people had come to church for her, to see Grace Marshall get married.

She imagined the presents they would bring, sheets and towels, maybe a small frying pan. All of these things would belong to her now. She was getting married. The people in the churchyard looked tired and wrinkled. Most of them had put the clothes back on they'd worn to church that morning.

The door from the hallway opened, and Mrs. Michaels stepped in, bobbing her head and smiling. The preacher's wife reminded Grace of a small child playing a game.

"Here you are," said Mrs. Michaels. "I've been looking for you." She held an orange flower by the stem, a poppy, and she wanted to pin it to the shoulder of Grace's dress.

"I guess it's okay," said Grace, wondering if her cousin Vivian would find the pin hole in the dress later and complain about it.

"Don't you look nice," said Mrs. Michaels. Grace hoped she was telling the truth. She wished she could keep her swollen feet out of sight.

"What's the matter? Don't your shoes fit?"

"They're Grandma's," said Grace.

"I've got some slippers," said Mrs. Michaels. "I'll run get them. Nobody will know."

"Is Orland here yet?"

"Who?"

"Orland. He's my, he's going to be . . . my husband." The word sounded funny. She hadn't used it before.

"He can't come back here," said Mrs. Michaels. "He can't see the bride until you're all in the church." She went out of the room after her slippers.

"I just wanted to know if he was here," said Grace.

It had been Tuesday night when Orland came again, and Esther brought her chair right out into the yard, though she couldn't rock half so well on the brown uneven grass.

"What do you want?" cried Grace, wishing she was brave enough to curse her grandmother. "Why can't you leave us alone?"

"So tell me," said Esther. She looked Orland in the eye. "Do you plan to marry this girl?"

"Marry?" said Grace, her voice rising too high.

"Well what if I do?" said Orland. He was staring right back at Esther. Grace could hear faint voices drifting through the night from the Jolly Kone, a country song on the jukebox that sat outside by the picnic tables where Grace and Orland had shared their milkshakes. "Yes," said Grace. "That's right. What if he does?"

"That's the way it is then?" said the old woman.

"What if it is?" said Orland.

"Let's set the date, why don't we?" said Grace's grandmother.

"Then will you leave us be?" cried Grace. "Then will you go away?" But Esther wasn't listening to Grace. All of her attention was on the boy.

"Hell," said Orland, "I'm ready right now."

"Sunday week," said Esther. "In the evening. We can wait till then. You get the license."

The jukebox had stopped playing. Now it started up again, the same song, the same woman's voice. It was somebody's favorite.

"I'll do it," said Orland.

"You can use our church," said Esther, "unless you have one of your own."

"Your church is fine," said Orland.

Grace felt her blood had turned to air, as if it was rushing up to escape through her ears and her eyes.

"Now go away," said Esther. "We'll see you a week from Sunday. Seven o'clock."

A woman laughed from the Jolly Kone, and a man said, "*Three for a dollar? I'll not pay that,*" his voice full of disbelief. Esther wasn't rocking anymore.

"Go away?" said Orland. "But I said I'd marry her."

"That's ten days from now," said Esther. "That's not tonight." She set her chair in motion again, the legs of the rocker creaking with the strain of her body, regular as the metronome Esther kept on the piano in the front room. Orland sat for another half hour, staring straight ahead angrily into the night, and Grace sat next to him, afraid to so much as reach out and take his hand.

"I'll be going now," said Orland, when he had stayed long enough to make his point. He pressed his watch into Grace's hand and stepped off the porch and out of the light.

The cloth slippers Mrs. Michaels brought were small, too, but if Grace bent the heels down and pulled the front of the slippers tight, she could get by. Mrs. Michaels had been a week in the hospital in Visalia, and Grace wondered if she had bought the blue slippers to wear after her surgery.

"Do you want me to play the piano?" asked Mrs. Michaels. "But wait," said the woman, "do you still play, Grace? Maybe you should play." Mrs. Michaels had given Grace piano lessons for four years. She gave all the children lessons, charging three dollars a week and leaving a plate of fresh cookies beside the piano at Christmas. "What am I thinking?" she said. "You can't play this evening. You're the bride."

"Could you play?" said Grace.

"I think I can," said Mrs. Michaels. "I'm better now." She pushed her hair into a small bun at the back of her head, and Grace noticed one or two gray streaks that seemed to have appeared only yesterday, looking as though they wanted to escape.

"I'll see if the young men have arrived," said Mrs. Michaels. She gave Grace a quick hug, and then, before she could slip away, the door was filled by Esther, who peered in at Grace as though she had never seen the young woman before.

"Whose dress is that?" said Esther. "Is that Vivian's?"

"It's Grace's dress," said Mrs. Michaels, "at least for today. It looks good on her too."

But it didn't matter what Lettie Michaels said. It was Esther's opinion that counted.

"Turn around," said Esther. "Let me see."

Grace turned around slowly.

"Don't you have a slip?" said Esther.

"No," said Grace. She thought she would cry because of it.

"You look fine," said Esther. The words surprised Grace. She threw her arms around her grandmother's neck.

"Is he here yet?" It was her grandmother who said that too. Grace heard the voice as if it came from deep inside the old woman.

"I'll go and see," said Mrs. Michaels.

In the room where she had first learned the stories of King David and Jonah and Judas Iscariot, Grace stood next to her grandmother, the woman who had raised her. The pastor's wife had returned just long enough to inform them that Orland had not arrived yet; then she had settled in at the piano, playing one of the sweeter hymns Grace sometimes sang in her room at night when her sister, Lisa, was at a friend's house. Mrs. Michaels wasn't the regular church pianist. She only played four songs, and she got flustered once and had to start over.

Pastor Michaels knocked on the door and waited until he was asked into the room. He wore a familiar gray suit with a handkerchief in the pocket. It made Grace wonder again what Orland would wear. When she pictured him, all she could see him in was his FFA jacket. The pastor's gray suit was nice, but she wished he would find a way to look happy. He might have been preaching at a funeral.

"We usually have a rehearsal," he said.

"What can go wrong?" said Esther. "Short and sweet. Let them say 'I do' and we can all relax."

"Esther Marshall," said the pastor, "I hope you know what you're doing."

Grace didn't know why that made the tears come again.

"Let her cry a little," said Esther. "A few tears at a wedding, that's nothing new."

"Do these children have rings for each other?" asked Pastor Michaels.

"Oh," said Grace. She had forgotten about rings. Orland hadn't said anything about them. She felt a swelling inside of her, as if she might burst.

"Here," said Esther. The old woman's face turned a muddy red as she handed the preacher her own thin gold wedding band. "That ring has been in the family," said Esther. "It's the best kind."

Grace hugged her grandmother, and the preacher slipped the ring into his coat pocket.

"Go see if the boy's here," said Esther. It made Pastor Michaels frown to be spoken to that way, but he went out into the hall without talking back. "As soon as he's here," said Esther, "we can get started."

At seven-thirty, after playing hymns for half an hour, Lettie Michaels played the first chords of the wedding march. Grace's heart leaped into her throat. She clutched Orland's watch in her hand and listened carefully for the familiar notes again, but the pastor's wife returned to the first of her four hymns. Mrs. Michaels played cautiously after that, and the more she played, the less it sounded like she was practicing for a future occasion. When she had played through all four songs once more, she began a new one, a song Grace knew well.

"That's 'Silent Night,'" said Grace.

"I guess it is," said Esther. She took a handkerchief out of her purse and wiped the sweat that had collected on her forehead.

"It's July," said Grace.

"I'm glad she's playing a different song," said Esther. "I was getting tired of those others."

They sat and fanned themselves until Orland's watch said a quarter to eight and Grace couldn't wait any longer. Esther led her down the hallway toward the sanctuary, where they stopped just outside the door so Esther could look in to see if the boy was sitting in one of the front rows, with or without one of his cousins or uncles for support.

"Oh hurry, Orland," murmured Grace, happy that she had the watch to hold tight in her hand. "Don't make people wait." She knew how much her grandmother hated to wait. It was the reason for the scowl on Esther's face.

Grace studied the watch. When nobody was looking, she set the minute hand back half an hour. But she knew what she had done, and she made herself reset it to the proper time. At one minute after eight, with Orland an hour overdue, Pastor Michaels passed her on his way out the side door for a breath of air. The children inside had grown restless, and their mothers sent them out front to play in the churchyard. Esther encouraged Mrs. Michaels to take a break from the piano, but Lettie didn't seem to want a break. She had been playing out of the new hymnal. Grace watched as she took out the old *Our Faith* hymnal and looked through it, hoping to find something else she knew how to play. Esther sent a boy to the Sunday school room for a folding chair.

"Get one for this girl too," said Esther.

A warm breeze filtered through the church. Someone had opened one of the large doors that led to the street. Grace stole a look out into the sanctuary again. It was only some of the men slipping away to have a smoke.

Grace had vowed not to look at the watch anymore until Orland came, but she couldn't help herself. It was exactly eight twenty-seven when Mrs. Michaels stopped playing and came to stand before her in the hallway, her voice trembling.

"Pastor says I have to quit," she said. "I don't care. I'll play a while longer if you want me to."

"Don't trouble yourself," said Esther.

"There has to be music for a wedding," said Grace. "What kind of wedding is it without music?" She looked from one of the women to the other. They wouldn't meet her eyes.

"There won't be a wedding," said Esther.

The words went straight to Grace's heart.

"Don't say that," cried Grace. "It's your fault. You shouldn't have said that. You've ruined everything."

"Straighten up, missy," said Esther. "We're not going to make a scene. He isn't coming."

But Grace refused to believe Orland wasn't coming. She wouldn't leave the church for another hour, long after the others had gone home taking their gifts with them, long after her grandmother had told Pastor Michaels off and demanded that he return her ring. Grace sat in the Sunday school room in her cousin's dress, half aware her sister had entered the room and was sitting quietly next to her. It was Lisa who helped Grace out of the white dress, who folded it neatly and put it in the paper sack, and who led her back toward the room they shared in their grandmother's house. Lisa didn't say anything when Grace threw Orland's watch across the road into the weeds, nor did she say anything when Grace spent an hour on her hands and knees looking for it in the dark.

• • •

Gerald Michaels hung his suit coat over the door to his closet. He took his trousers off and let them fall beside the bed. He had the feeling that if he didn't lie down quickly, he might never lie down, that he would be frozen in a standing position for whatever time remained of his life.

When he lay his head on his pillow and closed his eyes, he could see the boy named Orland again, how he had come up through the weedy lot at the side of the church. Michaels had been standing in the side doorway alone, and when he saw the boy, he instinctively edged out onto the steps and pulled the door closed behind him. He looked across the lot to the feedstore, all its windows dark, not even a night-light left on. Beyond that, he could see a barber pole, the one in front of Fergie's shop, still turning in the faint glow of a streetlamp. The boy had arrived an hour late for his own wedding, but he acted as if he wasn't late at all, as if he was there to do someone a favor. The coat he had on fit him in the sleeves, though it billowed out around his narrow waist. He had a white shirt and a tie on, and he smelled of cologne and beer.

"I'm Orland Newberry," he said. "I'm here to get married."

Michaels didn't smile at the boy. He didn't move off the top step.

"You're very late," he said. Inside, his wife had stopped playing the piano for the moment. Michaels was glad of that. When she started up again, she played a Christmas carol, which caused the boy's eyes to widen.

"I'm not that late," he said. "It ain't Christmas."

Michaels stepped down off the landing so he could stand next to Orland Newberry, wondering what family of criminals and idiots had set the boy loose to court a girl like Grace. He closed his eyes, filled with shame at his thoughts. He was here to take care of whoever came through the doors of the church, not just the handsome and talented ones. He wanted to reach out to Orland and embrace the boy. He wanted to believe in him. It had slipped away somehow, the old certainty. He thought about the quiet girl in Salinas, the one who was killed by a hit-and-run driver, and he wondered if the damage had been done to him then. God hadn't spoken through him that day. Michaels had been inept with the girl's parents, cowardly. He didn't believe God had spoken through him in a long time.

But even if he had lost faith in himself, he had always believed in marriage. Life wasn't easy for anyone; people who lived alone were the saddest of all. He had counseled many women, and men too, to stay with a poor marriage rather than risk living without another soul in the house. He thought about his own wife inside playing the piano so these two could marry. He hoped he had made Lettie happy, at least in their early years together. When he looked at Orland, at the way the boy's coat swelled out behind him, the insolent tilt of his head as he stood in the weeds between the church and the hardware store, Michaels thought about the life Orland and Grace would have, their children, the poverty of their purse and spirit. He wondered how much he, a pastor all these years, believed in anything.

"You listen to me," he said, though he didn't know what he was going to tell the boy. "You listen good," he said. Then the words formed

in his mouth without any effort on his part, and they came in a rush, and
he couldn't have stopped saying them even if he had known what he was
about to say. He spoke as though inspired, filled with a spirit.

"There's nothing for you here," he said. "You better go away." His
voice turned low and hoarse, surprising the boy and himself. "You'll live
to regret it. All of this."

"Go away?" said the boy. "I'm not going away."

"Don't be a fool," said the pastor. "Don't open the door to regret. It's
all regret after this, your whole life."

"I'm no fool," said the boy. "I'm here to get married."

"Why?" asked Michaels. "Just to get up next to that girl?"

"You got no call to talk that way," said Orland.

But Michaels knew the boy was wrong. If a man had no control over
what he was saying, then he had every right to say it.

"Run," said the pastor. "Go out across that vacant lot and run for
your life. It's your only chance."

"What are you saying?" said the boy. He was growing frightened.

"Here," said Michaels. "I'll give you money." He took sixty dollars
from his wallet. His wife was playing hymns again, and he could hear the
front doors of the church opening and closing as men went outside to
have a smoke. Michaels pulled the boy closer to him, into the shadows.

"Take this money and go to Los Angeles. Go to Mexico, go to Alaska.
You can't marry this girl. Not Grace. Not here. I won't do it."

"What do you mean you won't do it? What kind of preacher are you?"

"Can't you see?" said Michaels. As he spoke, he was in awe of himself. He wondered what he would say next. "I'm saving your life. I'm
keeping you from an awful mistake." He caught the odor of the boy's
cologne again and something else, a deeper smell of irrigation and dead
leaves, of the dust of the orchards, of the earth itself. "You'll never get to
sleep with her. The old woman already told me that."

"She told you that? I don't think so."

"Look, you little ass." Michaels gripped the boy's arm tight above the elbow. He wanted to shake him. It was hard not to. "Get the hell out of here," he said. "Run away just as fast as you can."

"A preacher's not supposed to swear," said the boy.

"Listen to me," said Michaels, and he struck the boy on the head with his knuckles. "This is serious."

He put all the money he had into the boy's hands. Orland looked as if he was about to cry.

"Go on now," said Michaels, gentle again. "Don't let her catch you. That old woman will have your hide."

The boy nodded, though he wouldn't have been able to say why. But he had taken the money. They both knew he would have to leave now. He wiped at his eyes with the sleeve of the jacket he had borrowed somewhere, from some older friend or brother probably dead or married himself. Orland started to speak, but Michaels shook him roughly. The boy's eyes rolled back into his head as the pastor gave him a shove toward the road. Michaels didn't move from the shadows of the church until Orland had crossed through the weeds to the asphalt. The boy was all but running, looking back over his shoulder in fear he would be followed. The door of the church opened, and Michaels looked up at Esther's large face staring out into the night.

"Who's out here?" she said.

He walked up the steps past the woman and into the church.

"Oh," said Esther, "it's just you. I thought it was somebody."

In his room, once the Reverend Michaels lay down, he didn't have the strength to pull the blanket over him. Lettie was in the kitchen, talking to the cat. He didn't want his wife to come to bed. He didn't want to talk about what had happened in the church. He thought about calling his oldest daughter, who sometimes could help him explain things to himself, and he thought about calling a minister he had known years ago, someone else who might understand, but he could remember speaking harshly of that minister when the man stopped preaching and took a job as a high school teacher. He thought about the heartbroken girl and wondered if there had been a time when he would have been able to comfort her, to say the words that would restore her faith. The grandmother was a fool, and the boy was no good. That was what the girl longed to hear. She didn't want to hear about God's mercy, God's love.

Michaels lay alone on his bed. He felt the heavy weight descend, pressing the back of his head into the mattress. And he tried to pray as he tried every night, this time for Grace.

If I'd Known You Were
• Going to Stay This Long •

IT'S PART OF HOW I GOT BACK HERE, the words, the language. My father, Ernie Foster, never swears. Before he retired, before he delivered milk for twenty years, even before he did farm work for a living, he was in the army. He fought from D-Day to the end of his war and he never said anything worse than *heckfire*, which is the word for him. I might put it on his gravestone if he loses this fight. Maybe it didn't happen like he said, maybe he boozed his way through Europe all the way to China, traded chocolate bars for women every night, maybe he raised hell, but I don't think so. Not Ernie Foster.

So, you're probably asking, what's the story? My father's eighty-three and fighting lung cancer, and me, I'm fighting the urge to go into one of the dark and dirty places on Main Street where I used to take the edge off, even when I was still in school, living at home. Everyone's got problems. I can hear you thinking that. You probably have some problems yourself.

Last year I was trying to be like him, Ernie straight and narrow. I wasn't drinking, and I was too old for fighting. I was taking my medication. I wasn't thinking about the others, about what happened to Troy and Darrel, not every day I wasn't. I had a job as the custodian of a grade school out in Missoula. They liked me there because, even if I'm white, I can work with Indians, Mexicans, queer people, anybody. I'm easy to get along with. But I couldn't control my language. I'd see some goofy kids knock their heels against the wall, leave black scuff marks I knew I had to clean up later, and I'd say, "Hey, don't make scuff marks on the goddamn wall." They'd turn pale as lizards, and then I'd realize what I said, and I'd try to make a joke out of it, but the kids were backward, some of them. They thought the world was flat, Jesus was a holy roller, all of that. They thought I was scary as a monster.

I watched two little brown kids try to ditch school one morning, waiting in the bushes until the bell rang and they could scoot downtown to the arcade. I didn't care if they skipped school. They weren't my kids, although if I think about how I never had a kid with Alice, who lives in Vermont now with a man who is not her husband, it will choke me up completely. I wasn't going to tell on the kids in the bushes. Why should I? When the bell rang and the coast was clear and the kids poked their heads out to dash across the street, a little Japanese car came around the corner, a quiet car. The Japanese make good cars. Even my father drives one now. Those kids were not paying any attention, and I yelled, "Look out, you little shits. You'll get your goddamn asses run over." The kids crapped in their pants, and so did the school's principal, who was standing outside on the sidewalk just waiting to nab them.

I was sunk. I went home and thought about what my father would have said. "Heckfire," is what he would have said. In fact that's what he did say when I told him I thought I was about to lose my job and maybe I would come home for a visit. I knew he was sick. I thought this could be our chance to get over some of the old business. I hadn't been in jail for years, and there were no warrants for my arrest in California. The way things turned out, I won't be getting either of my brothers in trouble again. I don't even write checks anymore. I thought my father would be glad to see me.

"Heckfire," he said. "Let me ask your mother."

I was sweating it then. I am nothing like my mother. This isn't even my mother's story. The story is about my father. She could have put an end to it right there if she wanted to remember all the items she had against me, starting with the fact that I was born two months prematurely and it cost her a good job at the Visalia Woolworths. Worse things than that.

That was then and this is now. My father got back on the phone and told me to come ahead. I guess my mother forgave me for everything, or forgot some of it.

"Are you bringing anybody with you?" he asked. "You currently married, anything like that?"

He was taking a lot of medication himself, so I didn't let it get to me, his own lack of memory.

"I'm coming alone."

"You can sleep on the couch," he said. "Unless you'd rather sleep in the recliner, the way you used to." Which was a jab at me because I used to stay out so late I would fall asleep any time I sat down for fifteen minutes. Now he's the one who sleeps in a chair. I could have made a comment about it, but I didn't.

I'll get to the point, but it isn't easy. I get home sometime last winter. It's after Christmas because there are little pine needles stuck in the carpet. Of course, that's not the only way I can tell it's after Christmas. I'm just sharing a fact with you. My father is glad to see me, I think. I don't ring the doorbell because we never had a doorbell, but I knock on the front door, and I can tell it's a big effort for him to get out of the recliner and meet me at the steps.

"So," he says, "the prodigal son." To this day, he makes those Biblical allusions. He knows I'll get them is why. I know what he'll say next, about buying a fatted calf down at SavMor.

"I got tired of eating corn husks," I tell him, and he smiles. He likes knowing some of Brother Slade's training didn't wear off so easy.

"Come inside," he says. "Your mother wants to see you."

She sort of does want to see me, too. She hugs me, but it's awkward.

My father sits in his chair again. He's got the game on, the 49ers, and this little smile as if he's done something clever. I come right out with it. "When's the operation?"

"It's not that easy," he says. "They have to shrink the tumor first."

"I've never heard of that," I say, because I really don't want to know. I don't want to know a lot of it.

"Chemicals," he says. He's wearing a ball cap with the word Ortho on it, and when he takes it off, I can see he isn't bald all over, but little spots here and there. The hair that's left is white.

"It could take a long time to shrink it," he says. "Maybe I'll die first."

"That's no way to talk," says my mother. "Your last son just got here."

"He don't have to stay," says my father. "Not for the duration. He can go back any time."

"I'll stay a while," I tell him.

"Good," he says. "I've got a tree in the backyard you can help me prune." He says it as if I've never been away, as if he isn't sick at all. As if I'll fall for anything.

Some time passes, days, maybe weeks. I'm not counting. It's afternoon and I'm in the kitchen looking for an ashtray, the television blasting my father's ball game through the house, when my cousin Frances calls. I tell her the TV is on loud because he doesn't hear so well, though I suspect I'm the one who can't hear anymore because of a lot of second-rate rock and roll in high school gyms and beer joints here and in Montana, everywhere. The beer joints of the world. I stand next to the kitchen sink and run my hand through my hair, which is getting a little spotty too. And this is the first time it happens. For a minute I don't know who I am, if I'm the son come home to take care of the father, or if I'm the old man himself about to tell some Baptist joke about the Arab and his camel. My cousin Frances on the phone says I owe her a hundred dollars for the trip out.

"Is that how I got here?"

"From Montana," she says. "Don't start that."

"I don't remember the trip." I'm not lying. A lot of my memory has drifted away.

"You slept the whole way," she says. "From *Montana*."

"That's a long time to sleep."

"Tell me about it. I was chauffeur to a zombie. You never woke up, even to eat. You made water by the side of the road. I think you were asleep then too. You almost got me arrested."

"Where?"

"In Oregon. By the side of the road."

I don't remember any of it. I tell her I must have been in a state, like once or twice before. Listening to her voice, all I can think about is a cigarette. There are no ashtrays in the cupboards of my mother's house, no ashtrays in the dishwasher, in the refrigerator, anywhere. My father knows what I'm looking for. He can read my mind.

"I don't know anybody who smokes anymore," he says from his chair in the living room. "Not even at church."

"You owe me a hundred dollars," says Frances. "For gas. Do you have any money at all?"

I decide to use my pocket for an ashtray again. I'm wearing an old shirt I think once belonged to my brother Troy. I light a cigarette just the way my father used to. He could put his finger against the head of a match and make it pop when he struck it. Then he'd take a long drag and look off at the wall, at a place where he plastered over some damage I did a long time ago with a basketball. He would stare at the place forty times a day, make me feel rotten through and through.

"I'll pay you for pruning the tree," says the old guy. It's as if he can hear my cousin Frances on the other end of the phone, her asking me for money, although he's not listening in. He's watching ice hockey.

"Tell her we're going to start on Monday."

I tell her.

"I know that tree," she says. "You'll both fall out and kill yourselves."

"Tell her you have to go," says my father. "Tell her I'm wandering in the street without any clothes on."

I tell her that.

"I don't believe you," says my cousin. "Him either." But she hangs up.

I go outside where it's February or it's March, and the grass wants to turn green, the backyard damp and so familiar to me it hurts to look at it. My father's got a peach tree that's just about bent over, all laden down with small green peaches. He hasn't been able to tend to it. Orange groves crowd the place on every side. The olives are gone now, pulled up a long time ago and replaced with more oranges. I smoke three cigarettes in a row while I check out the evidence from my father's life, these unfinished projects. The greenhouse against the fence where he started his tomatoes, a front end to a Chevy pickup. The shed is still standing, the one I tried to burn down when I was a kid. It needs a new roof. I look at it with a critical eye, but I don't make any plans to fix it.

And it hits me: I am so much like my father I can't keep us straight anymore. He's sitting in there in his recliner and I'll be sitting in the other recliner, which in truth belongs to my mother since I'm only visiting, but then all of a sudden when I get up to take a leak or go for a hopeless look in the refrigerator, I can't be sure if it's me walking across the room this time or if it's him. I take those first three steps bent over with grief, I pause at the window and look up at the sky, I clear my throat as if I'm going to speak, but I don't. These are moves my father has made for as long as I can remember.

I know why it is I've come home, if I can't remember how I got here. (It's a long drive from Montana, and I *should* remember five days in the car with my cousin. It's not so easy to remember yourself.) I'm here for the operation. He's the one having it, that much I am sure. They're going to cut the cancer from his lung. Just thinking about his tired old lungs makes me short of breath.

I check out the tree he is talking about. They always say, when you go back home, everything will be smaller than you remember it. But this tree is huge. Long after I stopped growing, this tree kept at it. The branches fork up toward the sun until, halfway between the earth and the sky, every limb ends in a gnarled ball of wood, higher than a man can reach from the top of a twelve-foot ladder. I think of tumors. A thicket of fresh branches grows from each stub, and it's this new growth he wants to cut off, long and wavy as fishing poles. When I was a boy, we did the job in a weekend, my father, Troy and Darrel and me. The tree was smaller then. Now it would take three grown men a week to cut it back, and another three days to clean up the mess.

"We'll get started tomorrow." My father has come up behind me, and when I hear his voice I can't get any taste from my cigarette. He makes a wheezing raspy noise from the least exertion. We shouldn't sound alike these days, but we do.

"If I'd known you were going to stay this long," he says, "we could have started sooner."

You don't need a reason to want to be different from your old man. I didn't think like him, and I didn't want to look like him. I didn't want to talk like him either. It was always this way. Certain people used to call up and ask my father when he was going to pay back the money he owed them. They asked that question because they thought they were talking to me. Or grown-ups would call the house and ask me to deliver extra milk for the holidays, thinking they had him on the line. If my father wasn't around, I knew how to take down the address and the number of bottles they wanted without letting on they were talking to the son, not the father. We'd help each other out. After a while, though, he wasn't any good at paying my bills. He had to draw the line.

"You better quit smoking those things," he says. He puts his hand on the tree. Maybe he's taking the damn thing's pulse. I wouldn't know. I stub out my cigarette. "I should have told you that before now," he says.

My ex-wife calls, Alice from Vermont, and I don't want to talk to her. Ever since she quit nursing, she wants me to send her money. It's money I owe her, but still.

"He can't come to the phone," says my father. I guess he never liked her much. "I wouldn't lie to you," he says. "The boy's sick in bed. They're going to operate pretty soon."

I can't hear what she says. I'm not the one with the receiver mashed up against my ear. But it's strange, that telephone. If you sit in my father's chair and turn the TV on real loud, you have a pretty good idea what someone is saying on the phone three thousand miles away. How long has this been the case? I think back on the phone calls from my youth, that time between when I got out of the group home and when I left for Montana, all those nights when the old man sat here in this very chair pretending not to know what I was talking about, and I am embarrassed.

"The boy doesn't feel as bad as he looks," says my father. He is talking about me. "I don't think that would be possible," he says. He is standing in the kitchen doorway next to the place where he used to measure my height each fall at the start of the school year, measure all three of us. The marks are still there on the jamb, mine a good deal higher than Darrel's last mark, a little shorter than Troy's. "They're trying to shrink the tumor," he says.

She doesn't buy any of it.

"I don't know," says my father. "Maybe you get this kind of cancer from your genes. He could have caught it from me. It could happen."

She tells him to hang on for a minute so she can go yell at her son, who is not my son. My heart breaks a little. I watch my father move to the doorway, and I wonder if we are still the same height, him and I.

"I thought you married a rich guy," says my father when Alice comes back to the phone. The game on television is college basketball, Fresno State against San Jose. Our money is on Fresno State.

"What?" he says. "Well, why don't you *get* married? Why do you need to bother my Johnny?" When the old man says my name, the room gets quiet, as if one team has walked off the court. "Okay, okay," says my father. "Then how about this—why don't you try paying your own bills?" He slams down the phone, and since I'm in his chair, he moves to my mother's recliner. My mother is in the back room folding laundry, so she doesn't mind if we use her chair. We sit that way for ten minutes without talking, watching Fresno State.

"Get up," says my father. I get up like he says and we change chairs.

"That's better," he says, putting his feet up on his own chair where they belong. I feel a little less confused too.

"I hope she doesn't call here again," he says.

"If she does," I tell him, "Mom can say we're outside. She can say we're pruning the tree."

The ladder he uses is a wonky old thing. He's got it strapped together with electrician's tape, and the third rung from the bottom is missing altogether, just a wire spoke where a wooden step used to be. He wants to climb up into the tree, but he can't even lift the pruning shears. It's as if I'm a kid again in the backyard, watching him fight those limbs and branches. I used to run around and grab the green shoots as quick as they landed on the grass. Now I'm the one on the ladder and he's down on the ground looking up at me.

I wonder what he's thinking about down there, and I wonder what I used to think about. Girls maybe, basketball games I was about to play, beer I hid in the hedgerow. Then there were the things I tried not to think about, all the mistakes I was aware of and a few I wasn't aware of. He gets a lawn chair from the shed and sits down.

"I never got to sit down," I tell him. I'm glad when he doesn't hear me.

"Heckfire," he says. "I'm tired of cancer."

I pull myself up onto the tree house he built for us when I was nine. He didn't put sides on it. It's a platform made of leftover boards, whatever was around at the time. Part of it is an old coffee table. He's repaired the tree house more than once, although I can't imagine why unless it's so he can stand on it the way I am standing on it now to prune the tallest limbs of the tree. I prune and I prune. I cut and I clip. There's a lot of work to do here. My arms ache from holding the shears over my head, and sometimes I get dizzy, but when I stop to take a rest, I have moments when my head gets clear. I can see Twin Buttes off a little ways in the distance, these two rock outcroppings that rise up from the orchards like nothing else for miles around. And I can smell the orchards. What I smell is a blend of orange blossoms and pesticide, a little diesel from the trucks, and that wet earth smell when they irrigate, or even better, when it rains. Tuesday after a rain, which was three days ago, the real mountains rose up as close as ever. Not Twin Buttes. The Sierras.

"It's next week," says my father. He sits below me in his chair, never taking the ball cap from his head, though his hair never did completely fall out. I've taken him to the hospital for treatments and checkups, and I know what cancer is now, how the body looks when chemicals eat away at whatever parts the doctors don't want.

"They're going to operate on Monday," he says.

I have nothing to say, so I cut another branch from the tree. It falls like a spear to the ground a foot from where he sits. He doesn't flinch.

"They're going to start pretty early in the morning," he says, "unless you kill me with a tree limb first."

"You should have cut this tree down twenty years ago," I tell him. I'm surprised he talks about killing people. He usually doesn't slip up that way. We've spent years not mentioning it. He takes the ball cap off and wipes his gray forehead with a handkerchief that's just as gray.

"You're full of shit," he says. I almost lose my balance hearing him say that.

"Say again?"

"Pay attention to what you're doing," he says, his voice a shovelful of gravel, but soft. Small gravel. When he was young, he had a nice singing voice. I used to stand on the pew next to him and listen to him sing before I could read half of the words myself. Then his voice changed, though I can't tell you why. One day he sings like the angel Gabriel, and the next day he's still moving his lips, but not much sound comes out. It's a Baptist way of singing. It shouldn't have surprised me when it happened. It happened to me too.

I was a kid once, and I could sing both loud and true back then, songs about love, songs about Jesus, songs about cruel war. I sang in the church choir and at the group home, and later when they let me come back to live with my parents, I sang in the high school choir. I hit every note. Sometimes I got asked to sing in other choirs if they didn't have enough male voices. Five years out of high school, I'm sitting in a little bar in the chair next to the jukebox, which is not a great jukebox. When I first started going to bars, I went for the music as much as the beer. A lot of places then, you could ask me, B-11? And I'd tell you it was the Beach Boys or Marty Robbins or maybe it was Otis Redding. But I'm sitting in this bar, and a song comes on, a nice slow Motown I liked to sing, and I open my mouth and nothing comes out. No volume. I knew all the words to that song, and I wasn't even drunk probably. I just lost my volume, the same way my father lost his one morning in the middle of "God Be with You till We Meet Again."

The next morning, he can't get out of bed. I'm standing in the kitchen with a cup of coffee. I've got my gloves on, and I'm ready to go out and do battle with a tree when my mother comes in to tell me he isn't up to it today. She sends me out by myself, and I work all morning, careful not to misstep, wondering if he's going to die. When she calls me in for lunch, he sits there at the table like it's Saturday morning and he's waiting for his pancakes. He doesn't look so hot, but he isn't dead.

"Something I ate," he says. I pretend to believe him. "Why don't you take the rest of the day off?" he says. "We don't have to finish on any certain day."

"I'll just work an hour this afternoon," I tell him.

"Gets in your blood, doesn't it?" he says, and he laughs until he coughs.

"I'm not like you," I say. "I can quit if I want to."

He can't talk, he thinks this is so funny. He waves at me across the table, and after a while I get up and go outside, where I work on the tree until dark. I watch the birds fly off the power lines in great swarms, black birds and gray ones, and some that look green in the last light of the day. I remember shooting at those birds with a pellet gun when I was a boy. I am sorry for each one I shot.

Later, we're in the living room resting up a little when the telephone goes off. I try to crank down my recliner, but the chair gets stuck at half-mast and my father gets to the phone first. It's a friend of mine calling, Isaac Franklin. We go way back, Isaac and me. I may owe him money, maybe not. I've made it to my feet by then, so I move over and settle into my father's chair and turn up the volume on the TV. We are watching golf, and they always whisper on golf. I have to turn the sound up.

"I been here a few months," says my father. I know what he's doing right away. He's pretending he is me. Even my friend Isaac won't know the difference. Some guy in green pants misses a long putt on the TV, and the living room shakes with the crowd's disappointment, but I'm not paying any attention to that. It's as if, in that crazy chair, I can *hear* Isaac, and he's in the room with us. He wants to know why I haven't called him.

"Oh, you know," says my father, looking at me as if I'm the invalid. "I don't go out much these days. I'm sober."

So? says Isaac. *Some of us never were drunk full-time.* That makes my father laugh, and the laughing makes him cough.

You still smoking those cigarettes? says Isaac.

"Actually," says my father, "I recently quit. I'm feeling better than I have in years."

That's good, says Isaac. *Know what we could do? We could drive up to the mountains to the park. See some snow. Or play some basketball? We don't run up and down the court anymore. Just shoot some, get some dinner.*

"Maybe later," says my father. "I'm trying to watch my spending." There's a pause on the phone, and that means Isaac is remembering the last time I was here, who paid for all the good times and who didn't, and my old man takes the opportunity to wind it up.

"We'll get together," says my father, "when things sort out." And he hangs up the phone, but nicely this time.

"What things?" I ask. The way my father is standing in front of me makes me think of George Washington in the famous painting, waiting for someone to get up and give him a place in the boat. I get out of his chair and take the other one.

"This is still golf?" he asks, meaning the television. "Isn't there anything else?"

"There's lacrosse on the other station."

"Slim pickings," says my father.

"I told you so," I say. And we both stand up and go out back to look at the tree.

There are only a few limbs left to work on when my mother and I take him to the hospital. I keep telling myself what the surgeon is going to do to my father is a kind of pruning job. I don't like the idea though. It means the bad stuff will grow back, and next year we'll have to do it again, and the next year, and so on. He's in the hospital for a lot of days—I lose count—and all the time he's there I don't work on the tree. I don't do much of anything.

When he gets out, he's old. Before he went in, he was past middle age (hell, I'm past middle age), but now he's getting up there in a serious way. When my mother brings him home from Visalia, he's wearing one of my shirts. It's okay. I give him back his fuzzy slippers, too, because his feet get cold. I can see all of this is hard on my mother, so I look for

247

ways I can help out. I cook mostly. I'm pretty good at it. He and I like the same stuff, macaroni and burgers, baked potatoes, so I cook what I like, and he doesn't complain. It doesn't taste as good as what my mother cooks. I lose a few pounds, but he shovels it in with a determined look on his face. He doesn't plan to stay sick forever. He gains the weight as fast as I lose it, and pretty soon we're the same size again. I go out and buy myself a new shirt exactly the same as the one my mother took from my closet, the one she gave to him. I get some fuzzy slippers, too.

I started growing a beard when he went into the hospital, but it doesn't mean anything. I'm just doing it. When he gets home and settled into his chair, he says he's too tired to shave. After that, I watch the whiskers come in on his chin, thin and white and no two of them pointing in the same direction. A week of it and I go out and buy a couple of razors, one for each of us. You would think he would appreciate the thought, but he doesn't mention it.

It's my cooking that makes the difference, or it's the way he eats. He tells me he can't control anything else, but he can make sure he doesn't starve to death. He comes along like a mule, and I stay out of his way. He starts taking walks in the evening after the day has cooled off. Brother Slade said the heat of July in the San Joaquin is a foretaste of the hereafter for some of us. Who knows? I'm glad to see him up. He measures how far he's walking in rows of orange trees. First, it's two rows of trees before he turns around and comes back to the house. Then it's four rows, and then ten. Pretty soon he's walking all the way down to the four-way stop, and I know it's time. One afternoon before the shadows grow long, I get him out of the recliner—we're watching women's sand volleyball—and we go out to the backyard and look at that shade tree. It's in full leaf again, but it's easy to see the longer branches, half a dozen of them, the ones I didn't cut before he went into the hospital.

"You left those?" he says.

"I didn't leave them," I say. "I saved them." And my voice breaks as if we're in some women's movie. We both get sloppy for a minute, reach into our pockets for the cigarettes that aren't there. I get a sniffle, and he blows his nose. He goes to get the pruning shears while I set up the ladder.

I help him climb it step by step, then steady the ladder so he can make the big step to the lowest branch. When he's halfway up the tree, I have a moment of sanity and wonder what the hell we're doing. But he gives me a grimace and gets a knee up onto the tree house. I push him up so hard he almost goes over the other side. Once I get up next to him, he is content to let me do the actual pruning. It's enough for him that he's up there. We can't see anything for the new growth, so I go nuts for a half hour hacking away leaves and branches until we get a clearing we can look out. Of course, we can't see the mountains in July, but we act as if we can. We just look at the horizon and breathe and sweat a little. I try not to think about how I'm going to get him back down on the ground.

"We should do something," he says. "To mark the moment."

"Like what?" I say, and he looks at me as if he knows me for the fool I am.

"I don't know," he says. The phone rings inside the house, and my mother comes outside to tell us who's calling. It could be for me. It could be for him. When she sees us up in the tree, she grabs onto the doorway as if she might faint.

"The two of you," says my mother, "who do you think you are?"

"Doesn't matter," says my father. "And whoever it is on that phone"— he's shouting to her louder than he needs to—"tell them we're up in the goddamn tree, and they can wait to talk to us when we're good and ready."

My mother adjusts her glasses to look at him better. Then she looks at me.

"I'm with him," I tell her. "Heckfire."

She goes back in the house, and it's quiet in the yard. The road he lives on is made up of people who hardly make any noise. It must be the heat.

"What should we do?" he asks. This time I know what he's talking about. We need an excuse to be up here so long. In a tree house.

"Maybe we could sing," I tell him, ignoring the fact that we don't have any volume anymore, either of us. The thought simply occurs to me and I say it out loud. I'm feeling pressed.

"Sure," he says. And then I'm worried he won't know any of the songs I know, and I'll have to sing one of his.

"You know this one?" he says. "This one has a little punch." He starts to sing "When the Roll Is Called Up Yonder," all faint and quavery, and it's so sweet up there I can't join in for a minute, but that's okay with him. He starts over at the beginning. We sing all the verses we know. We sing quiet and we sing loud. By then my mother has brought some neighbors over to talk us out of the tree. I see Isaac Franklin down in the yard. He looks a little old to me, a little worse for wear, but he's standing up straight like he's gotten over most of it. And Miss Whitefield is there. She's 160 years old if she's a day. She waves. Then I see she's not waving. She's going for a Rolaid.

It's not as hard to get him down out of the tree as I feared it would be. But we make them all go home first. Because this moment is private. This is ours.

In the house after dinner, he puts on his other shoes and gets ready for his walk. I think maybe this time I will join him, but then I decide, no, it's a good chance to slip into the back room, get a head start on packing. I pull my suitcase out from under the bed and see him standing in the doorway.

"There's no hurry," he says.

"I know that," I tell him. "Anyway, I'm not going far. Isaac says I should come stay with him a while."

He smiles and walks off toward the front of the house. I know he's going to stop at the kitchen window to look out at the evening, and he does. He nods at the sky the way we would nod at an old friend but not just any old friend, and I have that strange feeling again as if I'm outside my body watching myself walk across the carpet toward the door. I see a man who resembles me go around the coffee table, weaving between the recliners. A hand that belongs to one of us, it's his hand or it's mine, who knows, reaches for the doorknob, steels itself for the world on the other side. It will be an easy walk tonight over familiar roads. I am hoping we make it.

Ted Kitterman

BARRY KITTERMAN grew up in California's San Joaquin Valley and has lived and taught in Belize, China, Taiwan, Ohio, and Indiana. His novel *The Baker's Boy* (SMU, 2008) won the 2009 Maria Thomas Peace Corps Writers Award for Fiction. He lives in Clarksville, Tennessee, where he teaches at Austin Peay State University.